CHARLIE THORNE

THORNE

AND THE

LAST EQUATION

Also by Stuart Gibbs

The FunJungle series
Belly Up

Poached

Big Game

Panda-monium

Lion Down

The Spy School series
Spy School

Spy Camp

Evil Spy School

Spy Ski School

Spy School Secret Service

Spy School Goes South

Spy School British Invasion

The Moon Base Alpha series
Space Case

Spaced Out

Waste of Space

The Last Musketeer

A CHARLIE THORNE NOVEL

CHARLIE THORNE

AND THE

LAST EQUATION

STUART GIBBS

Simon & Schuster Books for Young Readers

New York   London   Toronto   Sydney   New Delhi

SIMON & SCHUSTER BOOKS FOR YOUNG READERS
An imprint of Simon & Schuster Children's Publishing Division
1230 Avenue of the Americas, New York, New York 10020

SIMON & SCHUSTER BOOKS FOR YOUNG READERS
is a trademark of Simon & Schuster, Inc.
For information about special discounts for bulk purchases, please contact Simon & Schuster Special Sales at 1-866-506-1949 or business@simonandschuster.com.
The Simon & Schuster Speakers Bureau can bring authors to your live event. For more information or to book an event, contact the Simon & Schuster Speakers Bureau at 1-866-248-3049 or visit our website at www.simonspeakers.com.
Interior design by Hilary Zarycky
The text for this book was set in New Caledonia.
Manufactured in the United States of America
0819 FFG
First Edition
2 4 6 8 10 9 7 5 3 1

Library of Congress Cataloging-in-Publication Data
Names: Gibbs, Stuart, 1969– author.
Title: Charlie Thorne and the last equation / Stuart Gibbs.
Description: First edition. | New York : Simon & Schuster Books for Young Readers, [2019] | Series: Charlie Thorne ; 1 | Summary: The CIA forces twelve-year-old Charlotte "Charlie" Thorne, a rebellious genius, to use her code-breaking skills on an epic global chase to locate Einstein's last equation before dangerous agents discover it and unlock the solution to harnessing energy.
Identifiers: LCCN 2018050572 (print) | LCCN 2018060315 (eBook) | ISBN 9781534424760 (hardcover) | ISBN 9781534424784 (eBook)
Subjects: | CYAC: Genius—Fiction. | Spies—Fiction. | Einstein, Albert, 1879–1955—Fiction. | Adventure and adventurers—Fiction. | Racially mixed people—Fiction.
Classification: LCC PZ7.G339236 (eBook) | LCC PZ7.G339236 Ch 2019 (print) |
DDC [Fic]—dc23
LC record available at https://lccn.loc.gov/2018050572

For Ciara, my niece; Suz, my sister; and Jane, my mother—
three of the toughest, smartest, coolest women on earth.
Charlie Thorne exists because of you.

I know not with what weapons World War III will be fought, but World War IV will be fought with sticks and stones.

—ALBERT EINSTEIN

PROLOGUE

Albert Einstein was dying.

In the great man's bedroom on the second floor of his white clapboard house, a young doctor held a vigil by his side.

It was a quirk of fate that the young doctor was even there. Einstein's regular physician, a man who had been his friend and confidant for years, was sick himself that night. The young doctor was filling in for him and had answered the emergency call, never expecting that he would end up witnessing history.

The doctor was at once awestruck and saddened. He couldn't believe he was here, treating Albert Einstein himself—and yet he knew the old man's time was quickly running out. Einstein was in agony, fading in and out of consciousness. There was nothing the doctor could do for him except try to ease his pain.

To the doctor's surprise, the housekeeper—a stern older woman named Helen—had argued vehemently against giving Einstein painkillers, even trying to throw them out the window. Ultimately, the doctor had to drag the old woman from the room and lock her out. He had felt guilty about this—especially when Helen had pounded on the door, desperately pleading for him to listen to her—but he had administered the drugs anyhow. His responsibility was to the patient. It would have been a violation of his oath to let Einstein continue suffering.

Eventually, Helen had stopped pleading and gone to make a frantic phone call.

Now Einstein seemed to be asleep, his head propped on the pillows, his breath coming in ragged heaves. However, his pulse was still racing, indicating that his body wasn't truly resting.

The doctor heard a car screech to a stop on the street outside and then Helen answering the front door downstairs. Whomever she had called had arrived. It hadn't taken long—perhaps five minutes. The doctor wondered if this new visitor would be more willing to listen to reason. . . .

Einstein's hand suddenly clasped the doctor's wrist, startling him. The great scientist snapped upright in bed, his eyes wide open but unfocused—the wild stare of a morphine haze. He pulled the doctor toward him with surprising strength and hissed, *"Die Gleichung muss geschützt werden!"*

"I—I'm sorry," the doctor stammered. "I don't understand."

Einstein stared at him, seeming both confused and aggravated. The doctor suspected delirium had set in, a side effect of the painkillers. Einstein probably had no idea where he was—or that he was even speaking German. And yet he spoke with startling conviction for a man who had been heavily sedated, as though his thoughts were so important, he was determined to express them at any cost.

"Pandorabüchse!" Einstein exclaimed urgently. *"Sie ist im Holmes. Die Gleichung muss geschützt werden!"*

The doctor could now hear footsteps racing up the stairs. He tried to lay Einstein back down in bed, to comfort him somehow, but Einstein remained upright, clutching him tightly.

"I don't speak German," the doctor explained. "Please. Try in English. . . ."

"Pandorabü . . . ," Einstein began again, but it was all he could manage. The light in his eyes faded. His pulse faltered. Then he collapsed back onto the bed, the final thought of his incredible life unfinished.

Ernst Klein burst through the door a second later, splintering the frame. He was the same age as Einstein, and they had been friends since they had met during their freshman year at the Federal Polytechnic in Zurich nearly six decades earlier. Ernst wore only pajamas with a raincoat hastily pulled over them. He hadn't even taken the time to put on a pair of slippers; his feet were still bare.

The moment he saw Einstein, Ernst knew he was too late. His knees buckled slightly, as if all his years had suddenly descended upon him. Tears welled in his eyes. But this was all the remorse he had time for. He fought his emotions aside and turned to the young doctor. "I heard him speaking to you. What did he say?"

"I don't know." The doctor was surprised to find his hands were shaking. He had already witnessed many deaths in his thirty years, but this one had been different. His final moments with Einstein had left him strangely unsettled. "It was in German—I think. I couldn't understand it."

"Can you repeat it?" It wasn't a question so much as a demand. Despite his years, Ernst had a commanding presence.

"No. I don't think so."

"Please!" Ernst seized the doctor by his lapels with such force that he nearly lifted the young man off the floor. "You must try!"

The doctor forced himself to concentrate. "It was something like 'pander abuse. . . .'"

Worry flickered in Ernst's eyes. *"Pandorabüchse?"*

The doctor gasped, surprised. "That's it! How did you . . . ?"

"Did Albert say anything else?"

"Yes, but I can't recall it. It sounded urgent, though . . . like it was an order. Like he wanted me to do something."

Ernst relaxed his grip on the doctor, nodding sadly, aware the younger man had no more information to share. If only he had been here a few seconds earlier! If he had just driven a little faster, maybe taken Chestnut Street instead of Maple . . .

No, Ernst told himself. There was no point to wishing that history was different. As Einstein would have pointed out, time moved in only one direction. There was work to be done.

An anguished cry rang out behind him. Helen stood in the doorway, clutching the jamb for support, staring at Albert's lifeless body.

Ernst felt a pang of remorse. He wanted to comfort the woman. He wanted someone to comfort *him*. He wanted to sit by the bed, hold his old friend's hand one last time, and cry.

But he couldn't. Not now. Not when Einstein had spoken about *Pandorabüchse* on his deathbed. The worst-case scenario they had always feared had come to pass, and now Ernst had to deal with it. He grasped the doctor's arm tightly, leading him from the room. "You must go," he said firmly.

"But I have to report the death. . . ."

"Do it tomorrow. Go home now. Get some rest. Then phone in your report. Say Albert died at seven a.m. . . ."

"I can't do that. It's against my oath. . . ."

"Do you know who that man is in there?" Ernst nodded toward the bedroom.

"Of course."

"Would you have ever questioned his judgment when he was alive?"

The doctor considered this, then shook his head.

Ernst fished an envelope from his pocket. It was creased and brown with age. "I'm not giving you *my* orders. They're *his.*"

The doctor reluctantly opened the envelope. Inside were two yellowing pages. The first was a letter, typed and notarized:

```
To whom it may concern:
    I, Albert Einstein, being of sound mind,
name Ernst Klein to be the supreme executor
of my estate. He is my closest friend and
he is to be given your complete and utter
trust.
    If you are reading this, I have passed
```

on. I beg you to do whatever Ernst requests. He is acting in accordance with my wishes. Do not waste his time asking why; he does not know himself. Only I do, and my reasons shall die with me. Suffice it to say, I have a very good explanation for such extreme precautions.

I beg you: Never speak a word of this to anyone.

Thank you for your understanding,

Albert Einstein

The doctor looked back at Einstein, stunned, wondering what the old man could have had in mind. He began to turn to the second page of the documents, but Ernst snatched them away.

"I'm afraid the rest of this is for my eyes only." Ernst took the doctor's arm again and steered him down the stairs. "Now, if you'll be so kind as to give us some time, we'd greatly appreciate it."

The doctor was surprised to find himself nodding in agreement. He couldn't explain why exactly; he simply had a sense that something far greater than himself was taking place. Something only an intellectual powerhouse like Einstein could conjure up—or comprehend. Before the doctor knew it, he was at the front door, shaking hands with Ernst, devising a plan to falsify the time of Einstein's death.

Ernst closed the door on him and turned all three latches. Then he made a beeline for Einstein's study.

It was on the first floor, wedged between the living room and dining room, but lacking any of their formality. This was the place where Albert could be himself, and it was strewn with the residue of a thousand ideas in progress. Notebooks and papers covered every available surface: they were piled on the desk, couch, and chairs; floor-to-ceiling bookshelves buckled under their weight; even the fireplace was being used for storage, with sheaves of paper stacked upon the andirons. A double-sided blackboard in the corner was coated with dozens of equations, many half-erased and then written over again. As Albert had aged, his organizational skills had waned, although he had never stopped thinking.

Looking at the study, all Ernst could think was that he had a great deal of work to do.

Even so, he quickly read the second page from the envelope, the instructions Albert had given him ten years before. Ernst knew what they said, but what he was about to do seemed so radical—so sacrilegious—that he needed Albert's reassurance before he began.

It made sense to start with the papers in the fireplace. He found a box of matches, struck one, and set it to the pile. Much of the paper was old and brittle; some might have been stacked there, forgotten, for a decade. The pile quickly burst into flame. Thousands of Einstein's calculations instantly turned to ash.

The next pages Ernst added to the fire were Einstein's instructions themselves. Then, working as quickly as his old muscles would allow, he began to burn everything else.

Over the crackle of the flames, Ernst heard two cars skid to a stop in front of the house. Men's voices echoed in the night.

They're already here, Ernst thought.

He was surprised. Not that Albert had been right about them—Albert was *always* right—but that they had arrived so quickly. They must have been stationed closer than he had realized.

Ernst stepped up his pace, throwing everything he could into the fire, racing to destroy as much as possible in the little time he had. He gave no thought to himself, only to the promise he had made to Albert, even though the fire was now blazing hot enough to scorch his skin and the smoke stung his eyes and filled his lungs. He continued feverishly stoking the flames, even as he heard the men break down the front door and shove Helen aside, even as they burst into the room and pulled their guns and screamed at him to stop, right up until their leader clubbed him from behind, crumpling him to the floor.

In the seconds before he lost consciousness, Ernst Klein prayed that, by some miracle, *Pandorabüchse* had been in the fraction of Einstein's work he'd been able to destroy—and that it was finally gone from the earth once and for all.

PART ONE

THE FATE OF THE WORLD

It has become appallingly obvious that our
technology has exceeded our humanity.
—ALBERT EINSTEIN

ONE

The director of the Central Intelligence Agency scrutinized the photograph of Charlie Thorne, then dropped it on the conference table and gave Agent Dante Garcia a hard stare. "You must be joking."

"I'm not," Dante replied solemnly.

"This is a twelve-year-old girl!" Director Carter exclaimed.

"She's not a *normal* twelve-year-old."

"I don't care if she can fly," Carter snapped. "I own pairs of *shoes* that are older than this kid. The fate of humanity is at stake here and you want me to rely on someone who's barely a teenager?"

"Desperate times call for desperate measures," Dante said.

"These measures aren't desperate. They're *insane*."

"Well, maybe it's time we tried something crazy. The

CIA has been using the same old techniques to find Pandora for almost seventy years, and they haven't gotten us anywhere. They certainly didn't work in Bern."

Director Carter's gaze went cold, making Dante think that he'd pushed things too far. But then Carter gave a slight nod, conceding that he was right, and sat back in her chair to think.

Dante had seen the director lapse into deep thought before, though never when he was the only one in the room with her. The previous times, he had been a junior agent, relegated to the background, expected only to observe and keep his mouth shut. Carter's long pauses to think in meetings were legendary at the Agency. She had been known to not say anything for up to ten minutes, during which she expected complete silence. This could be awkward for the other agents in the room, but they all greatly respected Carter—revered her even—and so they dealt with it.

Jamilla Carter was in her sixties, the rare CIA director who had risen to the job by being an exceptional agent rather than a political appointee. Her piercing brown eyes stood out against her dark skin. She had been an analyst, rather than a field operative, but then, most CIA employees were analysts, and Carter was one of the best.

Carter was in analysis mode now. She picked up the file Dante had assembled on Charlie Thorne and leafed through it for what was probably the twentieth time that day.

Dante grew uncomfortable watching her, so he let his gaze drift out the window. It was January and the sky was roofed with gray clouds. Squalls of snowflakes swirled outside the window. Even on a sunny day, the buildings of CIA headquarters were drab; today they looked ominous and foreboding.

Carter's eyes shifted from the file to the photograph once again.

Charlotte Thorne, aka Charlie, was a mix of many different races, although she didn't look like one more than any other. If Charlie had been ten years older, this would have been a huge asset. She could have passed for a very tan white person, a light-skinned black person, or Hispanic or Arab or Indian, or even partly Chinese. Looks like that would allow you to blend in anywhere on earth, to pass yourself off as almost any culture if you could speak the language.

But Dante hadn't suggested Charlie because of her appearance. It was because of her intelligence. Her IQ was off the charts. Director Carter had dozens of certified geniuses under her at the CIA, and none of them had IQs as high as Charlie Thorne's. Carter wouldn't have believed anyone could score that high if Dante hadn't provided three separate reports from respected psychologists to confirm it.

Carter flipped through the psych reports again. She

had read them twice already. The second time, she had marked them with a red pen, circling words or phrases that were important to her, for reasons that were good or bad. Finally, she looked back at Dante.

"She's brilliant," Carter said. "I'll give you that."

"She's *beyond* brilliant," Dante corrected. "She speaks at least twelve languages and can understand more. She's already been accepted to college, studying advanced math and theoretical physics. She has a photographic memory. . . ."

"There's no such thing as a photographic memory."

"Well, hers is as close as it gets. Her mind is wired differently than ours. She knows everything about everything. Science, history, art . . . you name it."

"Perhaps. But there are other characteristics of her personality that are more worrisome." Carter tapped some of the reports where she had made notes. "Rebellious. Headstrong. Conceited. Disrespectful of authority."

"Do you know who else was like that as a child?" Dante asked. "Albert Einstein. As well as Leonardo da Vinci, Isaac Newton, Charles Darwin, Benjamin Franklin, and every other groundbreaking genius you can name. Anyone that brilliant is going to chafe at authority. Because they're *smarter* than the authorities." Dante leaned across the conference table. "The CIA has been searching for Pandora ever since Einstein died, and we've gotten nowhere. So maybe we need someone as smart as Einstein to find it. And the closest person we have to Einstein right now is her." Dante thumped his finger on the photo of Charlie Thorne.

Carter's eyes fell to the photo again, then returned to Dante. Agent Garcia was mentally gifted himself; that was why Director Carter was even sitting here with him, considering his radical suggestion, when she had a thousand other things to do. Like dealing with the fallout from Bern.

Dante was only twenty-eight, but he had already proved himself in the field many times, rising rapidly through the ranks. Like Charlie Thorne, he was a blend of races, able to pass as almost any ethnicity he wanted, meaning he had served all over the world.

"Miss Thorne's disrespect for authority probably goes much farther than Einstein's ever did," Director Carter said. "As far as we know, Einstein never broke the law, whereas Miss Thorne has. And in rather spectacular fashion."

"That's exactly *why* she'll work for us."

Carter arched an eyebrow. "You want to blackmail her into helping us? That's not exactly going to make her respectful of authority."

"I can handle her."

Carter leafed through the file on Charlie Thorne

one last time, considering all the possible ramifications of bringing this girl aboard. The kid was a risky play, for sure. The chances were high that it wouldn't work. And yet, as Agent Garcia had said, these were desperate times. Carter's intelligence said the Furies were closing in on Pandora; meanwhile the CIA was no closer than it had been seven decades ago.

"This will have to be an unsanctioned mission," Carter said. "Completely off the books. There can't be any record that the CIA is coercing twelve-year-olds to work for us."

Dante smiled. "Of course not."

"That means a bare-bones operation as well. Only you and one other agent."

Dante's smile faded. "Only one other? That's crazy!"

"Weren't you just telling me it was time to try something crazy? If it helps, you can select whoever you want."

Dante didn't hesitate for a second. "Milana Moon."

Director Carter nodded. Even though she had thousands of agents working under her, she knew exactly who Moon was. The fact that Dante had named her so quickly simply confirmed his intelligence to her. "Fine. If she'll agree to it."

"I think I can convince her."

"Then we're done here." Carter snapped to her feet and slid the file back across the conference table to Dante. "Destroy that. And then go find Pandora."

TWO

Snowmass Mountain
Pitkin County, Colorado
One day later

No one had skied Deadman's Drop yet that year.

To begin with, it was illegal, lying outside the ski area boundary. Second, it was difficult to get to. After you took the Elk Camp lift all the way to the top of the mountain—11,325 feet above sea level— you still had to hike to get there. Up another mountain ridge. Through the snow. Struggling to get a breath in the thin air, lugging your skis or snowboard, until you finally reached the drop-in point.

But the real reason no one had skied Deadman's yet was because it lived up to its name and was extremely dangerous. Deadman's Drop was a couloir, a steep and narrow gouge in the rock, a sixty-degree slope flanked by sheer walls only a few feet apart. There was little room for error—and if you screwed up and busted your leg or tore an ACL, they couldn't send the ski patrol to get you. You'd have to claw your way out by yourself. And if all that wasn't scary enough, the couloir ended at a cliff. The ground simply dropped away, leaving a fifty-foot plummet down to the Grey Wolf ski run. There was no way out except over the edge.

Even if you did make it, and managed to stick the landing without breaking a leg or bashing your head on a rock, there was a decent chance the ski patrol would come after you—as you had now landed back on Snowmass property—and they'd yank your ski pass for the rest of the year as punishment for going outside the boundary. Unless you could outrun them, which was highly unlikely, because the ski patrol was staffed by incredible athletes who skied one hundred days a year.

But Charlie Thorne was skiing Deadman's Drop anyhow.

For her it was pure, unadulterated bliss. Two months' worth of virgin snow was piled up inside the couloir, and her skis floated over it as she fired through, whooping with joy. She didn't have the grace of an adult skier yet, slewing about like a rhino on roller skates, but she was a natural athlete with the devil-may-care attitude of a teenager, so she barreled ahead recklessly. Her long dark hair was tucked into a ski helmet, and her green eyes were hidden behind goggles, so all that was visible of her was her broad smile, which her friends considered a near-permanent fixture upon her face.

It was noon on a Tuesday. Charlie should have been in school.

Theoretical physics, to be specific.

But then, Charlie had shown up to her theoretical physics class only once this entire year besides exam days. She had arrived late on the first day of school, listened to fifteen minutes of Dr. Fromer's lecture, then grown bored and left to go mountain biking. Of course, Dr. Fromer hadn't been pleased about any of this. So he had thrown a bunch of extra questions into her most recent exam that weren't on anyone else's—on subjects that weren't even covered in the textbook—just to flunk her and teach her a lesson in humility while he was at it.

Charlie had aced the exam anyhow. She hadn't even needed the entire testing period. She had just sauntered in and casually done the math, the way other people might have jotted down a thank-you note, while all around her students ten years older than her—students who were *majoring* in theoretical physics—were tearing their hair out in frustration. It had taken her only thirty minutes, and she didn't even bother to check her work. And most infuriating of all, she had caught a mistake of Dr. Fromer's, circled it in red, and written, "Sloppy work. Try harder next time."

Similar things had happened in all of Charlie's classes. Charlie hadn't accepted her full scholarship to the University of Colorado for the coursework. She had done it to get away from her parents—and for the proximity to the mountains. The scholarship didn't mandate that she actually go to any of her classes, only that she pass them. So she spent her time hiking and biking and skiing with classmates, then showed up on exam days.

There *were* some courses that intrigued her, although they were all extracurricular and not for credit. Things like rock climbing, kayaking, and self-defense. Charlie was always on time for those, because they were fun.

The only real problem Charlie had was getting to the hiking trails and ski resorts. She might have been a genius, but she still didn't have a driver's license.

Luckily, Charlie wasn't the only student who had chosen the University of Colorado for its location. There were always plenty of others who were willing to skip a few days of school for some adventure in the mountains.

That was how she had gotten here, to Snowmass, even though it was four hours from campus. A few sorority girls had been thrilled to blow off class and give Charlie a ride out to the mountains in return for a free place to stay at a swanky ski-in, ski-out house. Charlie had claimed the house was her uncle's, when really she had rented it herself, because otherwise she would been stuck explaining *how* a twelve-year-old girl had enough money to rent a house that cost more than a thousand dollars a night, and Charlie didn't really feel like doing that.

The girls were cool, too. This was the second time Charlie had gone on a road trip with them. A lot of her fellow students didn't know how to behave around her, given her reputation as the tween who was ten times smarter than any of them. They were either condescending, treating her like she was a seven-year-old, or they were weirded out by her, whispering behind her back like she was a circus freak. However, these girls were fun and friendly—and they were rebellious, too. It was one of them, Eva, who had suggested skiing Deadman's Drop in the first place.

Eva probably hadn't thought Charlie would take her up on the challenge, but once Charlie agreed to it, Eva— and all the other girls—had been forced to agree to it as well. They couldn't let a twelve-year-old be braver than them, could they? They had been acting excited about Deadman's as they slipped under the boundary ropes and hiked up to it, but Charlie could tell that underneath the bravado they were all nervous and thinking that maybe Eva should have kept her big mouth shut.

Charlie didn't think it was such a big deal, though. She had gotten away with far more in her life than a little trespassing.

She whooped again as she came flying through the couloir.

Eva and the other girls followed, but much more

tentatively, worried about their safety—and Charlie's, too.

Charlie fired through a tight gap in the rocks, and the lip of the cliff came into view. It was as though the earth simply ended up ahead. There was a sharp white line where the snowpack stopped abruptly, nothing but bright blue sky beyond it.

The numbers instantly came to Charlie.

Her grin jacked up a few notches. She tightened her tuck and barreled straight for the edge.

Behind her, Eva and the other girls slid to a stop, cowed by the sight of the cliff—and worried that Charlie was heading right for it.

The girls all knew Charlie was an impressive skier for her age. The rumors around school were that she had grown up skiing somewhere back East, Vermont or Maine maybe. The girls had already seen her handle double black diamond runs with ease and had watched her pull double corks off the jumps in the terrain park. But this was different. This was Deadman's Drop. No matter how good a skier you were, you couldn't just jump right off a cliff. You had to check it out first, go to the lip and look down, figure out where you were going to take off and land, gather your nerve. You could *die* on this thing if you weren't careful—and it sure didn't look like Charlie Thorne was being careful. If anything, it looked like the girl had a couple of screws loose. Like maybe she wasn't as brilliant as everyone said; she might have had book smarts, but she obviously sucked at analyzing risk.

In truth, Charlie had already analyzed Deadman's Drop far more than any of the girls realized. She had carefully observed the end of the couloir from the ski lift down on the Grey Wolf run. She had assessed the height of the drop and the angle of the ground beneath it and worked out exactly how fast she needed to be going and where she needed to land and then rechecked her math two dozen times and memorized it all. Now all she had to do was enjoy the ride.

So while the other girls stopped in the couloir and held their breath, Charlie kept barreling forward, apparently unfazed by the sudden drop ahead, laughing like the happiest person on earth. And then she launched herself over the edge, into thin air.

As the ground dropped away from under her, Charlie was suddenly struck by a pang of fear and self-doubt. What if she had made a mistake in her math? She was five stories in the air above a ski slope. If she made any mistakes now, she could die.

So she focused on the numbers.

She saw them in her mind, etched onto the landscape of the earth before her. The numbers were the equations she had worked before, back on the ski lift. They told her how she needed to move, where she needed to land, what she had to do to survive. Better yet, they told her what she needed to do if she wanted to make this look *awesome*.

Her fear vanished and her confidence came flooding back. At exactly the right moment, she threw herself into a reverse somersault, whipping her shoulders back, arching her spine, watching the sky rotate in above her, then the cliff, then the horizon—and by then the ground had already rushed up to meet her, so she cocked her skis at forty-five degrees to match the slope, kinked her legs to cushion the impact, and nailed the landing. One second she was falling and the next she was skiing, glowing from the adrenaline surge, rocketing downhill for a few more seconds before dramatically skidding to a stop in a spray of snow.

The skiers on the Grey Wolf run stopped and gaped in astonishment at the young skier who had just appeared out of nowhere. The skiers on the Elk Camp lift who had witnessed the whole stunt burst into applause. Up in the couloir, Eva and the girls heaved sighs of relief that Charlie hadn't biffed the landing and killed herself. Charlie allowed herself a moment of grandstanding, flashing a smile to the spectators and taking a bow.

And then she saw Agent Milana Moon waiting for her.

THREE

Milana Moon and Dante Garcia had tracked Charlie with her phone. All phones had Global Positioning Systems in them, and the CIA had accessed that and triangulated Charlie's location. Dante had assumed they would be heading to Boulder, where the University of Colorado was, but they had discovered Charlie was in Aspen instead.

Due to the urgency of their mission, they had the use of a jet, albeit an outdated one the CIA had confiscated from some arms dealers twenty years earlier. Agent Moon, among her many other talents, was an instrument-rated pilot.

They landed at the Aspen airport, which was only a short cab ride from Snowmass. Dante and Milana could both ski, and they didn't want to sit at the bottom of the mountain for the whole day, waiting for Charlie to come down. Time was too precious in the hunt for Pandora. So they had rented skis and used the GPS to track Charlie more precisely.

It wasn't hard to blend in on a ski mountain. Far easier than it was to blend in on a city street, where people could be wearing anything from T-shirts and cargo shorts to three-piece suits. All skiers basically wore the same thing: heavy jackets, ski pants, helmets, scarves, and goggles. The helmets, scarves, and goggles had the added bonus of hiding the agents' faces.

They had fallen into the Elk Camp lift line behind Charlie and she hadn't even noticed. Or so they'd thought.

The plan was to apprehend Charlie nice and easy if they could: Wait for her to split off from her friends, maybe when she went to the bathroom. Then they'd grab her, badge her, and tell her she was under arrest. Hopefully she wouldn't try to run, but if she did, they'd cuff her and take her down. It should have been a cakewalk. It wasn't like they were bringing in a hardened criminal. Just a twelve-year-old girl. If anything, it seemed beneath their rank.

They had been a little thrown when Charlie and the girls had gone out of bounds, wondering how they could possibly follow them without drawing attention to themselves, but then Dante had talked to a ski bum, who had told them the girls were probably headed for Deadman's

Drop, and if so, that it would dump them right back onto Grey Wolf. The ski bum had even pointed out the exact spot where that would happen. So Milana Moon had posted herself there, acting like a normal skier waiting for her friends, while Dante had gone farther down the run to stand guard by the base of the ski lift, in case something went wrong.

Which was exactly what had just happened.

Dante knew a great deal about Charlie Thorne, but he had severely underestimated her ability to notice her surroundings, unaware that Charlie had made a point of honing that skill.

It was amazing how little most people really noticed in the world around them. All federal agents knew that eyewitness testimonies tended to be shaky at best. Most people could barely remember what they'd had for breakfast any given morning, let alone recall details about a suspect they might have seen for only a few seconds.

But Charlie Thorne was different. She had gotten away after breaking the law, but she didn't assume that would always be the case. Someday someone would come looking for her. Therefore, she always needed her guard up. She always had to be prepared for trouble.

Always had to be ready to run.

So she was constantly paying attention to everyone

around her, even here, at a ski resort. She had trained herself to focus on the people in the crowds, to notice what they were wearing, to look for patterns that were too statistically unusual to be a coincidence.

The woman standing downhill from where Charlie had landed on the ski run had been right behind her in the lift line on the way up the hill. There was nothing particularly unusual about her ski outfit, but this skier was tall for a woman, a few inches above average, and had the same distinct, strong jawline, so Charlie was sure it was the same person.

Charlie couldn't help herself; she started seeing the numbers.

It had been like this her whole life. Even when she was a little kid, well before anyone had tried to teach her math, the numbers had come to her. In fact, no one had ever *needed* to teach her math; she had simply worked everything out on her own. It hadn't been difficult. Instead, it had just seemed . . . obvious. It had all come so naturally, Charlie was five before she realized what she was doing was unusual. Until then she'd thought *everyone* instinctively knew how to add and subtract or how to calculate the volume of a box—or, for that matter, how to understand a foreign language by merely concentrating on its syntax and patterns as it was spoken.

To understand coincidence, you simply had to understand probability. For example, people were generally surprised if, in a group of thirty people, two turned out to share a birthday. But there was a greater than 70 percent chance this would happen. You just had to do the math:

$$1 - \left(\frac{(365-1) \times (365-2) \times (365-3) \ldots \times (365-29)}{365^{30}} \right) = 70.6\%$$

So now Charlie worked out the probability that someone who had been behind her in line on the way up the lift would be standing here thirty minutes later, at the exact spot where Deadman's Drop emptied back out onto the run. To do this Charlie considered a variety of factors, like the number of lifts at Snowmass, the amount of skiable terrain, and the approximate number of skiers there were on the mountain that day. She calculated a 0.08 percent chance, which was certainly within the realm of possibility, but still slim enough to be of concern.

But there was one way to definitely tell if this woman was following her.

Up in the couloir, Eva had finally gathered her nerve to make the jump off Deadman's Drop. It was hard for Charlie to tell where the suspicious woman was looking, given that she was wearing ski goggles, but her attention—at least for the moment—appeared to be on Eva.

Without even bothering to wave to her fellow skiers, or to see if Eva managed to land safely, Charlie turned and fled.

. . .

Milana Moon didn't notice Charlie had run for a moment. She was watching the next girl jumping off the cliff, unable to believe someone would risk her life for a stupid stunt like that, thinking there was a good chance the idiot was going to wipe out badly and snap her spine right there in front of everybody. As it happened, the girl *did* wipe out, tumbling down the slope, her skis and poles flying everywhere, but somehow she was okay. She lay there on the ski run, laughing at herself, then sat up and yelled to her friends, "Well, I really screwed that one up, didn't I?"

Then Milana returned her attention to Charlie—only Charlie wasn't standing there anymore. She was well down the ski run, in a racing tuck, going for speed.

Milana swore, then grabbed her phone and alerted Dante. "Dagger! It's Coyote! The rabbit's on the run!"

Dante was waiting down the hill, near the base of the ski lift. It was cold, just standing there, and a chill had started to seep into his bones. He was in position to catch Charlie if she ran, but the ground here was flatter, so he'd need ample warning from Milana to get up to speed. Now, as he saw Charlie flying down the hill toward him, he swore under his breath as well. Milana's warning hadn't come fast enough; Charlie had gotten the jump on her somehow.

Milana was coming too, but Charlie had a big lead on

her, at least thirty seconds. Dante dug his poles into the ground and moved into the middle of the ski run, blocking Charlie's path, ready to tackle her if he had to.

Only Charlie didn't stay on the run. Before she got to Dante, she suddenly veered to the right, into the trees.

She spotted us, Dante thought. *How on earth did she do that?*

Up the mountain, Milana changed course and followed Charlie into the woods.

Dante dug his poles into the ground again and took up the chase.

Charlie shot through the trees. Her hunch had been right. Someone had found her. She didn't know *who* exactly, but she wasn't going to wait around to find out. She had seen the second person down below, moving to block her escape, forcing her to take evasive action. And the one she had spotted on the ski run was coming after her too.

The problem now was that she was on tricky, unpredictable terrain. She had spent plenty of time studying the trail map for Snowmass, picking out potential escape routes in case of trouble, but she couldn't possibly scope them all out. She could only hope that she was skilled enough to handle them.

The forest was thick here, full of trees, and Charlie was certainly moving too quickly through it to be safe. She had no choice though. The female agent was coming after her just as fast, and whoever had been waiting down below— she couldn't even tell if it had been a man or a woman— was certainly coming as well. So Charlie skied through the trees as quickly as she could, reckless as it was.

It struck her that the forest was incredibly silent compared to the ski resort. The runs at Snowmass were filled with the noise of other skiers and the clanking machinery of the lifts, but here in the woods that sound had faded almost instantly, muffled by the canopy of branches and the deep snow on the ground. Every sound Charlie made—every swoosh of a turn, every grunt of exertion— sounded as loud as a cannon, but she could also clearly hear the woman pursuing her.

The woman was catching up.

Charlie might have been an excellent skier, but she was still only twelve. The woman was bigger and stronger than she was. And in addition to the trees, there was another big problem with fleeing on skis. Charlie was leaving tracks. Perfect, easy-to-follow tracks in the snow. Which was allowing the woman behind her to stay on her tail. Charlie needed to do something to slow her down.

So, in addition to looking for the best route to speed through the forest, she also had her mind racing, analyzing the gaps between all the trees ahead, estimating the distances between them, assessing which route would be optimal for what she needed. Finally, she spotted what she was hoping for. As she shot through the gap in the trees, she ducked and held a ski pole above her head, turned perpendicular to her. It wedged perfectly between the tree trunks, which yanked it from her grasp and held it there, suspended four feet above the ground.

Charlie didn't risk a look back to check her work. She could only plow ahead, hoping the pole would blend in with the forest and that the agent pursuing her would be too focused on following the tracks in the snow to be looking at the trees.

A startled yelp rang out through the quiet woods from behind her, followed by the sound of a skier getting clotheslined by a ski pole and then wiping out badly.

Charlie grinned, proud of her trick.

And then the ground dropped out from underneath her.

FOUR

Dante came upon Milana so fast he almost skied right into her.

She was sprawled directly in his path, having lost control for some reason and smashed into a tree. Dante swerved and nearly crashed himself, then stopped to check on her. Yes, that meant Charlie was widening the gap between them, but he feared Milana might have knocked herself unconscious, and he couldn't leave her behind. By the time he found his way back to her, she might have frozen to death.

"Moon . . . ," he began.

"I'm all right." She groaned. Although she was trying to hide the pain, he could hear it in her voice. "Go get her."

"Are you sure?"

"Yes! Go get that little jerk!" Milana pointed down the mountain.

So Dante went after Charlie. Only he'd lost some time and a lot of speed. It took him a while to get moving again, but the slow pace turned out to be a blessing in disguise. If Dante had been going much faster, he might have gone over the edge of the cliff.

It wasn't a huge cliff, but it came up fast, the lip of it hidden by a thick stand of trees. Even at his relatively slow speed, he almost pushed through the branches and went right off the top.

His fear for his own safety was immediately overwhelmed by his fear for Charlie Thorne. She probably wouldn't have seen the cliff coming either, and she would have been going fast. Dante didn't want the kid dead. He skidded to another stop and cautiously sidled to the lip, peering down over the edge.

The cliff was only thirty feet tall, but there were plenty of rocks at the bottom and only a narrow patch of snow to land in. To Dante's relief, Charlie wasn't splayed out on the rocks below. Instead, there was a pair of ski tracks leading through the snow into the trees, indicating that somehow, by incredible luck or incredible skill, the kid had nailed the landing and continued onward.

So she was still alive.

The problem was, there was now a cliff between Dante and Charlie, and Dante sure as heck wasn't about to ski off the top of this thing. He looked around and spotted an area to the side where the rock face gave way to a narrow slot filled with snow. That, he could handle. It wouldn't look good, but he could manage it. The bigger concern was that it would eat up more time. Dante had no choice though. He needed to bring in Charlie Thorne. The fate of the world depended on it.

Charlie was now well down the mountain ahead of Dante. The slope had grown steeper since the cliff, but Charlie wasn't going as fast now, exercising more caution. The cliff had caught her by surprise and shaken her. If another sudden drop came up, she wanted to be ready for it.

She knew she was lucky to have weathered the cliff as well as she had. She had been skiing recklessly, too focused on what was behind her instead of what was ahead. One moment there had been ground beneath her and the next there wasn't. There hadn't even been time to see the numbers before she hit the ground. She simply had to go on instinct. Somehow she had landed all right, though she had barely made it a few feet into the woods before catching a shoulder on a tree and getting knocked on her butt. Fortunately, she had been able to recover from that quickly and set on down the slope again, although her shoulder throbbed and she now had about five pounds of snow down her pants, freezing her rear end.

She had come down at least a thousand feet in elevation since Deadman's Drop. The thick stands of ever-greens were giving way to forests of aspen, and the bare branches of those trees were easier to pick out a path through. That was good news, as Charlie was growing tired. Fleeing her enemies was exhausting.

She was also starving. Skiing burned a ton of calories, and she and her friends had been planning to get lunch after Deadman's. Now Charlie was thinking that, in addition to being tired, she might be hypoglycemic as well.

As Charlie sliced through the trees, her phone rang in the pocket of her ski parka. It was probably Eva or one of the other girls, wondering where she was, annoyed at her for taking off without them and now making them look for her. There was no time to answer it though. They would have to just keep wondering where she was.

It made Charlie think about the mess her life had suddenly become. She had been hoping no one would have ever caught on to what she'd done. Hoping that she could continue coasting through college, then maybe do the same thing in graduate school, until she was eighteen and legally free from her parents. Then she could do whatever she wanted with the money she had socked away—as long as she was smart about it.

But now someone was onto her. Maybe they worked for the government and were technically the good guys. Or maybe they weren't good people at all. Either way

Charlie couldn't go back to college. That life was over. She would have to figure out something else.

She had money to get by in the meantime. She always carried money on her in case of trouble. A lot of money, in cash. And her passport, too. It was in a special belt strapped around her waist underneath her ski clothes.

As for Eva and the other girls, she would never see or speak to them again. They would probably sit around for the next fifteen minutes, getting more and more annoyed about her, and then they'd start to get worried, and then they'd probably notify the ski patrol, who'd notify the police, and then the rest of the afternoon would be everyone trying to piece the puzzle together of what had happened to her, a puzzle no one would ever fully figure out. . . .

There was a noise ahead.

Charlie stopped and listened.

She heard the sound of a motor in the distance. Then she heard it cut out, followed by the sounds of someone talking on a cell phone.

Charlie smiled. According to the ski map she had memorized, she had a good idea what lay ahead.

She continued down the slope, confident enough to move faster now. The ground flattened out a bit, and she carved quickly through the trees until she saw what she was looking for.

A house.

It was enormous. A mansion. Anyone who could afford the millions of dollars to buy a ski-in, ski-out property could also afford plenty of house. There were probably eight bedrooms and twice as many bathrooms, a gourmet kitchen, a grand dining hall, and a few rooms the owner didn't even know what to do with. And given that it was a second home—or maybe even a third or a fourth home—chances were the owners weren't even here.

The house sat at the end of a road that Charlie had seen from the ski lift at the bottom of the mountain. There were lots of enormous houses on the road, houses very much like this one. The road was gated and had a security post to keep people from coming in uninvited, though the guards wouldn't be that concerned with people going out.

A pickup truck was parked in the driveway, the truck of a local pool serviceman, probably here to check the hot tub. Any mansion by a ski run would certainly have a hot tub. Maybe two.

The truck would do nicely.

Charlie skied up to the house, popped off her skis, and abandoned them in the snow. She pulled her goggles up off her face but didn't bother taking her ski helmet off.

Then she checked the pickup to see if the keys had been left in it. It would save her some trouble if the pool guy was careless and had left them there. He hadn't though. So Charlie worked her way around the house, following the fresh footprints in the snow.

Sure enough, there was a hot tub, filled with heated water. The pool guy had just flipped the lid up, and steam was billowing into the air.

The guy was young and busy talking on his phone, the buds jammed in his ears, barely even focused on his work, so he didn't hear Charlie coming before he saw her. Then he stopped in midsentence and stared at her, trying to figure out what she was doing there. The dazed look in his eyes indicated he wasn't too bright.

Charlie knew she didn't appear threatening. She was tall, so she looked older than her twelve years, but she was still obviously only a young teenager at most. "Can you please give me the keys to your truck?" she asked, nice and easy. "It's an emergency."

The pool guy yanked the buds from his ears. "What kind of emergency?"

"The kind that requires your truck. Could you please just give me the keys?"

The pool guy laughed, like maybe this was a joke. "You want me to hand over the keys to my truck? Just like that?"

"Exactly," Charlie said. "I don't have the time to explain this in any more detail, so . . ."

"What happens if I don't give you the keys?" the guy

asked, taunting her. "Are you gonna take them from me, girlie?"

The guy's attitude was upsetting to Charlie. Instead of being concerned for what trouble she was in, he seemed amused, which wasn't cool. But she did her best to remain calm and said, "Thank you."

"For what?"

"I would have felt bad about taking your truck. But now that I realize you're a sexist jerk, that's not the case anymore."

The pool guy glowered at her, then gave her a little shove, knocking her back on her heels. "You think you can take my keys from me?"

Charlie sized the guy up. He was nearly a foot taller than her, but she had learned in self-defense class that size wasn't everything. In fact, big guys were often over-confident in their abilities. "Yes."

The pool guy laughed condescendingly. "I'd like to see you try."

"All right." Charlie hadn't expected things to come to this. She'd never had to fight anyone outside the dojo and wasn't completely sure she had what it took. But she needed that truck, fast, and now this guy was in her way. So she thought back to her martial arts classes and put everything she had learned into action.

Step one: When confronting someone bigger than

you, use their size against them. She lashed out a leg and swept the pool guy's legs out from under him. On the icy deck, it was easy. He slipped and landed flat on his back.

Step two: Incapacitate your enemy as quickly as possible. Charlie knew she wasn't strong enough to punch the guy's lights out, so instead she dropped onto his stomach with her knees, knocking the wind out of him.

Step three: Be prepared for a counterattack. Sure enough, it came. The pool guy made a lame attempt to try to swat her off him, but she caught his hand and wrenched two of the fingers backward. The pool guy wailed in pain and stopped fighting.

Charlie was surprised how easy it had all been. "The keys," she said. "Now. Or you'll need an ambulance."

With his free hand, the pool guy quickly fished the keys from his pocket and held them up to her.

Charlie snatched them away. "Give me your phone, too." She didn't want the guy calling the police the moment she left.

The pool guy wavered about ceding his phone, but another yank on his fingers made him change his mind. He handed that over too.

Step four: Make sure your challenger is down for good. According to Charlie's martial arts instructors, a lot of jerks would pretend to be down for the count and then attack again the moment you turned your back. So to be safe, she shoved the pool guy into the hot tub. He wasn't going to be able to run after her soaking wet in this weather. His clothes would freeze solid on him.

The guy howled and then called her a whole bunch of really offensive things.

"This could have been a whole lot easier on you if you hadn't been such a creep," Charlie said, and then ran for the truck, hoping she hadn't been delayed too long. There was no time to kick her bulky ski boots off to drive—she didn't remove her ski helmet or her gloves, either. She simply climbed into the truck and started it up.

Charlie had driven only once before; a few weeks earlier Eva had let Charlie tool around a supermarket parking lot in her car late at night in exchange for help with her homework. It hadn't been that complicated, and all vehicles worked pretty much the same. Charlie found the gear shift, put the truck in reverse, backed into the road, shifted into forward, and floored the gas.

Charlie had expected that driving on an icy road was considerably more complicated than driving on a dry parking lot—but she hadn't been prepared for how much more powerful the truck was than Eva's crappy car—or that it would be difficult to use the gas and brake pedals with ski boots on. The truck leapt forward and nearly plowed right into an aspen tree. Charlie swerved away, flattening a shrubbery, and then almost skidded right off the other side of the road. She swung back in the original direction, took out the neighbor's mailbox, and finally managed to wrest the truck under control. She hit the gas again and sped downhill, hoping she was on her way to freedom.

Suddenly, the second of her pursuers, the one who'd been at the bottom of the ski run, shot out of the trees, sliding into the center of the road ahead. At this range, it was now evident that he was a man, and a big man at that. He reached under his jacket, going for his gun.

Charlie knew what she needed to do. If she hit the accelerator, she could mow the agent down before he got the gun out. It'd be the idiot's own fault for doing something reckless like throwing himself in front of a truck on an icy road. By the time anyone found the body, Charlie would be long gone.

She willed herself to floor the pedal.

But she couldn't do it. She couldn't kill anyone. So she slammed on the brakes instead. The tires locked and the truck spun on the ice.

The man scrambled to the side of the road, dodging the bumper as it swung past, allowing Charlie to get her first good look at the man's face.

Dante Garcia, she thought. *I should have known.*

Then the truck nailed a snowbank and upended, and everything went black.

FIVE

Somewhere over Missouri

Charlie knew she was on a private jet before she opened her eyes. She had never been on a jet before, even though she could afford it, because chartering a jet as a twelve-year-old would have gathered attention she didn't want. But she knew enough about what a jet would be like to put the pieces together.

She could feel the vibrations of flight and hear the telltale purr of the twin engines. That meant she was on a plane. And yet she was facedown on a couch. It felt like fake leather against her face. Commercial planes didn't have fake leather seats. Or couches, for that matter.

Plus, it was relatively quiet. A commercial flight would be full of chatting fellow passengers, flight attendants doing food and beverage service, maybe a crying baby or two. The only noise Charlie could hear besides the engines was the occasional rustle of paper. It sounded like someone was reading.

Her captors had removed her ski helmet and pried the boots off her feet, but she was still wearing her other cold-weather clothes, so she was hot inside the plane. However, she didn't move. Instead, she remained still and kept her eyes closed, not wanting anyone to know she had regained consciousness yet, trying to piece together what she could.

First things first: She had been apprehended by the CIA. That's who Dante Garcia had worked for the last Charlie knew, and Dante would rather die than leave the Agency.

Second: Despite the wreck she had been in, she was feeling fine. She had lost consciousness, which was a concern, but she had no headache at all, which was good. Lucky she had kept that ski helmet on.

Third: She hadn't been handcuffed or bound in any way. Her wrists were free. Although something was wrapped around her left forearm. A Velcro strap with a tiny piece of metal placed over her median antebrachial vein. A pulse monitor.

Nuts, Charlie thought. She instantly willed herself to relax, but she knew it was too late. The pulse of someone awake was inevitably faster than that of someone asleep. Which meant . . .

"You can stop pretending," Dante said. "I know you're awake."

Charlie could actually hear him smiling.

"I'm not pretending," Charlie replied, keeping her eyes closed. "I'm recovering from that car wreck. I nearly killed myself trying to save your stupid butt. What kind of idiot jumps in front of a moving truck?"

"Twelve-year-old girls shouldn't be driving trucks in the first place. Or stealing them, for that matter." There was a slight rustle as Dante set down whatever he had been reading. "Although for you, stealing a truck is small potatoes, isn't it?"

Charlie chose not to answer that question. Instead, she said, "I could have a concussion. I should be in a hospital."

"That's not necessary. Agent Moon and I both have extensive medical training. We've been monitoring your vitals this whole time. You're fine."

Charlie reluctantly opened her eyes. Other than the split-second glimpse she had caught before wrecking the truck, this was the first time she had seen Dante in years. He looked almost exactly the same. Thick brown hair, gleaming hazel eyes; people had always said he was handsome. He had always been in good shape, too, but now he appeared stronger than ever, his wrestler's physique straining his clothes. Dante had changed into khakis, a blue button-down shirt, and an old sports jacket that was fraying at the collar. A loaded shoulder holster peeked from under his right armpit. A briefcase sat by his feet. He held his phone, which was relaying Charlie's pulse rate to him. He was grinning smugly, proud of himself.

Charlie said, "I could have run you over, you know."

"Don't flatter yourself. I would have shot the tires out first."

"Yeah, right. If I weren't such a nice person, you'd be roadkill right now and I'd already be halfway around the world. . . ." Charlie trailed off, suddenly concerned. She dropped her hand to where her money belt had been wrapped around her waist. It wasn't there. "Where's my passport?" she demanded. "And my money? And my phone?"

"They're in a safe place," Dante replied.

"They were already safe. Can I have them back?"

"Eventually. If you behave."

Charlie sighed. "You are such a schmuck."

She sat up, jammed her hands in her pockets, and pouted, doing her best to act like a petulant twelve-year-old. It wasn't that hard, as she was already ticked off. But the show was really designed to hide the fact that she was checking her jacket to see if they'd found *everything* she'd had on her.

They hadn't. Charlie felt a small, hard object tucked

into one of the pockets in the liner and suppressed a smile. This was something she could use to her advantage. When the opportunity presented itself.

In the meantime, Charlie took in her surroundings. The jet looked as if it hadn't been remodeled in decades: The upholstery was done in faded pastels, and the thick-pile carpet had been trampled bare in patches. The couch Charlie sat on stretched along the left wall of the cabin toward the rear of the plane. Dante sat across the narrow aisle in a seat that faced the couch. There was a small table next to him, flanked by another seat. Between them and the cockpit were four more seats, these ones standard airline seats, two facing forward, two facing back. At the rear of the jet was a small kitchenette and a door to what must have been the bathroom.

The window shades were up. The sky was glowing orange. Sunset. According to Charlie's watch, it was only three o'clock back in Colorado, so they must have been heading east.

The woman who had chased her was in the pilot's seat, the cockpit door open so she and Dante could stay in contact. The jet was on autopilot, so the woman didn't have to pay attention to what was in front of her. She was swiveled around, looking back toward Charlie.

This was the first time Charlie had a good look at the woman's face unobscured by ski goggles or a helmet.

She was striking, with wide cheekbones, raven hair tied back in a ponytail, and dark eyes that shone with intelligence.

"Hi, Agent Moon," Charlie said, nice and friendly.

"Hello, Charlotte," Milana said.

"Please don't call me that. My friends call me Charlie."

"I'm not your friend," Milana replied. There was a coldness to her voice that said she wasn't joking.

"Your loss," Charlie said, which provoked the tiniest trace of a smile from Milana. Charlie studied the features of her face. "Are you Native American?" Charlie asked.

Milana blinked. She tried to hide it, but she seemed impressed that Charlie had picked up on this. "Yes."

"What tribe?"

"We don't have time for small talk right now." Milana swiveled back around in her chair and resumed flying the jet.

Charlie returned her attention to Dante. "Do we have time to eat? I missed lunch, seeing as I've been unconscious."

"We picked up some sandwiches before we got on the plane." Dante nodded toward the kitchenette.

Charlie stood and headed to the back of the jet. She didn't feel dizzy or wobbly, which was a good sign. She was concerned about the fact that she had been knocked unconscious, but her brain seemed to be working all right. She did a few advanced calculus problems in her head, just to confirm this.

There was a small refrigerator. Inside were sandwiches wrapped in plastic. One of them was tuna fish and roast beef on rye bread. With pickles.

"Ugh." Charlie groaned. "Dante, I see you still have the most disgusting sense of taste on earth."

"You don't have to eat it," Dante replied. "There's one for you in there."

Charlie found a turkey with Havarti cheese on sourdough and smiled despite herself. Dante had remembered it was her favorite.

In the cockpit, Milana Moon perked up at this exchange, trying to understand Dante's connection to Charlie Thorne. There was apparently more to it than he had let on. He obviously hadn't learned about this kid's existence recently. He *knew* her somehow.

There was also a can of Cherry Coke in the fridge. Another of Charlie's favorites. She returned to the couch with it and the sandwich and flopped down. "Just so we're clear here, you're making a mistake. I haven't done anything illegal."

"Well, there we have a difference of opinion," Dante replied. "Yours versus everyone else in the world's. Most people would say that stealing forty million dollars is illegal."

Despite her best intentions, Charlie couldn't hide her reaction. Dante had the number almost exactly right. Which meant he knew all about Barracuda. Her face filled with worry, but then she caught herself and tried her best to recover her calm facade. "I didn't steal anything," she said coolly. "I simply took back what they had stolen from me."

"You never had forty million dollars."

"I added some interest." Charlie took a bite of her sandwich. "Not that it really matters. I'm obviously not under arrest."

Dante arched an eyebrow, which he had always done when Charlie said something that got his attention. "Why do you say that?"

"First of all, I'm sure you know where I'm going to college. I made the national news when I picked Colorado over Harvard and Yale and all the other schools that accepted me. So if you really wanted to bust me, it would have been much easier to do it there, rather than coming to Snowmass and ambushing me on a ski mountain."

Even though Charlie was right, Dante didn't give her the benefit of admitting it. He merely stood, went to the back of the plane, and got his own sandwich from the fridge.

"Next," Charlie went on, "*if* I had stolen this money— and I'm not saying I did—that isn't the CIA's jurisdiction anyhow. So you wouldn't even be making the bust."

"Agent Moon, are you hungry?" Dante called.

"Starving," Milana replied.

Dante grabbed a sandwich and a Diet Coke and walked them up to the cockpit for Milana.

Charlie took another bite of her sandwich and spoke with her mouth full. "Finally, I know this probably isn't the snazziest jet in the CIA's fleet, but still, it's a *jet*. And I've heard that jet fuel is really expensive. So I'm betting the Agency doesn't loan jets out at the drop of a hat. Busting a kid like me certainly doesn't qualify as a national emergency. Therefore, something else must be going on. Something serious. Because you wanted me fast. The question is: Why?"

Dante returned to his seat, considered Charlie a moment, then laid his cards on the table. "We want you to work for us."

Charlie nodded, as though she had expected this all along. "And your plan is to use my supposed crimes to blackmail me into it?"

"The thought had crossed my mind."

"Even though I'm not exactly spy material?"

"You have certain gifts we believe would be helpful in this particular case."

Charlie took a sip of her soda, then said, "I pass."

Dante's eyebrow arched again. "What?"

"Thanks, but no thanks. I don't want to be a spy. It

sounds like a lousy job. The pay stinks, you answer to the government, and people occasionally try to kill you. Plus, your blackmail plan isn't going to work. I'm only *twelve*, Dante. You can't force me to do anything I don't want to. It'd make the CIA look like a bunch of slimeballs."

Dante said, "I'm not going to force you to do anything, Charlie. You're going to *choose* to help us of your own free will."

"And why is that?"

"Because if you don't, your life—and the lives of billions of other people—will be in danger."

SIX

Why don't you tell me what all this is about?" Charlie said.

"How much do you know about Albert Einstein?"

"Plenty. I've read a couple books about him. Did you know he never wore socks? He hated it when they got holes in them."

"Have you ever heard of something he developed called Pandora?" Dante asked.

"No," Charlie replied, although she was intrigued. It surprised her that there could be anything Einstein had come up with that hadn't been in any of the biographies she'd read.

"Sometimes it's referred to by its German name: *Pandorabüchse*."

"I still haven't heard of it. Contrary to popular belief, I don't inherently know *everything*."

Dante checked his phone to see if there had been a change in Charlie's heart rate. That might have happened if she was lying. But it held steady. Charlie seemed to be telling the truth.

"Pandora is an equation," Dante explained. "Related to the theory of special relativity. I'm assuming you know about that."

"Duh. *Everyone* knows about that."

"So, why don't you tell me what you know about it?" Dante took a bite of his roast beef, tuna fish, and pickle sandwich.

"Could you stop eating that in front of me?" Charlie asked. "I'm getting nauseated just watching you."

"I'm hungry. I had to skip lunch today to apprehend you."

"You know how the CIA does really annoying things to force bad guys to give up? Like blasting them with awful music at high volumes? They should just send you in and have you eat that sandwich in front of the bad guys. And maybe let them smell your breath afterward. I'm sure they would surrender in droves."

Dante's smile faded slightly at the mention of his breath and he glanced toward Milana, as though worried she had overheard this. She was still focused on flying the plane though. So Dante made a show of setting the sandwich down and said, "Satisfied?"

"Yes."

"Now tell me what you know about special relativity."

"Okay. Einstein published it in 1905—and the world has never been the same. Essentially, Einstein deduced that matter and energy are the same thing, which led to the most famous equation in history: $E = MC^2$. The amount of energy in something (E) is equal to the quantity of matter within it, which is its mass (M) times the speed of light (C) squared. Which is the speed of light multiplied by the speed of light." Charlie settled back on the couch and dug back into her sandwich.

Dante stared at her. "That's all you've got?"

"How much more do you want?"

"If I were your professor, I'd give you a D for that."

"Well, you're not my professor. What's the point of all this?"

"I want to make sure you know what the equation *means*. Give me more than just the elementary school version."

Charlie sighed. "Fine. Just about everyone has heard of $E = MC^2$, but what most people don't realize is exactly how big 'C squared' is: The speed of light is nearly three hundred million meters per second. Square that and you're at over a quadrillion. That's a massive number.

A quadrillion seconds ago, the earth was just forming. Multiply the mass of something by a number that large and . . . Well, what Einstein's equation really means is that inside even the tiniest bit of matter, there's a staggering amount of energy. For example, in one teaspoon of plutonium, there's enough energy to run a single lightbulb for a hundred million years—or better yet, to power all of Manhattan for a day."

Dante smiled, looking pleased. "Very good."

"Gee, thanks, Professor," Charlie said mockingly. "Do I get an A now?"

Dante ignored her and grew serious. "With relativity, Einstein handed us the power of the atom. But there were always rumors that he was never satisfied with the equation. It's obviously correct, but not easy to use. It's not hard to obtain energy from coal or petroleum—you just burn them—but to get energy from something as small as an atom is immensely complicated. Even after Einstein developed the theory, it took hundreds of the world's greatest minds several decades to figure out how to put it to practical use."

"You mean nuclear bombs?"

"Nuclear energy too. But even now our methods to extract that energy aren't very efficient—or safe. Well, the story goes that at some point in his life, Einstein proposed there might be a shortcut: another equation that would make the process of converting mass to energy considerably easier. He called it *Pandorabüchse*—or Pandora's box, though it's usually just referred to as Pandora. You know the myth of Pandora, right?"

"Of course," Charlie replied. "In Greek mythology, Pandora was the first woman. Her story mirrors that of Eve in the Bible, in that both women are blamed for humanity's fall from grace. In a lot of those old myths, women were nothing but trouble. I'm betting men wrote them."

"Let's focus on the story," Dante said.

"Fine. Originally, the world was paradise—and then Pandora came along. She was given a box and told never to open it, but curiosity got the better of her. The box contained the Furies—great evils that were then unleashed upon the world. Which was a total setup. Honestly, what jerk gives someone a present and tells them they can't open it?"

"But the box also contained hope," Dante added. "In Einstein's view, his new equation would have a similar impact. There was hope: With Pandora, the world's energy problems would be solved. But on the flip side, there was a very significant danger that—"

"Any jerk with an ax to grind could build a nuclear weapon." Charlie's cocky attitude vanished. Her face was now full of concern.

"Exactly," Dante agreed. "The only thing that has kept nuclear power out of the hands of dangerous people is the difficulty of using it. But if it was easy . . . well, the world would be a very scary place. Anyone who got ahold of Pandora would have the capacity for incredible destruction. Which is why, according to the story, Einstein decided to stop looking for it. He lost his faith in humanity and decided that the rest of us simply couldn't be trusted to do the right thing."

Charlie sat forward on the couch, her eyes now riveted on Dante. According to her heart monitor, her pulse was rising with excitement. "I'm guessing that's not the only version of the story."

Dante held her gaze for a moment before admitting, "No. The other version says that Einstein let everyone *think* he stopped looking for Pandora—but he didn't. Despite his reservations, he couldn't keep himself from unlocking the secrets of the universe. And, being Einstein, he succeeded. Only once he figured out the equation, he knew humanity wasn't ready for it, so he hid it."

"Where?" Charlie asked.

"I don't know. No one has ever been able to find it."

"No one?" Charlie burst into laughter. "Then it probably doesn't exist."

"The CIA thinks it does."

"Really? It's been nearly seventy years since Einstein

died. How many agents have you sent looking for this equation?"

"I don't know the exact number. . . ."

"Well, I'll bet it's big. And the CIA can't be the only organization that's heard about Pandora. I'm sure someone leaked that info to the Russian KGB or British MI6 or who-knows-what-else along the line. So hundreds, maybe thousands of agents have been scouring the earth for this thing for seven decades and come up dry?"

"Yes."

"Then you don't have anything to worry about. Pandora's a myth."

"I don't think so. . . ."

"Like I said, I've read plenty about Einstein. There's no record of Pandora. Einstein never wrote anything about it. He never said anything about it. Not once, in his entire life."

"Actually," Dante said, "that's not quite true."

Charlie's pulse grew even faster. "What do you have?"

"Proof that Pandora existed. And a clue to where it might be hidden."

"From where?"

"Einstein himself. The night he died."

Charlie frowned. "The CIA has had a clue to Pandora's location for all this time and has never been able to find it?"

"Apparently we don't understand the clue."

"And you think *I* can figure it out? When all those other thousands of people couldn't?"

"Why not? You're as smart as Einstein. . . ."

"*No one* has ever been as smart as Einstein!"

"Well, we need you to be."

Charlie stared at Dante, struck by the harsh tone of his voice. Suddenly she understood the urgency of the mission. She knew why the CIA had sent a jet for her, why they couldn't even wait for her to finish her day of skiing before apprehending her.

"Someone bad has found Pandora?" she asked.

"Not yet," Dante said. "But they will soon. Because unlike us, they already know where it is."

SEVEN

Limassol ferry port
The Isle of Cyprus

The people on the docks never saw it coming.

The nuclear bomb detonated without warning. Although it was barely the size of a suitcase, easy to smuggle aboard a passenger ferry, it created a staggering amount of devastation.

Everything within a mile radius was vaporized. In the three miles beyond that, buildings shattered, cars were tossed like leaves, and people were killed in an instant by the shock wave. Those were the lucky ones. The people farther from the explosion found their world destroyed, their cities devastated by blast winds, their bodies scorched by heat and poisoned by radiation. As the mushroom cloud rose into the sky, they all saw that the End of Days had come.

Alexei Kolyenko blinked, and the fire and carnage vanished. Before his eyes, reality returned. Life continued on the docks as before, thousands of people unloading cargo, shuttling between ferries, lined up at customs. They went about their lives in blissful ignorance, assuming they were safe, thinking that the punishment Alexei had imagined would never come.

But it would. Alexei would bring it to them soon.

Not to *these* people, of course. Limassol was too small, a mere maritime crossroads. No, when Alexei and his men set off the real bombs, they would target much larger cities, places teeming with people of inferior races. Cairo. Tehran. Karachi. Tel Aviv. Bombay.

He would destroy them all.

The day was close. Alexei knew it. God had willed it. Pandora hadn't been in Bern, but now, thanks to a fortuitous twist of fate, he knew where Einstein's equation was really hidden. After ten days of arduous travel, Alexei and his team were almost there.

They filed through the crowded docks, passing from one ferry to the next, two of them pretending to be friends on holiday, the others going solo, acting like businessmen anxious to get home. All were respectful and courteous at customs, cautious not to arouse suspicion.

After Bern, Interpol would be hunting for them—and the CIA, too. But Interpol and the CIA were like blind men fumbling in the dark. They had no idea where Alexei and his men were. The manhunt was probably still focused on Switzerland, the authorities assuming his team couldn't possibly get this far. But it wasn't hard to pass from one European country to another if you put a little effort into it.

Even in these days of heightened security, there were still giant holes on the borders of most countries. And even if they were patrolled, the guards were far more worried about refugees funneling into the west than white men heading east.

Refugees, Alexei thought hatefully. Europe was teeming with them these days. They were streaming in by the millions, leaving their own wretched countries behind to ruin others. They were disgusting, foul, uneducated people who brought nothing but trouble. Their customs were abominable, their languages shrill—and when they assimilated, they were even worse. Then they stole jobs that should have gone to *real* people.

Alexei had seen it happen time and time again. In Germany, his home country, he had lost many jobs to immigrants, as had his friends. The cities of Berlin and Munich and Nuremberg, which had once been beautiful and respectable, were now cesspits. Everywhere you looked, there were people of inferior races: working in stores, repairing appliances, driving cabs. Restaurants filled with immigrants served repugnant food from far-off lands instead of the food Alexei had grown up with. And unless someone did something about it, the surge would never stop. These people bred like rats, overpopulating their own countries. There were now millions of them with no place to go except Europe.

But Alexei knew how to deal with rats. You couldn't merely kill the ones who had invaded your home. More would keep coming. But if you found their nests and wiped them out there, then your rat problem would be done.

Alexei knew he was the one who would do this. God had chosen him to do it. How else could you explain how fate had pointed him to Pandora?

It had happened twice in his life.

The first time had been two years earlier. He had been at a bar in his hometown, grumbling with his friends about how they couldn't find work, about how the immigrants had taken all the good jobs. The bar was crowded, even though it was the middle of the day. There were many men like him in Europe these days, idle and angry. Alexei was at the bar most days, and most days were like one another. Until the day fate changed everything.

An old man sat beside him at the bar. A man Alexei had never seen before. The old man was angry too.

Alexei was complaining about the immigrants, as usual, when the old man suddenly interrupted him. "Do you really want to do something about these people?" the man demanded. "Or do you want to just sit on a barstool all day, wasting your life away?"

"I want to do something!" Alexei told him.

"Then I have a job for you," the old man said, and proceeded to tell Alexei an incredible story. He had been drinking too, and at first Alexei thought the story might be the ravings of an alcoholic. It seemed the man had tried to tell the story to many people in the bar that day, only to be shunned. But Alexei didn't turn the man away. He listened. And the more he listened, the more excited he became.

The old man had been a KGB spy in Eastern Europe for many years, undermining the Americans. Somewhere along the line, he and his team had captured an American spy. The penalty for espionage in their country was death, and the American was a man of weak nature. He cowardly offered secrets in return for his life. The old man and his fellow agents listened as the American spilled his guts—and then they killed him anyhow.

One of the secrets the American had told was about the night the great scientist Albert Einstein had died. The American had been a junior agent back then, on an assignment he considered pointless, monitoring Einstein's house. For months it had been dull and boring. It was almost as if Einstein knew he was being listened to. But on the night he died, Einstein was given morphine—

and with his defenses down, he had finally said something of interest. He had spoken of an equation called Pandora. The most dangerous equation of all time. And what was more, he had given a clue to its whereabouts.

The CIA hadn't been able to make sense of the clue— and, as it turned out, neither had he and his fellow spies in the KGB, although they had followed dead ends for years. However, the old man now had one more idea as to where the clue might lead . . . but he was too elderly to follow through with it. He was looking for a younger man, or really a team of younger men, to complete what he had been unable to.

He believed Pandora was in Bern, Switzerland.

Alexei was intrigued, and he had friends who were interested in Pandora as well, but they didn't have the money to go to Switzerland at the time, even though the country was right next door to Germany. It had taken months to scrape the funds together, working the few lousy part-time jobs they could get, thanks to the refugees. The old man had died in the meantime.

Alexei and his team called themselves Das Furii. And they eventually made their way to Bern to see if Pandora was where the old man had said it was.

It wasn't.

But then the second twist of fate occurred, when the next clue to Pandora's location presented itself. Which was why Alexei and the rest of Das Furii were now here, in Limassol, crossing the Mediterranean.

It had been difficult to get here from Bern. He and his friends had to make it over the Alps, in winter. But they were all strong men of the superior race, built for survival and devoted to their cause. They had made it over the mountains into Italy, then taken a train to the coast, where they boarded the ferry to Limassol.

Technically, they weren't even entering Limassol; they were merely passing from one ferry to another at the ship terminal. Alexei was the first to reach the boat that would take them to their final destination. The customs agent gave him little scrutiny. He merely checked Alexei's boarding pass and passport, then stamped both and waved him toward the gangplank.

As Alexei headed up it, a great commotion grabbed his attention. A fishing boat had arrived at the dock, filled with Arab refugees. Alexei had learned much Arabic over the years, from the people who had flooded his homeland. He wasn't fluent, but he could piece together their story. In desperation, they had tried crossing the Mediterranean in a boat that was too small for all of them, with no training for the sea. The boat had sunk, of course. Many had drowned, and those who had survived had floundered in the water for days until the fishermen had rescued them. Now they were barely alive, their bodies shrunken, their skin blistered, begging for help.

Alexei turned his back on them in disgust, angry at the fishermen for taking mercy on them. They should have been left to drown. The world would have been a better place without them.

Alexei would make the world a better place once he found Pandora. A much better place.

Behind him, the final member of Das Furii ascended the gangplank, the last passenger to board the ferry. The others were already aboard. There had been no troubles. None of the customs agents had given them a second glance.

The ferry pulled out of the harbor, leaving Europe behind and heading into the Mediterranean, taking Alexei toward the place where Einstein's last equation was hidden.

Soon, the power of God would be in his possession, and he would no longer have to imagine what Armageddon would look like. He would make the whole world see for itself.

EIGHT

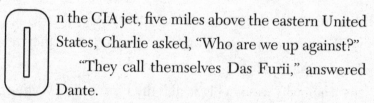n the CIA jet, five miles above the eastern United States, Charlie asked, "Who are we up against?"

"They call themselves Das Furii," answered Dante.

"The Furies," Charlie translated.

"Correct. They're a small terrorist sect from Eastern Europe. White supremacists, anti-immigration. The members are from a few different countries: Poland, Austria, Germany—but they're based in Germany and communicate primarily in German. Until recently they were working on a small scale, attacking immigrants: smashing windows, throwing Molotov cocktails into refugee camps, a few cases of assault."

"Quality people," Charlie said sarcastically.

"Sadly, there are plenty of groups like that in the world. We can't even keep track of them all. But then, a few months ago, the Furies shifted their behavior. They stopped their usual attacks and headed for Bern, Switzerland."

"Where Einstein lived when he developed the theory of relativity. There's a museum about him there, in his old house."

"Exactly. In fact, the Furies were paying a lot of attention to that museum. They rented an apartment close by and started making visits to the museum archives."

"Surely if the CIA has been looking for Pandora all these years, they've searched that museum."

"Dozens of times. Hundreds maybe. And they've always come up dry."

"Then why was it a big deal if the Furies were visiting the place? It's a dead end."

"It's a big deal because they were the first terrorist cell to ever show an interest in the archives. So Interpol started paying attention, which made *us* start paying attention. We alerted our agents in the area. And they reported back that the Furies weren't merely interested in Einstein. They seemed to know about Pandora."

"Which was also a first?"

"Yes."

"How'd you find out?"

"We eavesdropped on their conversations. Not only did we hear them discussing Pandora, but it became evident that they had"—Dante paused, choosing his words carefully—"sensitive information about the equation. Information they shouldn't have had."

"What kind of information?"

"Knowledge of some recordings that, until that point, the CIA thought they had kept secret."

"How'd they get the recordings?"

"We don't know."

Charlie polished off her sandwich, considering all this. "These guys are chasing a dead end, and they did such a lousy job of it that they tipped off Interpol and the CIA and then blabbed about their top-secret information. They don't sound like a very effective terrorist cell. They sound like a bunch of stupid thugs."

"Most terrorist cells aren't exactly full of Einsteins. They tend to be mostly angry young men who just want to lash out at the world. . . ."

"*Men*," Charlie repeated pointedly.

"Yes," Dante agreed. "And their methods tend to be blunt and primitive. They use pipe bombs and other rudimentary explosives. The 9/11 attack on the World Trade Center, the deadliest terrorist attack in US history, was carried out with box cutters. But just because these people aren't brilliant doesn't make them any less dangerous. In fact, you could argue that it makes them *more* dangerous, because they don't realize the full consequences of their actions. And if they get ahold of Pandora, then they'll be *really* dangerous."

"Are they still in Bern?"

"No." Dante broke eye contact with Charlie as he answered, indicating he was hiding something.

Charlie didn't call him on it—for the moment. "Where are they now?"

Dante's gaze returned to hers. "We don't know. They vanished from the city ten days ago. Interpol set up a dragnet, but somehow they slipped through."

"Why did they leave so suddenly? Did they figure out you guys were watching them?"

Dante's eyes flicked away again. "Of course not."

Charlie looked toward the cockpit, checking to see what Agent Moon's response to all this was. Moon didn't appear to be paying attention to the conversation at all, and seemed completely focused on flying the plane. Charlie suspected that Moon *was* listening to everything she said, however. She got the idea that Moon was the type who observed far more than she spoke and who didn't miss much.

Beyond Moon, on the ancient tech of the jet's instrument panel, Charlie could see they were closing in on eastern Virginia, where the CIA was headquartered.

Charlie returned her attention to Dante and asked, "So now you want me to help you figure out where the Furies went?"

Dante said, "I want you to help me figure out where they're *going*. So we can beat them there and keep Pandora out of our enemies' hands once and for all."

"I have a demand first."

"You're in no position to make demands."

"Actually, I'm in a *great* position to make demands. You're in no position to deny them."

"We're talking about the safety of the free world here," Dante snapped. "You'd put your own interests before that?"

"I would prefer not to go to jail," Charlie said. "Or juvenile hall or wherever else you're thinking of sending me."

"I thought you said you were innocent."

"I *am* innocent, but the CIA doesn't seem to agree with that. So, if I'm going to do you a solid here, I want a guarantee that you'll get off my back and let me be. Forever. I want a signed letter from the director of the CIA claiming there's no evidence for any government agency to convict me of *any* crime. There will be no attempt to punish me in any way. After I locate Pandora for you, I'm a free person, legally entitled to all my assets."

Dante chewed on that for a while before admitting, "I suppose we could manage that."

"Can you manage it *now*?"

Dante sighed, then picked up the briefcase by his seat,

unlocked it, removed a letter, and handed it to Charlie.

Charlie read it over. It was exactly what she had just asked for. "You weren't going to give this to me unless I demanded it?"

"CIA policy is to not make offers like that right away. If the criminals in question don't think to protect themselves, that's their fault."

"I'm not a criminal," Charlie said heatedly.

"Well, if you can find Pandora, then the CIA will agree with you."

Charlie stuck her tongue out at Dante.

He laughed at her. The kid might have put up a mature front, but behind it all she was still twelve.

Charlie folded the letter and put it in her pocket. Then she looked back at Dante and said, "So, are you ever going to tell me what this 'sensitive information' the Furies has is?"

Dante opened his briefcase again. "What I'm about to show you is classified. I can't tell you how many strings I had to pull to get you clearance to see it. As far as the CIA is concerned, it doesn't exist." He took out some papers and passed them to Charlie.

Charlie took a look at them and gasped in surprise.

NINE

The pages Charlie held were photocopies of photocopies, so many generations down the line, the paper was gray and the print was barely legible. It was a typed transcript of a conversation, although it began halfway through:

```
MIC#5-MASTER BEDROOM (CONT'D)

DOCTOR: I doubt he'll make it through

the night. He's beyond anything I can

do . . . although I could ease his pain

with some morphine. . . .

HELEN DUKAS: No! He gave me strict

orders. No painkillers . . .

DOCTOR: Please. He's in tremendous pain.

He's running a 104-degree fever . . .

(OBSCURED) . . . a violation of my oath

to refuse such care.
```

Charlie looked up at Dante, stunned. "This is from Einstein's house the night he died. The CIA had it bugged?"

"Why do you assume it was us?"

"Besides the fact that you have this transcript? The US government was always uneasy about Einstein. He was a big agitator for peace. Even though he originally pressed President Roosevelt to begin the Manhattan Project, he refused to work on it. During the Red Scare, he publicly called on scientists to refuse to testify to Joseph McCarthy. He was outspoken and popular. And he was theoretically working on Pandora, the world's next great weapon. How could the CIA resist?"

Dante raised his hands. "Okay. Yes. The Agency bugged him."

Charlie swallowed her annoyance and returned her attention to the transcript. She read it carefully, piecing together the events of the night, looking up only when she came to Einstein's final words:

Pandorabüchse. Sie ist im den Holm. Die Gleichung muss geschützt werden.

"Do you understand it?" Dante asked.

"Of course. It's only German. 'Pandora's box. It's in the railing. The equation must be protected.'"

"Correct."

"Did the CIA search the railings in the house?"

"Every last one," Dante replied.

"Did they try . . . ?"

"Finish reading it," Dante said. "Then we'll talk."

Charlie turned back to the transcript. She read the rest, up until the strange men arrived and stopped Ernst Klein from destroying Einstein's papers, at which point the transcript ended abruptly. Charlie set the papers aside, astonished by everything she had learned. "Wow. The CIA really screwed this up, big-time."

"Why do you say that?"

"Hiding Pandora must have been kind of a Hail Mary pass for Einstein. He was assuming that if he made the equation extremely difficult to find, then anyone intelligent enough to locate it would also be wise enough to use it properly. Therefore, there's no reason for Einstein to ask anyone to destroy it—unless you know two things: Einstein suspected his house was bugged, and he spoke under the influence of morphine."

Dante leaned forward intently. "Why?"

Charlie explained. "From what I understand, Einstein was always extremely cautious about remaining in control of his thoughts. He rarely drank and never used drugs. Because alcohol and drugs make people do stupid things. But then, on Einstein's deathbed, his regular doctor—a man he surely trusted—isn't there. Instead, some naive kid shows up, disobeys the housekeeper's orders, and gives Einstein morphine. Einstein loses control and talks about Pandora—but since he's whacked out on drugs, he speaks in German, the language of his childhood. The doctor doesn't understand him. Meanwhile, the housekeeper calls Ernst Klein, whose worst fears are confirmed: Einstein has revealed that Pandora exists. Klein knows it's in the house—but he doesn't know where. Therefore, he has only one choice: to destroy everything. But a goon squad stops him before he can finish the job. That's the CIA, I assume?"

Dante reluctantly nodded.

Charlie tossed the transcript back to him. "How's the story end?"

Dante said, "The Agency impounded everything Klein failed to destroy—although they quickly replaced most of the documents. That way, Princeton, which had claim to anything Einstein produced while employed there, wouldn't realize anything had been taken. Klein and Helen Dukas, the housekeeper, threatened to go to the police, but the Agency was able to prevent this from happening."

"How?"

"A private meeting with President Eisenhower was arranged. Miss Dukas's concerns were assuaged. Klein wasn't so easy. He didn't go to the police, but it was evident he never got over the belief that he'd failed Einstein. He died in a car wreck a few months later. Alcohol was involved."

"That seems awfully convenient for the CIA."

Dante let this slide. "Given Einstein's final words, every railing in the house was examined. Over the years, they were all removed and replaced, one by one. They were checked for engravings, x-rayed, taken apart splinter by splinter. There was nothing inscribed on or hidden inside them."

"'*Holm*' can also mean 'shaft,'" Charlie pointed out. "Did the CIA check the fireplace?"

"They took the whole thing apart brick by brick. And checked out every other shaft they could think of. Air vents. Heating vents. Then they went over the entire house with a fine-tooth comb, just to be on the safe side. Over the years the whole building was practically taken apart and put back together again. Nothing was ever found."

Charlie asked, "How much of Einstein's work did Klein destroy before the CIA got there?"

"Very little. A tenth at most."

"Pandora could have been among that."

"True. But why would Einstein say Pandora's box was in the railing if it was actually in his papers?"

Charlie nodded agreement—and then sat upright, excited. "Maybe he *didn't* say it was in the railing. Maybe he said something else entirely."

Dante frowned at her. "That transcript distinctly says '*holm*.'"

"Well, who's to say that the transcript is correct? Who-ever transcribed this was eavesdropping on a hidden microphone almost seventy years ago. No offense, but the technology back then was crap. It was probably hard to make out what anyone was saying at the best of times, and on that night there was a lot going on. So maybe whoever was transcribing heard something wrong. Or wrote it down wrong. Or maybe Einstein mumbled a bit in his delirium."

Dante's frown slowly shifted to a look of intrigue. "What do you think Einstein said instead?"

Charlie considered that, trying to remember her German. And then her eyes lit up again. "What about 'Holmes'? As in Sherlock Holmes? It would be much eas-ier to hide something inside a book than a railing."

Dante shook his head, killing her excitement. "The Agency thought of that. There was a Holmes anthology among Einstein's books. The CIA took it apart, scanned every page for imprints, and compared it to other copies of the book to see if Einstein had altered it in any way. He hadn't. They didn't find a thing."

"That was the only copy they checked?" Charlie asked. "The one in his house?"

"It was the only one they found. They searched his office and his classroom as well."

"That's it?" Charlie sighed. "I thought you Agency guys were supposed to be smart."

Dante's eyes narrowed. "So enlighten me, genius. What'd we do wrong?"

"The CIA went through Einstein's belongings only at the time of his death."

"So?"

"Who says Einstein didn't find Pandora until he was *old*?"

Dante bit his lip, unsure of the answer.

"Mathematicians and theoretical physicists tend to peak early," Charlie explained. "Look at me. I'm already in college and I'm not even allowed to drive yet. Lots of big names did their landmark work before they turned thirty. Einstein published his theory of special relativity when he was twenty-six. He published three other major papers in *that same year*, including one on the photoelectric effect that won him the Nobel Prize. He was at the top of his game *then*."

Dante scratched his chin, intrigued. "You think Einstein found Pandora as early as that?"

"Maybe not in 1905, but I'll bet you there's a far better chance he found it within ten years of relativity than fifty. Old people don't think nearly as well as young people. Look at us. I'm, like, half your age and I'm the one with the brains in this operation."

Dante ignored the insult. "Would the timeline still hold up?"

"Absolutely. Einstein didn't have to wait until World War Two to see humanity wasn't ready for something like Pandora. All he had to do was know human history: the Crusades, the Inquisition, slavery. . . . So Einstein hid Pandora shortly after finding it—and never saw anything in the rest of his life that made him have any more faith in us."

"But why would Ernst Klein have destroyed things in the house when the book wasn't even there?"

"Klein didn't hear what Einstein actually said that night; only the doctor and the CIA did. All Klein knew was that Einstein mentioned Pandora. Maybe there was another clue in the house to finding the equation. Something that pointed to the Holmes book. Something Klein *did* destroy. But it didn't matter, because Einstein accidentally spilled the beans about the book in his delirium."

Dante nodded thoughtfully, realizing this all made sense. "Einstein lived in a dozen cities in six different countries after 1905," he said, concerned. "He traveled all over the world. If he had fifty years to hide Pandora, it could be almost anywhere on earth. . . ."

"I'd start with Jerusalem," said Charlie.

TEN

Alexandria, Virginia

amilla Carter knew she would never get back to sleep.

It was the nature of the business, the curse of this job. Evil never slept—and therefore, it often seemed, neither did she.

The work was what got you out of bed, but the fear kept you awake.

That's how it had played out tonight. The call from Dante Garcia had come only minutes after Carter had fallen asleep, revealing that there was a good chance Pandora was in Jerusalem.

According to Dante, the kid had figured it out. It had taken her only minutes to find a lead that had escaped the CIA for decades.

Pandora was in a book, and that book was probably in Einstein's archives. Einstein's archives were at the

Hebrew University in Jerusalem. The great scientist had been one of the university's founders, as well as an ardent supporter of the creation of Israel. Einstein had raised funds for the university's establishment, delivered the first scientific lecture there, been chairman of its academic committee and a member of the board of governors. At one point, he had even been asked to be the president of Israel itself. (He had refused the offer, claiming not to have "the natural ability or the experience necessary to deal with human beings.")

The archives included many famous items, like the original $E = MC^2$ formula, Einstein's scientific notebooks, and his personal letters, which were on display for the public—but what most people didn't know was that Einstein had donated far more than that, periodically sending troves of documents and other items to the university from the moment it was founded. All of this was preserved in a climate-controlled vault there. It made sense that if Einstein had something he really wanted to keep safe, like the hiding place for Pandora, then he had sent it there, where it would be protected for centuries, rather than keeping it in his home, which was susceptible to fire, mold, bookworms—and the CIA.

The CIA had known about the archives, of course. They had gone through the scientific papers and diaries dozens of times over the years. Maybe hundreds. But no one had ever thought to look for a mundane Sherlock Holmes book, which was probably tucked away in a box and forgotten.

The lead was good news, to be sure, but it meant more work for Carter. The CIA couldn't just waltz into Hebrew University, flash their badges, and invoke the Patriot Act. The Israelis didn't know about Pandora, and unless Carter wanted to cut them in on it—which she didn't—she had to make the acquisition look like routine research. That required tracking down the proper administrators, concocting a reasonable fake story about the reason for the visit, and greasing the wheels so Garcia could operate. After which, Carter had to deal with the fact that there were already CIA agents stationed in Jerusalem.

In part, that was beneficial, because Garcia needed support. But it was also tricky, because agents could be very territorial. If word got out as to what was at stake, any senior agent worth their salt in Jerusalem would want to run the show, rather than handing it over to Garcia. However, at the moment, all the senior agents stationed in Jerusalem were out in the field on covert operations. There were only a few young agents available, which was good for territoriality issues but bad for field experience. They had to be briefed on the mission, sworn to secrecy, and ordered to let Garcia be in charge.

Carter could have pawned most of the work off on

her staff, but half the reason she had the position she did was because she knew how to get results. By the time she was done with the calls, it was well past midnight and she knew sleep was out of the question.

So she did what she always did when this happened. She walked.

Carter lived in a gated community of tree-lined streets and three-car garages, close to Langley and far from the hustle and bustle of Washington. It was one of the few places in the world Carter felt comfortable at night without her gun. And yet, even out here, she couldn't escape the fear, because the fear was about things that could be done to you from a long distance away.

As she circled her neighborhood, Carter stared at the silent homes where fathers, mothers, and children slept. People who thought their biggest problems in life were traffic jams and office politics. People who had no idea what was really going out there in the world, how thin the line between calm and chaos could be. They all could afford this ignorance, Carter thought, because she and her agents were doing their jobs. But if they failed, that ignorance would end. The world would quickly become a very different, very dangerous place.

There were so many things that could go wrong with Pandora at stake. Maybe Charlie Thorne wasn't as smart as Garcia thought; maybe she was wrong about Pandora being in Jerusalem. Or maybe she was right and the CIA would get there too late. Maybe the Furies were too far ahead of them. Maybe they already had Pandora. In any of those scenarios—and a hundred others—death for millions of innocent people was a possibility.

Thorne.

Her presence in all this bothered Carter almost as much as the Furies did.

Garcia had probably been right to bring the girl in, but it was a devil's bargain. Charlie Thorne was a criminal, even if she was a young one, and criminals could never be trusted. They didn't see the world the same way Carter and her agents did. They looked out for only themselves. And given Charlie's incredible intellect, there was no telling what she was capable of. Carter didn't want someone like that getting her hands on Pandora.

Carter had been uneasy all along about Charlie's involvement, but beating the enemy to Pandora was the priority here, and Carter was prepared to do whatever it took to ensure that happened. But once the CIA had the equation, Charlie would need to be dealt with.

Carter knew Garcia couldn't be counted on for that. There were things Garcia hadn't told Carter about his connection to Charlie Thorne, but Carter knew them anyhow. She was the head of the CIA after all; it was her job to know things.

However, there was someone Carter *could* trust to take care of things, someone who could guarantee that after this was all over, Charlie Thorne would no longer be a threat.

Standing on the corner outside her house, only a few yards from where her husband slept, Carter sent an encrypted text and gave the order on how—when it was time—to take care of Charlie Thorne.

ELEVEN

Thule Air Base, Greenland

The CIA jet came in low and skidded across the icy tarmac.

Dante and Milana had decided to change route in midair, after Charlie explained why they should be going to Jerusalem.

They had veered north. The distance from the United States to Israel was actually shorter if you went over the arctic, rather than the central bulge of the earth. However, their small jet didn't have enough fuel to make it the entire way, so the CIA's transit division arranged for them to stop in Thule, Greenland, at the northernmost US Air Force Base.

Charlie had spent her time en route looking at everything the CIA had on the Furies. Dante provided her with dossiers on each member. Charlie started with the surveillance photos, which had all been taken in Bern.

There were six members of the terrorist cell and there were many similarities between them. They were all Caucasian men, in their twenties and early thirties, but they looked older due to tough lives, bad choices, and festering anger. In the photos, not a single one of them was ever smiling. Instead, their faces were locked into permanent scowls.

They wore cheap workmen's clothes and old boots, their winter jackets threadbare. When there were photos of them eating, it was always fast food, because fast food was cheap.

The photos were rarely head-on shots, and they were usually taken from a long distance, so they tended to be grainy. But there were enough for Charlie to get a decent idea of what each man looked like and commit his face to memory.

After that, she turned to the background information the CIA had amassed on each member. Overall, none of the Furies seemed particularly impressive—or even above average—in any way. They weren't the brilliant, erudite bad guys you saw in spy movies. They didn't have much in the way of specialization: There were no suave ringleaders, resourceful munitions experts, or deft break-and-enter men. They were all simply angry young thugs committed to a terrible, sadistic cause. They barely seemed capable of supporting themselves, let alone hatching a plan to kill millions of people. Two of them had done military time, and both had been dishonorably discharged. One had applied to be a policeman and been rejected. None of them were married or seemed to have much success with women, though all had been in a relationship at some time or another, which had all ended badly.

The only thing the Furies had been good at was ending up in jail. It happened time after time. Petty theft. Vandalism. Drunken driving. Bar fights. Domestic abuse. Public urination. The kinds of things that built up thick police files but didn't make for long incarcerations. The men usually spent a day or two in the drunk tank and were then spit back onto the streets.

The only one who seemed even remotely intelligent was the leader, Alexei Kolyenko. Alexei was a competent man who'd had a lot of bad breaks. His family was originally from Russia, but he had been born in a poor suburb of Berlin. He had gone to university for three years, doing well, only to have to quit due to financial issues. He was a half-decent mechanic, knew how to weld, and could do construction, but he still couldn't seem to find a long-term job. He had done far less jail time than the others—only two separate nights, both for public intoxication. The CIA believed he spoke three languages, including English.

However, Alexei looked the angriest of all of the Furies. He was thirty-two years old and built like a lumberjack, with broad shoulders and thick arms. He had short blond hair and blue eyes and a swastika tattoo on the biceps of his left arm. There was one photo in particular that struck Charlie. Alexei was passing a girl on the street, a Middle Eastern woman who looked somewhat like Charlie. Alexei was glaring at her with pure, unadulterated rage, as though he despised her for merely existing. It was the type of look that sent a shiver down Charlie's spine, a look that indicated Alexei Kolyenko would have no concern with engineering the deaths of millions of people. Maybe he would even be happy to do it.

The other men were merely his followers. Though the Furies didn't seem particularly impressive on paper, Charlie knew not to underestimate them.

Charlie had read quite a bit about criminals. Contrary to what movies showed, most of them weren't particularly intelligent. The greatest heists in history hadn't been conducted by brilliant criminal masterminds, but by dumb men who got lucky. The world's most infamous serial killers had all been unimpressive losers who had been unsuccessful at just about everything except murdering random helpless people. Even Adolf Hitler, the most horrible person in recent human history, had been a failure for much of his life.

So Charlie read everything the CIA had on each of the Furies, just in case it turned out to be important later.

Alexei. Marko. Oleg. Fez. Hans. Vladimir. Six men who looked ordinary but who were determined to cause pain and suffering for millions.

After she finished with that, there were two more files Dante had given her.

They were about agents Dante Garcia and Milana Moon. The idea being that Charlie ought to know who she was working with. No doubt Milana had also received quite a file on Charlie. Dante wouldn't have needed a file; he knew plenty about Charlie already.

Similarly, Charlie knew plenty about Dante. But she skimmed his file anyhow: born and raised in Miami, statewide wrestling champion, nationally ranked debater, full ride at Georgetown University in DC, recruited by the CIA before he'd even graduated. No surprises there. There wasn't any information on what she *really* wanted to know about: his cases. But all that was certainly top secret.

So Charlie turned her attention to Milana Moon.

As she had guessed, Moon was Native American. Blackfoot tribe, to be specific, from the reservation in northern Montana, just outside Glacier National Park. She had grown up poor, but had worked hard in school and had been a star athlete in track, earning herself a full scholarship to the University of Pennsylvania. She had excelled there as well, attracting the attention of the CIA, which had hired her right after graduation and placed her in the agent training program at Camp Peary, aka the Farm. Milana had been one of the top recruits in her class and then quickly proved herself in the field as well. She had excellent marksmanship, spoke Arabic and Mandarin Chinese, and was cool under pressure. The file made it obvious why Dante had selected her for this mission. Although Charlie suspected there was one other factor that had influenced Dante's decision as well.

He had the hots for Milana Moon.

Charlie had seen it in the way Dante looked at her. She had noticed how, when he had brought her a meal on the jet, he hadn't asked what she wanted to drink. He had just known her well enough. But Charlie was sure Dante hadn't said anything to Milana yet, and maybe he never would, because dating a fellow agent was probably against the rules at the CIA—or at the very least it was frowned upon. And Dante wasn't the kind of guy who broke the rules, even if it meant having an unrequited crush.

Charlie thought this was ridiculous. But then, she had always thought that rules were for other people.

Now, as the jet taxied across the tarmac in Greenland, Charlie set down the files and peered out the window. The base sat on the edge of Baffin Bay, but it was a winter night in the arctic, and Charlie couldn't even see as far as the water. It was pitch-black outside—and probably had been since noon. A howling wind was blowing so hard that the plane shuddered and the snow whipped sideways. Stands of klieg lights were arrayed along the edges of the runway, but even their powerful beams barely made a dent in the darkness. All Charlie could make out were a few Quonset huts, a fuel truck, and an air force man swaddled from head to toe in winter gear, obviously wondering what he had done wrong to end up assigned to this godforsaken place.

The jet came to a stop, and Milana shut down the engines. The airman waddled toward the plane, looking miserable, signaling to Milana that she should stay inside but open the door for him.

Charlie, Dante, and Milana zipped their ski parkas back on. Charlie pulled on her gloves and jammed her feet back into her ski boots too, preparing for the door to be opened.

Milana unlocked the door from the inside. A gust of subzero wind and snow instantly rushed through the gap, making Charlie shiver despite her heavy clothes.

The airman stepped inside, and Milana shut the door behind him, cutting out the frigid winds again. The airman looked like he was fresh out of the academy, maybe twenty-one years old, and his face was raw from the cold. "Greetings, Agents," he said. "Welcome to Thule Air Base." Then his gaze fell upon Charlie and he gawked, wondering what a girl her age could possibly be doing there.

"It's bring-your-daughter-to-work day at the CIA," Charlie told him. "Dad and Mom here are taking me on a covert mission to thwart some illegal arms dealers. They say if I help they'll give me a lollipop."

"Ignore her," Milana said, and then started to discuss the fueling procedures with the raw-faced airman.

The airman got on his walkie-talkie and talked to the driver of the fuel truck, who drove it over to the jet, then got out into the cold and started moving the gas lines about. He looked even more miserable than the first airman. Through the icy window, Charlie saw a dozen signs warning people that the tanker was flammable and there should be no smoking or open flames anywhere near it.

She slipped her hand into her parka, clutching the item hidden away in the pockets, the item the CIA had missed.

There was a *thunk* as the gas line was connected to the jet.

The young air force guy kept talking to Milana, drawing out the discussion. Charlie figured he was excited to see a woman, as there probably weren't many stationed up here in Thule. Even more likely, he was looking for an excuse to stay inside the warm jet and not go back out on the freezing tarmac.

Charlie returned to her files, finding herself drawn once again to the unsettling photos of Alexei Kolyenko.

Finally, the air force guy seemed to run out of things to say. He had Milana sign some forms on a clipboard, then said, "You folks ought to be finished in a few minutes. Good luck on your mission. I apologize, but it's about to get nasty cold in here again." Then he turned around and opened the door.

In the next instant, Charlie sprang from her seat, shoved the air force guy aside, and dove out the door.

The cold hit her like a truck. It was far worse than anything she had ever experienced, certainly well below zero, and then there was a brutal windchill as well. It made her muscles tense and sapped her strength, but she willed herself forward anyhow. It was hard going. Her ski boots weren't made for running, and the tarmac was icy, but then, she wasn't planning to go far.

As she had expected, Dante was right behind her. He had probably been keeping a close eye on her, hoping she wouldn't do anything stupid, but prepared just in case.

Although he probably hadn't expected she would do anything nearly as stupid as what she now planned.

"Charlie, freeze!" Dante shouted. "I'll shoot you if I have to!"

Charlie stopped beside the fuel tanker and turned around. Dante was only fifteen feet away, but it was hard to see him through all the blowing snow. She could still make out the gun in his hands, though.

The wind was so loud, Charlie had to yell over it. "I know you won't shoot me, Dante!"

"What are you thinking here?" Dante asked. "There's nowhere to run. There's no one else here but military personnel, who'll hand you right back to me the moment they catch you—and if, by some miracle, you got past all of them, there's nothing but a thousand miles of snow, ice, and polar bears in every direction."

Charlie took her hands from her pockets. In her right, she was holding the object the CIA hadn't found on her. A cigarette lighter.

The lighter wasn't a cheap plastic one from a convenience store. It was carved from jade with an intricate dragon etched into it. The kind of fancy family heirloom that got passed down from one generation to another.

Dante's eyes went wide at the sight of it.

The airman stepped out of the jet behind Dante and freaked out.

"Whoa!" he cried. "Do not light that! You'll blow us all to bits!"

Milana emerged from the jet door. She had her gun stiff-armed, aimed directly at Charlie.

Charlie ignored her and kept her gaze fixed on Dante. "Tell me what *really* happened in Bern. The truth this time." The air around her was thick with the stench of fuel exhaust. "Or I flick this and we see what happens."

"Dang it, Charlie!" Dante said. "Would you just get back in the jet? Stop screwing around out here before you kill us all!"

Charlie placed her thumb on the plunger of the lighter.

"Okay!" Dante held up his free hand, palm out, signaling Charlie to be calm. "Fine! I'll tell you everything!"

"It's about time," Charlie said. "I was really hoping I wouldn't have to resort to crap like this." She took her thumb off the plunger but didn't put the lighter away. "I'm all ears, Dante. Start talking."

TWELVE

Charlie had been outside for less than a minute, but it was so cold on the tarmac that she could already feel her core temperature dropping and her extremities going numb. Still, she stubbornly stood her ground, facing off against Dante. "What went wrong in Bern?"

"The Furies *did* make one of our men," Dante admitted. "About ten days ago. I don't know the full details, because I wasn't on the mission. The guy had been working to infiltrate the group for weeks. He'd even made some progress. But he messed up. He made a mistake in his German that tipped them off that he was a spy. Or, heck, maybe they'd made him weeks before. I don't know. But it blew the mission."

"What happened to the agent?" Charlie demanded.

Dante didn't answer for a few seconds, weighing his options. Finally, he said, "They killed him."

This didn't really surprise Charlie, but having Dante tell her the truth still shook her. Deep down inside, she had been hoping she had guessed wrong, but now the reality of it was overwhelming. Her legs suddenly felt weak. "What was the agent's name?" she asked.

"I don't see why that matters. . . ."

"What was his name?" Charlie shouted.

"Russo," Dante said. "John Russo."

"Was he a good agent?"

"Yes. He was one of our best."

Charlie felt panic beginning to set in, in a way she had never experienced before. She felt the cold and the dark closing in, like they were going to crush her. She fought to keep her tough facade up, but she couldn't do it. Instead she screamed at Dante, "You weren't going to tell me? Didn't you think I deserved to know?"

"I thought you'd be better off if you didn't." Dante sounded genuinely sad about this. He replaced his gun in the holster under his jacket. "Why don't you get back in the jet, where it's warm?"

"That jet is taking me to some place even more dangerous than here!" Charlie yelled. "People are getting killed over this equation! Good agents with plenty of training! And I'm only twelve! How could you possibly drag me into this?"

"I didn't think I had a choice! If the Furies get

Pandora, a lot more people will die than that one agent!"

"And your only choice was *me*? You ought to be protecting me, Dante! Not putting me in danger!"

Charlie was still holding the lighter in her hand, though in truth she had forgotten all about it.

Milana Moon hadn't. She kept her gun trained on Charlie, just in case the girl did something stupid. Dante turned to Milana and gave her a slight shake of his head. Milana reluctantly lowered her gun, although she didn't holster it.

Dante slowly approached Charlie through the blowing snow, his hands up where she could see them. "I'm sorry," he said. "I should have been honest with you. You deserved that. So know this: I'm being honest with you now. I will do everything in my power to keep you safe on this mission. I am only asking you to help advise us. I am not going to put you in harm's way. I promise I will protect you."

He was directly in front of Charlie now. She looked into his eyes and saw he was telling the truth this time.

Her own eyes were hurting from the cold. Her cheeks stung, and she realized there was ice on them. She had been crying, and her tears had instantly frozen to her skin.

Dante reached out to her and took the lighter from her hand. Then he examined it closely, intrigued. "This was Granddad's?"

Charlie nodded, then stuffed her hands inside her pockets. The little bit of warmth made no difference at all. Her hands were freezing. *She* was freezing. She was starting to shiver uncontrollably.

Dante wrapped an arm around Charlie's shoulders and led her back to the jet. On the way, he noticed the young airman was still staring at them, unsure what to do.

"Get back to work," Dante told him.

The young airman nodded and scurried off across the tarmac, disappearing into the snowstorm.

As Dante and Charlie neared the jet door, Milana asked, "How is she, Dagger?"

"She'll be fine," Dante said. He led Charlie back up the steps and past Milana into the jet. In the brief amount of time the door had been open, the temperature had dropped like a rock; inside, the jet was now as frigid as a meat locker. Snow had blown through the open door and piled up on the carpet.

Charlie looked at Dante, curious. Though she would have never admitted it, having his arm around her had made her feel a lot better. Her panic had subsided, and she was beginning to feel normal again. "Dagger?" she asked teasingly. "Oooh. Very macho code name."

"It has nothing to do with macho. It's from my initials. Dante Alejandro Garcia. DAG. Dagger."

"That's right. You never did like Dante." Charlie

shuffled back to her usual seat, blowing on her hands to warm them.

Dante was still holding the lighter. He stared at it thoughtfully, running his thumb along the inlaid stone dragon. Then he noticed something. He shook the lighter but didn't hear any liquid sloshing inside. "There's no fuel in this."

"Nah," Charlie said. "It ran out years ago. But I don't smoke."

"So you were bluffing out there?"

"Of course. I'm not stupid enough to blow us up. I'm a genius, remember?"

Milana Moon stepped inside the jet, closing the door behind them, cutting out the howling wind and the snow. She hadn't heard *everything* Dante and Charlie had said outside, but she had heard enough. Enough to finally make sense of the dynamics between them and to be upset at Dante for not being honest with her about it all.

"She's your sister?" Moon asked angrily.

"*Half* sister," Dante corrected, cramming the lighter into his pocket. "Now, let's turn the heat up and get the heck out of here."

THIRTEEN

Even though Dante and Charlie had the same father, they hadn't really considered each other family. There was a sixteen-year age gap between them, and they had grown up far apart, Dante in Miami, Charlie in Burlington, Vermont. They had seen each other only three times in their lives before Dante had shown up in Snowmass.

As far as Dante was concerned, the only thing they really had in common was a hatred of their father. Larry Thorne was an accountant who had abandoned Dante's mother when she was three months pregnant. She had punished him by not even passing his last name on to her son, using her own surname instead.

Larry remained married to Charlie's mother, but Charlie always wished that wasn't the case. Not that she was a big fan of her mother, either. Which was why she had hightailed it to college as soon as possible. Her father had always been a jerk, and her mother was vain and neglectful. Neither of them had been interested in spending much time with Charlie until they realized she was unusually intelligent—a revelation that it had taken them a disturbingly long time to reach. Charlie had continually told them that the reason for her rowdiness in preschool and kindergarten was that she was bored. They had ignored this and simply assumed she was a bad student and a liar. For a while they had even thought she might be mentally deficient.

Finally, a kindergarten teacher named Mrs. Peacock hadn't just listened to Charlie, but had thought to give her an IQ test. And then Mrs. Peacock had given her three more, just to confirm that the staggering scores weren't a mistake. When confronted with the evidence that Charlie was a genius, her parents had finally taken an interest in her—but not as a daughter so much as a meal ticket. Their first instinct had not been to try to get her into a school where she could thrive and be challenged, but to call talent agents. They had spent most of her elementary school years trying to make her the star of her own reality show.

However, to the chagrin of her parents, Charlie wasn't merely intelligent; she was also socially adept. By then she had discovered that not everyone was as impressed with her unusual mental abilities as her parents were. In fact, those abilities often seemed to alienate people. So Charlie had learned to keep them a secret.

While this served Charlie well with her peers, winning her plenty of friends, it was intensely frustrating for her parents. When they trotted Charlie out before other adults and tried to make her do tricks, like she was a trained monkey, Charlie refused to play along. When they convinced psychologists to give her new IQ tests, Charlie purposefully answered every question wrong. When they finally managed to get a TV network interested in a show about a young genius, Charlie played dumb in front of the executives. The pattern repeated itself throughout Charlie's childhood: While Charlie was perfectly happy to feed her enormous intellect everything from calculus to Mandarin in private, she stubbornly pretended to be normal in public.

This was infuriating to Charlie's parents, who retaliated with punishment. They grounded her. They took away her toys and her books. They refused to get her the puppy she longed for. And when that didn't work, they berated her and said things no parent should ever say to their children. None of this encouraged Charlie to show her true genius; it only made her more determined to get away from her parents as soon as she could.

Going to college early was only part of that plan;

Charlie also hoped to be independently rich by the time she left home, so she would never have to ask her parents for anything.

She had never set out to do anything illegal. It was the Lightning Corporation that *really* behaved badly, by taking advantage of a child.

Charlie's original plan was to make her money through computer programming. She was naturally gifted at it, and it was something she could do at home, alone, which was just about her only option for a hobby, as her parents kept grounding her and were refusing to let her do any extracurricular activities as further punishment. At the age of eight, Charlie created her own security program and upon hearing that Lightning, one of the biggest software companies on earth, was looking to get into the security business, decided to send it to them.

Unfortunately, for all Charlie's smarts, she was still young and naive where people—or at least corporations—were concerned. She simply sent the entire program on a flash drive, with a handwritten note asking that Lightning pay her a fair price for the program if they liked it. (Charlie added that she estimated a fair price would be at least ten million dollars.) She did not approach a lawyer or any other business professional to aid in the deal.

Charlie never heard back from Lightning, which was upsetting to her—although she was considerably more upset a year later when Lightning announced it had developed a new security system called Barracuda. The release had a multimillion-dollar advertising campaign. The reviews for Barracuda were stellar, and Lightning's stock skyrocketed.

Barracuda was Charlie's program.

She knew this for sure, because when she had developed it, she had built a back door into the code, a way to let her circumvent the security system. She hadn't done this for any nefarious reasons; she had simply thought it would be fun. Barracuda had the exact same back door—which was ample evidence that it had been stolen—but it also gave Charlie access to Lightning's entire computer network. Charlie hacked in, examined the code, and determined that Lightning had made almost no changes at all to what she had sent them. They had blatantly swiped it and were now making millions of dollars from something that belonged to her.

Charlie didn't want to tell her parents about this, because they would doubtlessly try to gain access to all the money themselves. She *did* approach lots of law firms, but none took her seriously. They all thought it was laughable (if somewhat adorable) that an elementary school girl wanted to sue the world's most powerful computer software company. Worse, Charlie didn't have any evidence to back up her story. Since Lightning had never responded to her letter, there wasn't even a paper trail of correspondence.

So Charlie decided to take back what rightfully belonged to her. She was no longer as naive as she had once been. She learned everything she could about banking and finance and figured out how to establish a secure Swiss bank account. After that, through Barracuda, she hacked into Lightning's corporate bank accounts, siphoned out a considerable amount of money, and deposited it in her own account. And then, because she couldn't help herself, she enacted a little more vengeance on Lightning.

On the company's homepage, she altered the slogan to "Committing Evil for 120 years" and animated their lightning logo so that it struck a kennel and set several cartoon dogs on fire. She also removed all the software products for sale on their website, replacing them with particularly horrible items like elephant tusks, rhino horns, and giant panda skins. Finally, she wiped out all of Lightning's access codes.

It was a massive black eye for Lightning. First, the news that Barracuda could be hacked killed the product, costing the company millions. But it was also incredibly embarrassing when one of the world's preeminent tech companies couldn't get into its own system to fix its own website. It took them six days to repair the damage, during which their stock price tanked. It never fully recovered.

The mischief Charlie had caused cost Lightning far more than what she had actually stolen. In fact, the company was so worked up about the mischief that several days went by before they even realized they had been robbed as well. After the horrible publicity of the hack, Lightning covered up the story of the theft, but they did reach out to the FBI.

At the time, Dante was still a young CIA agent, struggling to prove himself. There were plenty of leaks between the FBI and the CIA, so word got through about the Barracuda case. The moment Dante heard about it, he had a pretty good idea who was behind it because Charlie had once told him about sending a security program to Lightning and never hearing back from them. But Dante kept it to himself for several reasons:

1) He couldn't prove it.

2) It wouldn't look good for him to reveal that his own half sister was behind one of the most public crimes of recent years.

3) It wasn't his jurisdiction.

4) The Lightning Corporation probably deserved what Charlie had done to them anyhow.

The first time Dante had even met Charlie, she was four. He had been in college and had come to see Larry, thinking maybe there was a way to have his father in his life. Within minutes, he had realized that was a mistake, but he had been intrigued by his half sister, sensing that she was a lot smarter than her parents realized. The next time he had seen Charlie was when she was eight, at a family wedding, and then when she was ten, at the funeral of their uncle. (Their father might have been a tool, but his brother had always been a decent guy.)

By then Dante had used his CIA access to uncover Charlie's IQ tests for himself and confirm how brilliant she was—although he didn't tell Charlie he knew. Their next two encounters were prickly and uncomfortable. Charlie had a bad attitude and problems with authority, most likely stemming from the fact that the main authority figures in her life—her parents—deserved contempt. And yet Dante had always suspected that deep down Charlie was a good kid who had simply been dealt a bad hand. True, her incredible intelligence was a gift, but her despicable parents had been an even bigger burden. Even after the Barracuda incident, Dante didn't have the heart to bust Charlie—and he was quite sure that she wouldn't end up getting arrested anyhow. Instead, the FBI would get angry at him for overstepping his bounds and the CIA wouldn't look kindly on the family connection.

So Dante kept his theories to himself, hoping the time would never come when he needed to take advantage of them.

And then he heard about Pandora.

Pandora wasn't his case. He wasn't anywhere near Bern when everything went wrong and John Russo got killed. But the CIA's failure worried him. So Dante had gone to Jamilla Carter and told her almost everything about Charlie, showing her the IQ tests and the other data he had dug up, revealing Charlie's crime against Lightning and how it could be used to force Charlie to help the CIA. He hadn't told the truth about *how* he knew about Charlie, keeping the family connection a secret, although he figured Carter would piece that together sooner or later—if she hadn't already. It was a risk, but if there was any time to take a risk, it was now. Pandora needed to be kept out of the hands of the Furies—or any terrorist group—and Dante felt obligated to suggest his own plan, no matter how unorthodox it was.

Now he just had to hope it worked.

PART TWO
THE NAVEL OF THE WORLD

The world is a dangerous place to live, not because
of the people who are evil, but because of the
people who don't do anything about it.
—ALBERT EINSTEIN

FOURTEEN

Israel

Halfway between Tel Aviv and Jerusalem

I want a code name," Charlie said.

They were in a black SUV, heading along Israel's Highway 1 to Jerusalem. It was ten minutes past one in the afternoon. The CIA had lost eight hours flying east.

After Greenland, Charlie had spent her time on the jet boning up on Einstein—Dante had brought three books on the scientist and his work from the CIA's private library—until exhaustion overcame her. Then she had curled into a ball on the couch and slept until they touched down at Ben Gurion Airport in Tel Aviv. Dante had done the same, slumped in the chair across from her. And even though Milana was technically flying the plane, she had set the autopilot again and dozed herself en route. When you were CIA, you learned to get your sleep when you could.

There was a separate terminal at Ben Gurion Airport for private jets. Two agents from the Jerusalem office had met them there when they landed. They were parked right on the tarmac and facilitated a fast transit through customs. The Israeli team had also provided Charlie with new clothes, seeing as ski gear would have looked ridiculous in Jerusalem, where the closest snow was a hundred miles away. The clothes were tourist-casual, designed to blend in: shorts and a T-shirt for Charlie. All the adults were already wearing khaki pants and neutral button-down shirts. Charlie had changed in the bathroom at customs. The clothes fit perfectly. Someone had guessed her measurements to a tee, probably Milana, as Dante didn't seem like the type who would know anything about girl's clothing sizes.

One of the Jerusalem agents was a short, stocky guy with a crew cut who looked like he could have been Israeli but was really Sri Lankan. The woman actually *was* Israeli by birth, but looked stereotypically Californian, with blond hair, a dark tan, and a lithe, limber body. The guy was driving. His name was Agent Ratsimanohatra, but that was a mouthful, so everyone called him Rats. The woman sat in the passenger seat. Her name was Agent Bendavid, but since she looked like a Barbie doll, everyone called her Barbie.

As Charlie had learned, Garcia was Dagger, and he had revealed that Agent Moon was called Coyote. The three of them were all crammed into the back seat of the SUV, which was big, but not quite big enough to share with someone as bulked up as Garcia. Garcia and Milana were at the doors, intently staring out the windows, like they were expecting trouble at any moment. Charlie was wedged between them.

"Those aren't code names," Barbie said curtly. "We don't use them on missions. They're just nicknames."

"Fine," Charlie said. "Then I want a nickname."

Rats gave her a hard look in the rearview mirror.

It was clear that neither Rats nor Barbie liked anything that was going on here. Charlie had expected a certain amount of humorless, down-to-business attitude, but these two had been cold and brusque since the jet had landed. Charlie wasn't sure if they were upset about the mission itself, Charlie, or something else altogether, but they were definitely being jerks.

"I've come up with a good name for myself," Charlie said.

"I'm sure you have," Barbie grumbled.

"Prometheus," Charlie announced.

Milana Moon turned from the window to look at her. "That's a man's name."

"So? You're named after an animal. Dagger's named after a weapon. There's no rule that says I can't have a masculine code name."

"All I meant was there are a lot of cool women's names," Milana said. "If you wanted to go mythological, I would have thought you'd want one of those. Like Athena. Or Artemis."

It struck Charlie that this was the first thing Milana had said to her that could count as a conversation rather than discussion about the mission. She smiled in response. "I like Prometheus just the same. And besides, he wasn't really a man. He was a Titan."

"He was also a thief," Dante said. He kept staring out the window, looking away from Charlie as he spoke. "He stole fire from the gods and gave it to man. Prometheus thought what he was doing was a selfless act, but the gods didn't agree. As punishment, they condemned him to have an eagle rip out his liver for eternity. Is that what you think is going on here, Charlie? That you're being punished unfairly? Because your theft wasn't exactly selfless."

"I donated a lot of that money to charity," Charlie replied.

"But not all of it, I'm sure."

"I want to be Prometheus," Charlie said flatly.

"If you want to be mythological," Dante said, "I think 'Eris' would be more fitting for you. She was the goddess of chaos."

"Maybe we should change your code name to Hemorrhoid," Charlie shot back. "Because you're being a real pain in my rear end."

Charlie noticed Milana crack a smile at this for a split second before catching herself. Dante noticed too and reddened around his ears. Charlie couldn't tell if this was due to embarrassment or anger. Probably both. "We're done with this conversation," he said, and then turned his attention to responding to e-mails on his phone.

Charlie looked past her brother to the scenery outside the window. She had never been to Israel before and was fascinated by what she saw. The highway from Tel Aviv to Jerusalem wasn't long—Israel was a very narrow country— but it was choked with traffic the entire way. The highway slowly gained elevation as it went east from the coast, passing through hills that were green from recent winter rains, covered with grass that would be brown in only a few weeks. Even from the highway, Charlie could see a bizarre clash of time periods from Israel's fifty centuries of civilization: brand-new bridges arced over ancient Roman ruins; Bedouin families grazed their goats outside recently built suburbs; decades-old military vehicles sat rusting next to modern convenience stores. Although it was winter, the desert sun was beating down from a cloudless sky.

While Charlie was at once excited and frightened to have joined the hunt for Pandora, being in Israel brought another emotion to her, one that surprised her. She felt like she was suddenly part of history in a way that she never had been before. Her hometown in Vermont was only a few hundred years old. Boulder, Colorado, where her university was, was only one hundred and fifty, while Snowmass, where she had started the day, had been founded only five decades earlier. But people had been living in Israel for thousands of years, since even before biblical times. They had cultivated this land, built civilizations, razed them, and built new ones. Too many wars to count had been fought over it. Charlie wondered if there was a single hill within sight that someone hadn't died on.

The SUV crested a rise, and the city of Jerusalem came into view. Thousands of buildings perched at the top of a mountain, each built from the same white limestone, glistening in the sunlight.

Charlie's sense of anticipation grew stronger. Jerusalem was the city that had been luring people to the region ever since its founding, five thousand years before. Pilgrims, crusaders, prophets, and tourists. Charlie had once heard that the city was known as the navel of the world, since all life seemed to spring from it. At the time that had seemed silly to her, but now she felt it might be true.

Dante checked his watch impatiently. "Call the archives again," he told Agent Bendavid. "It shouldn't take this long to find one stupid book."

Agent Bendavid didn't follow the order. Instead, she said, "From what I understand, there are *a lot* of books in those archives."

"There are *sixteen million* books in the Library of Congress," Dante replied. "And the librarians there can find anything you need in minutes. Did you explain to them that this is a priority?"

Bendavid turned around in the front seat, not even bothering to hide her annoyance. "I'm trying to walk a fine line here. I know you don't want me telling them the *real* reasons that we want that book. I haven't even told them that we're CIA. But I've already pressed them as much as I can. If I push harder, they're going to suspect something is up. And when Israelis get suspicious, you know who they call?"

"The Mossad," Charlie said. Which was the national intelligence agency of Israel. Their equivalent of the CIA. Except with a tougher reputation.

Barbie looked at her, like she might have been the tiniest bit impressed that Charlie knew this. "Exactly. And I'm guessing we don't want the Mossad to know about Pandora."

"Of course not," Dante confirmed.

"Then we need to be cool," Barbie said. "We'll be at the university soon. As far as the archivists know, you're a visiting literature professor working on a book about how Sherlock Holmes influenced the thoughts of great scientists throughout the twentieth century. I told them you want to examine the book to see if Einstein made any notations in it. They're already bending over backward to carve out time for us on short notice. I don't think I should push any harder than that."

Charlie watched her brother think that through. A bad leader would have bristled at an underling questioning his orders—especially in the cocksure tone Bendavid was using—and doubled down, getting angry and insisting on his way. But Dante wasn't like that. He obviously didn't like Bendavid's attitude, but he still graciously conceded she was right. "Good point. I'm obviously just concerned about the Furies getting to this book before we do."

"That's not going to happen," Rats assured him. "If Pandora's in that book, then it'll be in our hands in less than thirty minutes."

Dante frowned, not ready to be optimistic about this yet.

"We'll get it," Milana told him, then gave him a reassuring smile.

Dante looked back out the window at the approaching city, wishing they were already at the archives, the equation in their hands. As much as he wanted to believe Milana, he had a nagging feeling that this wasn't going to be that easy.

FIFTEEN

Safra Campus
Hebrew University, Jerusalem

Despite Charlie's genius, since she was only twelve, there were still large gaps in her knowledge. She was surprised to discover that while the Old City of Jerusalem had been continuously inhabited for more than five thousand years, the part of the city outside the ancient walls was less than a hundred years old—far younger than London or Paris. Younger than New York or Philadelphia. Even younger than Albert Einstein himself.

The Old City had been built atop a mountain peak, designed to impress pilgrims and repel invaders, and the surrounding landscape was filled with steep hills and deep valleys. The Safra Campus of Hebrew University, where Einstein's archives were located, sat on one such hill, facing another upon which Israel's main government buildings were arrayed.

The center of the campus was at the crest of the hill, a wide lawn flanked by 1950s buildings and abutted by what had once been the National Library of Israel but was now just the library for the university. After driving through two separate security checkpoints manned by armed guards, they were directed to a parking lot just outside the library.

It was one thirty in the afternoon.

As Rats steered into the lot, Bendavid told Dante, "You'll have to leave your weapons in the car."

Dante cocked an eyebrow at her. "With Pandora at stake?"

"You're supposed to be a visiting professor, not a CIA agent," Bendavid reminded him. "And there are metal detectors at almost every building here. You don't want to make waves, remember?"

Dante reluctantly removed not just his gun, but the entire shoulder holster from underneath his jacket, and handed it to Bendavid in the front seat.

Milana did the same thing.

Bendavid took off her weapon as well, then placed everything in the glove compartment.

Rats pulled into a parking space. The library sat directly in front of them, a dull, squat rectangle built into the hillside. The main entrance, and the central lawn, lay up an outdoor flight of stairs.

Dante and Milana barely even waited for the SUV to

stop moving before they leapt out, eager to get the book.

Charlie started to follow her brother out of the SUV, but Dante held up an open palm. "Sorry, kid. I need you to wait in the car with Rats."

"You have to be kidding," Charlie said.

"Barbie was right," Dante told her. "We don't want to do anything that will raise suspicion. It's a hard enough sell that I'm a visiting professor. We don't want to have to explain what a twelve-year-old is doing here too."

"Tell them I'm your niece!" Charlie argued. "I'm a fellow book fanatic, tagging along with you. If anything, my presence will probably make them *less* suspicious. You guys look so much like CIA agents you might as well just have it tattooed on your foreheads."

The agents looked from one to the other, sizing themselves up, wondering if Charlie was right.

"I promised you I'd keep you safe," Dante told her. "So that's what I'm doing."

"Can I at least wait in the library?" Charlie asked. "So I can find a book to read?"

"No," Dante said. "It could be dangerous."

"It's a *library*," Charlie said petulantly. "The worst that can happen in there is I'll get a paper cut."

Dante simply shut the door.

Before Charlie could open it again, Rats engaged the automatic locks, trapping her inside the vehicle. Charlie jiggled the handle angrily, then banged on the window. "Dante!" she yelled. "This isn't cool!"

If Dante heard her, he didn't show it. Instead, he, Milana, and Bendavid headed up the library steps without so much as a glance back at the SUV.

Charlie turned to Rats. "Seriously? You're okay with them leaving us like this?"

"I'm not okay with *any* of this," Rats replied grumpily. "But orders are orders."

Charlie sullenly slumped in her seat. "I flew halfway around the world to get here and now I'm supposed to just wait in the car? This sucks."

Rats didn't respond. He remained facing forward, staring alertly out the front windshield at the library.

Charlie watched Dante, Milana, and Bendavid disappear over the top of the stairs, hoping she was right that Pandora was actually here.

The headquarters for Einstein's archives were in a tiny, unassuming office on the second floor of a building just off the main lawn. The door was flanked by two glass cases, one of which held replicas of awards that had been given to Einstein, while the other held a toy Einstein doll. Dante regarded them curiously, wondering if any other Nobel Prize winners had children's plush toys modeled after them. He doubted it.

A prim middle-aged woman answered the door within seconds of their knocking on it, as though she had been eagerly awaiting their arrival. "Hello!" she said cheerfully. "I'm Golda Solomon, director of the archives." Like most Israelis, she spoke English fluently, even though Hebrew was the official language of the country. She looked to the women. "I must have spoken to one of you on the phone . . . ?"

"That was me," Bendavid replied. "I'm Leah Bendavid. And this is my good friend Professor Dante Garcia, from Georgetown University."

"Thanks for taking the time to see me," Dante said graciously. There was no point to creating an alias for something like this. His passport and all his other ID had his real name on them. The CIA could provide any fake academic credentials he needed, not that a library or archive would even ask for them. "This is my associate Milana Moon."

"It's a pleasure to meet both of you," Golda said. Although she was conservatively dressed in a suit, Dante got the sense that she, like most Israelis, could handle herself in battle if needed. Almost everyone in Israel had to do at least two years of mandatory service in the army, and it made everyone tough and capable, even years afterward. Golda stepped into the hallway and locked the office door behind her.

"We're not going into the archives?" Dante asked.

"These are only the administrative offices," Golda explained. "Professor Einstein left far more to the university than we could store in this little space." She started back toward the staircase.

"So, where are the books?" Bendavid asked.

"In the library, of course." Golda grinned over her shoulder as she led the way down the stairs. "Including the one you're looking for."

"You found it?" Dante asked excitedly.

"Yes," Golda said proudly. "I must admit, this was an unusual request. I don't think anyone has ever asked to see this particular book before. I'm a little surprised we could find it on such short notice."

"Really?" Milana asked. "I'd have thought that all of Einstein's belongings would have been cataloged long ago."

"That's exactly the problem," Golda explained. "The book arrived long ago." They reached the bottom of the stairs and passed out the door back onto the main lawn. "Over his lifetime Einstein willed hundreds of thousands of items to the archives. To be honest, we're *still* not done going through them."

"Still?" Bendavid repeated. "It's been nearly seventy years since he died."

Golda said, "There are a staggering number of items that need to be conserved in this country, and to be honest, these haven't been the highest priority. The Dead Sea Scrolls have a full-time staff of conservators working five days a week, with the government footing the bill. We don't have that luxury."

The lawn was crowded with students, like that of any other university on a warm winter day. They were eating lunch, sipping coffee, lazing on the grass while they read or did homework or simply basked in the sun. At the far end of the lawn, a game of Ultimate Frisbee was underway, while closer by, a group of students strummed guitars in the shade of an enormous oak tree.

"We have to make do with volunteers," Golda continued. "Working when they can, on a very small budget. Priority was given to Einstein's personal documents. His notebooks, his manuscripts, his letters. But his books . . . Well, to be honest, while it's nice to have them, they've been a bit of a burden."

"Why is that?" Dante asked.

At the end of the lawn, there was a medium-size cement plaza in front of the library entrance. Half the plaza was given to a fountain. Five college boys were doing tricks on their skateboards along the edge of it.

"I'm sure it wouldn't surprise you to hear that Einstein was a voracious reader," Golda said. "He owned more than fifteen thousand books during his lifetime. Not every one of them was an important work, but they all ended up here. Normally, if someone wills books to a library, the idea is to share them with the readers. We go through them, pick the ones we think people will want to read, and throw the rest away."

"Throw them away?" Milana gasped, horrified by the thought.

"Sadly, we can't take every book people donate," Golda said.

As they crossed the plaza in front of the library, Dante could see their SUV parked in the lot below, Rats still at the wheel, keeping an eye on Charlie. Dante held the main doors of the library open for the women, and they passed inside.

There was a security station with a metal scanner. It wasn't nearly as advanced as what they had passed through to enter the campus—only a metal detector, an X-ray machine for bags, and a bored security guard watching over it all—but Dante still realized they had made the right call leaving their weapons in the car.

Golda set her keys and phone in a plastic bowl, then passed through the scanner. "The library even purges its own stacks every few years. If a book hasn't been checked out in a decade, it gets tossed to make room for books that people *do* want to read. But that wasn't the case with Einstein's. It didn't seem right to throw anything of his away. But his books were all deemed too precious to loan out as well. So they've just ended up sitting in a vault in the basement here, taking up space."

Dante also placed his keys and phone in the bowl and then passed through the scanner. "So that's where the book I'm looking for has been?"

"Yes," Golda answered. "It came to us in 1947, eight years before Einstein died, along with a thousand other books from his youth. They were all cataloged once, then put aside and basically forgotten. The records for them haven't been updated since, although they were computerized back in the 1990s."

Milana and Bendavid passed through the scanner without incident. While the main stacks of the library lay directly ahead, Golda led them toward a door marked LIBRARY STAFF ONLY.

Dante noticed there was no security system on the door. No keypad entry or card reader. There were no cameras in the halls either. The library appeared to have been built in the 1950s and had little modification ever since.

Golda led them through the staff door, to yet another staircase, this one descending into the basement level of the library. "I expect you're very excited to see this book," she said.

"Extremely," Dante agreed. "I promise, I'll take very good care of it while it's in my possession."

Golda stopped in the middle of the stairs, surprised. "Oh. The book can't leave the archives. That was Einstein's stipulation for all of his donations."

Dante frowned. "Yes, but this is an unusual case. . . ."

"There can be no exceptions," Golda said firmly. "Books are extremely delicate. Our vault has a specifically designed climate to protect them from mildew, mold, and pests. If they were removed from there, even for a minute, the effects could be devastating."

Dante wasn't surprised by this, but he had hoped exceptions might be made for a lesser-known book like Einstein's Holmes collection. However, he still didn't want to play his hand by revealing where he was really from. Reviewing the book inside the vault might be time-consuming, but he could still keep it safe there.

He told Golda, "If that's the case, I need to call in another analyst." He turned to Bendavid and said, "Phone Rats. Tell him to bring in Charlie."

SIXTEEN

Sitting in the SUV outside, Charlie said, "I have to go to the bathroom."

"No, you don't," Rats replied. "You're only saying that so I'll let you out of the car."

"No, I'm saying it because I have to go to the bathroom," Charlie told him, although this was in fact a lie. She was going stir crazy in the car. Rats had guessed correctly, but she wasn't about to let him know that. "I had a bunch of water on the plane, and I've been sitting in this car ever since the airport. My bladder is so full it hurts."

"I'm sure you can hold it."

"I've been holding it for more than an hour! Maybe all you CIA guys have some sort of advanced bladder control training, but I'm just a kid. I need to pee like forty times a day. If you don't let me go, I'm going to ruin all the nice upholstery you have back here."

"Go ahead," Rats said, calling her bluff. "This isn't my car anyhow."

Charlie flopped back in her seat, annoyed. She briefly considered urinating all over the SUV, just to teach Rats and everyone else at the CIA a lesson about how to treat kids, but decided it wasn't worth the embarrassment and the wet pants. In truth, she didn't really have to go at all. She had even been carefully monitoring her water intake so that, in case there *was* an emergency, she wouldn't have to pee.

She stared back out the windows again, looking at the campus she wasn't being allowed to set foot on.

As it was the afternoon, there were plenty of people around. The parking lot was nearly full, but most people were coming and going from the campus by foot or bicycle. Students and professors were moving up and down the stairs to the library at a steady rate.

The students looked pretty much the same as Charlie's fellow students had at the University of Colorado; fashion all over the world had conformed. The students wore the same style of clothes and sweatshirts with the university name on them. They carried the same style of backpacks. They had all gone to Starbucks.

Up at the top of the stairs, she could see the kids on their skateboards, attempting their tricks along the fountain, despite the NO SKATEBOARDS sign clearly posted nearby. There were skateboard guys at Colorado who did exactly the same thing and would have fit right in there. And just like the Colorado guys, these guys were failing at every trick they attempted, their boards clattering on the plaza.

Charlie was a much better skateboarder than these idiots. Or the ones back in Colorado. It had to do with seeing the numbers and then being skilled enough to put them to use. Skateboarding was how Charlie had first realized she could see the numbers in the first place. When she was seven, she had received a hand-me-down skateboard and used it all the time. (Even when her parents grounded her, she would often sneak out and practice tricks in the neighborhood.) She had honed her gift over the years, getting better and better at putting the numbers into practice, and thus, better and better at sports as well. She still boarded a lot. Mostly, she kept to herself, although sometimes at her university she would stop by the skateboard guys and pull off a few tricks to put them to shame.

She wanted to do that with these guys now. She wanted to be with Dante looking for Pandora. She wanted to be anywhere but held prisoner in this stupid SUV.

Rats's phone rang. He answered it, then listened for fifteen seconds. "All right," he agreed. "I'll bring her in." He hung up and turned to Charlie. "They need you inside."

Charlie sat up, excited. "Why?"

"They've got the book, but it can't leave the vault." Rats locked everyone else's gun in the glove compartment but kept his own tucked in his holster.

"They're not going to let you take that in," Charlie warned.

"I'm not bringing you in. I'm only walking you to the door. Then I'm going to keep an eye out for trouble. Let's go." Rats climbed out of the SUV.

Charlie quickly leapt out herself, excited to finally have something to do. She ran up the steps, forcing Rats to chase after her, then turned toward the door of the library . . .

And froze in her tracks.

She turned back toward the plaza, knowing that something had triggered a reaction in her subconscious. Even in her haste, her mind had been working furiously, taking in everything about her surroundings. Now she looked closer, taking the time to really focus.

By the fountain, the skateboarders were still attempting their tricks and failing. Other students were crossing back and forth through the plaza on their way to class or the library, while others sat on benches in the sun.

Rats came huffing up the stairs behind Charlie. "What's the matter?" he asked, sounding even more annoyed than usual. "I thought you were all excited to get moving. So move."

"Something's wrong." Charlie kept staring at the plaza, analyzing everything. One of the skateboard guys was attempting an ollie off the edge of the fountain and making a mess of it. Two college employees, most likely professors, given their manner and dress, were glaring at the skateboarders disdainfully as they passed, but not actually saying anything, as though their harsh glares alone would be enough to get the point across. . . .

There.

At the edge of the lawn, a man sat on a bench. He had a newspaper in his hands, but he wasn't reading it. He was looking *past* the newspaper, unable to keep his focus on it, as if it were merely a prop. Unlike everyone else, he was sitting in the shade, where it would have been chilly, when there was a perfectly good vacant bench in the warm sun across the plaza. However, the bench in the sun faced the opposite direction. So it seemed that the guy hadn't chosen the bench for comfort but for what it gave him a view of—which was the entrance to the library.

Rats didn't seem concerned by Charlie's belief that something was wrong. Instead, he said, "Dante wants you *now*."

"There's a guy casing the library on the bench over there," Charlie said. "If you make a scene, you're going to spook him."

Rats was a good enough spy to not immediately turn

and stare, which might have given them away. Instead, he kept his focus on Charlie and said, "Which bench?"

"The one in the shade. Can I borrow your phone? I want to use the camera."

Rats didn't want to make a fuss and draw attention, so he handed the phone to her.

Charlie acted like she was taking a photo of the fountain. Instead, she used the zoom on the camera to focus on the guy on the bench. He didn't seem to notice her. He was fixated on the library, and besides, Charlie looked like just another teenager with a phone, rather than a CIA agent. The phone's camera wasn't as good as a pair of binoculars, but it worked. The image was grainy, but still better than what she could see with her naked eyes.

The guy was wearing the same kind of clothes the CIA agents had: khakis and a button-down shirt, the kind of clothes you wore to blend in. He had a beanie cap pulled down low on his forehead and sunglasses, but with the camera, Charlie could make out the features of his face well enough to confirm her worst suspicions.

She knew this man. She had committed his photographs to memory only a few hours before.

"That's Alexei Kolyenko," she said. "The Furies are here."

At that moment, the alarms in the archives started ringing.

SEVENTEEN

Fate had played right into Marko's hands.

Marko was the youngest of the Furies, the same age as most of the students at this university, but while the students all had the luxury of taking four years to study for high-paying jobs in medicine and law and engineering, Marko had been scrounging for menial work ever since he was fourteen and his mother had died. He hadn't even known his father, who had abandoned his mother before he was born, never contributing a cent to his son's life.

The Furies had arrived in Haifa by ferry that morning, direct from Limassol. It had taken a long time to funnel through customs and rent a van, and then they had come right here to the library.

They hadn't parked at the university, because there were security booths at all the parking lot entrances, with armed guards and cameras that recorded license plate numbers. So they had parked at a movie theater a few blocks away and walked over, scoping out routes of escape as they crossed the campus.

Marko had been disgusted by everyone he saw, not because they could afford college when he couldn't, but because he hated everyone from this part of the world. The Jews and the Muslims had all come from the Middle East to his country and ruined it, just as they had ruined this country.

The Furies had split up upon reaching the library, as a group of foreign men was far more noticeable than several individuals on their own. Marko, Hans, Fez, and Vladimir had entered the building at separate times, a few minutes apart, while Alexei sat outside, keeping watch over everything. Since there were metal detectors, they had left their weapons behind. But beyond the detectors, it was easy to get in; no one even asked for ID. The library was open to everyone.

Marko had milled about in the library for a few minutes, acting like a student as he wandered deeper into the stacks, and then slipped through a door into the staff area of the building. Not only was there no security on the door, but the staff didn't seem even remotely concerned with security themselves. No one looked at him suspiciously. One staffer noticed that he seemed lost, but then naively offered to help him find his way around. The idiot had even pointed the way to the vault when he'd asked.

From what Marko knew, the vault wouldn't be easy to get inside. It would most likely require force, which he could still exert, even without his gun. There were many ways to cause someone pain.

The idea was to wait near the vault until some of his fellow Furies joined him, then force their way in and get the book. But when Marko arrived, fate had a surprise in store for him.

The vault wasn't what he had expected. There *was* a large steel door, behind which precious items like Einstein's books and other artifacts were protected—but before you reached that, there was a room with a wide window along the hallway. The room was brightly lit and filled with several tables. A few archivists were already seated at some of the tables, carefully examining books and documents. Obviously, the room was a regulated space to examine things from the vault. It appeared to be climate-controlled to protect the documents, and there was a sign in multiple languages on the hallway door explaining that artifacts could not leave the examination room without permission.

The examination room had more security than the rest of the library; the door had a coded-entry keypad and the window was thick and reinforced with thin steel wires.

But Marko could easily see inside through the glass. And there, sitting on one of the tables by the door, was the very book he was looking for. He was sure of it.

It was an aged Sherlock Holmes anthology, so old the spine was coming apart and the pages had turned brown. A young male archivist stood beside the table, shifting from one foot to the other nervously, like he was waiting for someone important.

Marko immediately assessed the situation. It appeared that someone at the archives must have realized the importance of the book. Given the behavior of the young archivist inside, Marko guessed that he had retrieved the book for someone else and was expecting them soon. Which meant that Marko had to act fast.

There was no time to wait for any of the other Furies to help him. He had been lucky, arriving here at such an opportune moment, but his window of opportunity was probably going to be very narrow. Whoever was coming—the CIA, most likely, but for all he knew it could be MI6 or KGB or Mossad—was going to be here soon.

Another archivist was entering the room at that very moment, typing her access code into the security keypad. Marko stepped behind her as she pulled the door open. The woman paused in the doorway, sensing something was wrong, and turned to him with a stern look. "I'm sorry. This room is restricted. . . ."

That was as far as she got. Marko backhanded her with a powerful swipe of his arm, sending her stumbling into the wall.

The other people in the room turned to him, startled.

Marko was already on the move. He ran to where the book lay on the table. The young archivist instinctively moved to protect it. Like a lot of Israelis, he knew how to fight, but so did Marko, and Marko had the element of surprise. He punched the archivist in the face, then drilled a fist into his stomach as he reeled backward. The archivist went down, whacking his head on a table, and by that point Marko had grabbed the book and was running for the door.

By the time someone tripped the alarm, Marko was already racing down the hall, holding Einstein's book in his hand.

The moment Dante heard the alarms, he suspected the worst. He, Milana, and Bendavid were still in the stairwell with Golda Solomon, heading back to the library entrance to meet Charlie. Until that point, Dante had been doing his best to act the part of a visiting professor, explaining why the analyst he was bringing in *looked* young but was actually much older than she seemed and hoping Golda would buy it. But now there was no longer any time to pretend. He wheeled on Golda and demanded, "Get us to the archives! Now!"

"But the alarms . . . ," Golda protested. "It might be an attack."

In Jerusalem, a terrorist attack was probably far more likely than someone stealing a book from the archives, but Dante presumed that wasn't the case right now. He grabbed Golda's arm with a firm hand and said, "It's not an attack. Someone's after the book!"

There was a forcefulness in his voice that Golda didn't question. She broke into a run, leading him down the stairs and into the basement hallway. "That way!" she exclaimed, pointing to the glassed-in examination room ahead.

Dante raced there, Milana and Bendavid on his heels, but as he reached the room, he knew it was too late. He saw the two archivists who had been overpowered, other people having already come to their aid, while the door to the room hung open.

He raced on down the hallway. Whoever had come for the book must have been going that way, because otherwise he'd have run into them. He reached a T junction into another hall, but it was empty in both directions.

Whoever had grabbed Einstein's book had a big head start on him.

Pandora was gone.

EIGHTEEN

Up in the plaza in front of the library, everyone froze in fear when the alarm rang. This surprised Charlie. Back in America, if an alarm had gone off on campus, people would have ignored it and kept going about their day. Because almost every time a campus alarm went off, it turned out to be false. The Americans might have looked around to see where the noise was coming from, but they wouldn't have been worried. Here in Israel, things were different. Everyone stopped in their tracks to determine if the alarm was the warning signal for an incoming missile attack. When they realized that wasn't the case, they were slow to return to what they had just been doing, because the alarm had reminded them that when you lived in the Middle East, you couldn't afford to be complacent.

Alexei was the only exception. Charlie had turned

toward the library when she heard the alarm go off—as had Rats—and when they looked back toward Alexei, he was no longer on the bench. His newspaper lay crumpled on the ground and he was racing across the main lawn, away from the library.

Rats swore in Hebrew, spun toward Charlie, and ordered her, "Stay here! Leave this to me!" Then he ran after the terrorist.

Charlie let them go. She had no intention of following Alexei. Pandora was what was important right now. She returned her attention to the library.

Since the library was built into a hill, half of the basement level was exposed. The only doors on that level appeared to be emergency exits, but Charlie figured that if *she* had stolen the book, she wouldn't be coming back out the main entrance. Not if she had triggered the alarm. To Charlie's left, a long ramp led down from the plaza, skirting the edge of the basement level, heading to another campus lawn.

As Charlie watched, an emergency door flew open alongside the ramp and a young man raced out, clutching a thick book in his hands.

Charlie recognized him. Marko. The youngest of the Furies.

Which meant the book in his hands was probably Einstein's Holmes anthology.

Charlie's immediate response was excitement—she had been right about the book being here—but that was quickly replaced by concern. She had expected to see Dante and Milana emerge closely behind Marko, but they didn't. Which meant they didn't know where Marko was. Only she did. And since Dante had confiscated her phone, she had no way to contact him. Charlie was hesitant to go after Marko, knowing it could be dangerous, but she had no choice. If she didn't do *something*, Marko was going to get away, and then the Furies would have Pandora.

Beside Charlie, one of the skateboarders was still listening to the alarm, cautiously watching the skies for any sign of an attack. His board lay on the ground at his feet.

Charlie snatched it and ran toward the ramp. "I just need to borrow this for a few minutes!" she yelled back to him.

"Hey!" the boarder yelled after her. "Not cool!"

"I'll bring it back!" Charlie shouted. "I promise!" As she reached the ramp, she dropped the board in front of her and leapt onto it in one fluid motion, using her momentum to give her an extra burst of speed. She sped down the ramp, keeping her eyes locked on Marko.

The lower lawn beyond the library was narrower and less crowded than the central upper lawn. A few students were lounging on it, but mostly people were just crossing it to get from one building to another. In the midst of it stood a statue of Einstein himself. The statue was positioned so that Einstein was walking away from the library, but even so Charlie could recognize the man's iconic mop of hair.

Marko sprinted past the statue, running like his life depended on it.

Charlie surfed down the ramp on the skateboard, moving fast enough to make her hair fly in the breeze; she had to brush it from her eyes as she rode. A concrete path meandered across the lawn, forcing her to weave back and forth to stay on it, dodging all the people as well. She shot through a game of Smashball and sliced between two professors in the midst of a heated discussion. She was closing the gap on Marko when he veered onto a staircase that angled downward between two buildings.

Charlie took a hard look at the railing and saw the numbers.

As she reached the top of the stairs, she performed a huge ollie, springing herself and the board into the air and landing the deck across the railing. Then she rode down quickly, grinding along the rail, bearing down on Marko.

At the base of the stairs was another parking lot. Charlie pounced off the railing, hitting Marko with the full force of her body. The two of them tumbled across the asphalt. The book went flying.

Charlie handled the fall better, as she had been prepared for it. She had taken enough spills on her skateboard over the years to know how to protect herself. She curled into a ball, arms covering her face, rolled, and snapped back up into a standing position next to the board.

Marko snapped to his feet as well—and immediately charged Charlie.

The suddenness of the attack caught Charlie by surprise. Before she even had time to shift into her fighting stance, Marko had lowered his shoulder and rammed into her. The young Fury was far more powerful and agile than Charlie had expected. He knocked the wind out of her while sending her reeling backward into the trunk of a parked car. The trunk caught her in the small of her back, sending a lightning bolt of pain up her spine. And then Marko's fist was sailing toward her face.

Charlie dodged to the side as fast as she could, although it wasn't quite fast enough. She avoided a direct blow to her nose, but Marko still clipped her chin, slamming her teeth together and making her reel.

Charlie used that momentum and spun away from the next blow, but her head was ringing.

She realized she was out of her league.

The instructors in her self-defense classes had been going easy on her. She was only a beginner, able to take down an uncoordinated lummox like the pool guy back in Snowmass—but she was in serious danger now that she was facing a brutal, talented fighter like Marko.

The Fury was powerful and angry. If he landed

another blow to her head, he could certainly knock her out, if not kill her.

Charlie knew she should run—but she also knew she couldn't. Because if she did, then she'd be leaving Pandora to the enemy.

So she ducked away from Marko as he attacked again, dodging another fist by a fraction of an inch, wondering how on earth she could defeat this guy.

She certainly wasn't going to overpower him. And she was too tired and banged up to keep dodging his attacks. She was already hurting so badly she thought she might throw up.

Marco paused, sizing her up, taking a moment to focus before he assaulted her again.

Charlie saw the numbers.

She ran past Marko, catching him by surprise, although he recovered quickly and spun around after her. That still took him a few moments, however, and in that brief space, Charlie kicked the skateboard back toward him, hoping she had timed things just right.

She had. The skateboard rolled directly under Marko's foot, and he slipped on it. The skateboard shot out from beneath him and he flew forward, the rage on his face now giving way to surprise—and then fear as he saw what was coming.

Marko plowed headfirst into a lamppost, hitting it

so hard that the sound rang across the parking lot. He fell to his knees, seeing stars, and tried to stand again, but before he could, Charlie was right behind him. She grabbed a handful of his hair, and with a surge of adrenaline and rage she'd never known she had, she slammed his head back into the lamppost again.

Marko collapsed facedown in the landscaping.

Charlie bent over and threw up.

She felt dizzy and wiped out and in more pain than she could ever remember. She just wanted to sit down and cry.

But she couldn't.

She threw up once more, then wiped her mouth with the back of her hand, swept the hair back from her face, and started to search for the book.

It was lying at the end of a row of cars, close to the rear bumper of one. *The Adventures of Sherlock Holmes.* Einstein's book. The cover had torn off in the fall, but overall the book was still intact.

Charlie staggered over to it.

When she bent to pick it up, a wave of exhaustion swept over her and she sank to her knees. As she did, something whistled over her head, moving so fast she could feel it searing the air, and then the rear windshield of one of the cars shattered.

Someone was shooting at her.

NINETEEN

There was no time to grab the book. Instead, Charlie dove between the two cars closest by, hitting the ground so hard that it jarred her already battered body. The impact stung, although not as much as getting shot in the head would have.

Another window shattered, glass raining down on her, but for the moment she was protected from the shooter.

Despite this, Charlie found herself gripped by a fear unlike any she had ever felt. She realized she had made a big mistake and let her guard down. Of course Marko would have backup. There were six of these guys.

She had never been shot at before. No one had ever wanted her dead. She was only twelve, for Pete's sake. She should never have been in this position. Where was Dante now that she needed him?

Charlie knew she was on the edge of a full-blown panic

attack. Her heart was racing. She was hyperventilating. Her thoughts were scattered. She had to pee—for real this time. She wanted to cry.

But none of that would get her out of this mess. If the CIA didn't know where she was, she would have to take care of herself.

Even though Charlie apparently hadn't learned enough about defending herself in her martial arts classes, she *had* learned how to be calm and to focus. That had been one of the first lessons. So she willed herself to take deep, slow breaths. Her heartbeat slowed. She focused on her surroundings and used logic to figure out her situation.

Given the gap in time between the shots, she could assume there was only one shooter. She hadn't heard the gun, so it must have had a silencer. And given the angle with which the bullets had struck the cars, she could guess the shooter's location. This portion of the campus was built onto the slope of a relatively steep canyon. On the other side was the Jerusalem Botanical Gardens, thick with trees and shrubs. The shooter was probably in there somewhere, positioned to cover Marko's escape.

Charlie lay on her belly, looking under the car beside her. Einstein's book was still in the parking lot, only a few feet away from her, and yet there was no way she could get to it without exposing herself to another gunshot. In fact, she couldn't go *anywhere* without exposing herself to danger.

She was away from the heart of campus now, far from the crowds, and it was surprisingly quiet. She could hear birds chirping, insects buzzing—and, in the distance, footsteps moving across the asphalt.

Looking beneath the cars, she saw feet coming her way. Decent shoes and pant cuffs. A professor. Someone who had arrived too late to witness her fight with Marko or hear the gunshots. The professor was walking without any concern at all.

The feet stopped by a car and climbed in. The car started and backed out of its spot.

Charlie realized this was her chance.

She got to her hands and knees and turned around, so she was now facing the way she'd come, looking toward the book. Not far away, the skateboard lay upside down where it had landed after Marko slipped on it. Charlie ran the numbers in her head, figuring out exactly how fast she had to move to make this work.

The professor's car was coming her way, moving slowly through the parking lot. The professor apparently didn't see the unconscious terrorist hidden in the landscaping; he didn't brake at all.

As the professor's car passed the line of vehicles Charlie was crouched in, shielding her from the sniper, Charlie sprang from her hiding place. Staying low, she grabbed the book with her right hand while flipping the skateboard onto its wheels with her left. Then she belly flopped onto the skateboard while grasping the underside of the car, directly below the passenger door. Her timing was just right. She didn't reveal so much as a glimpse of her body to the sniper.

The professor, unaware she was hitching a ride, slowly drove out of the parking lot, towing her to safety.

Beyond the lot, on the campus road, the professor picked up speed. Charlie did her best to hang on, but the skateboard wasn't in great shape and started to wobble wildly. The last thing Charlie wanted was to escape a sniper and then get run over in a dumb skateboarding accident, so once she felt she was well out of the sniper's range, she let go of the car and veered away from it, cruising to a stop behind the cover of a building.

A sign over the door announced what was studied in the building: THEORETICAL PHYSICS. Charlie took that as a good sign.

If the sniper was at the botanical gardens, they would have to come through campus security to get anywhere close to her now, which she doubted would happen. She hopped off the skateboard, sprang to her feet, and turned her attention to the book.

It was old and weathered, though it had probably been in that shape *before* being sent to the archives. Due to the perfect climate control of the vault, even after being in storage for more than seven decades, it didn't have a hint of mustiness or mold.

Charlie flipped open the cover and gasped with excitement. There, on the front page, in faded pencil, were the handwritten words "Property of A. Einstein."

When the book had fallen from Marko's hands, the cover had pulled loose from the binding, revealing a small tear in it. It looked as though a slit had been made in the inside of the cover, then painstakingly patched up again. It might have escaped even Charlie's notice if the damage to the book hadn't reopened it.

She jammed a fingernail into the slit and pulled backward, tearing away the inside of the cover, revealing a piece of paper hidden beneath it.

Before Charlie had a chance to look at it, someone grabbed her from behind.

Charlie twirled, breaking free from her attacker's grasp and bringing her elbow up high, intending to break their nose.

Her attacker anticipated the move, sidestepping her and wrenching the book from her grasp as she spun.

Dante.

Milana and Bendavid were with him.

"Why didn't you bring this to me?" Dante asked, annoyed.

Charlie felt annoyance blossom in herself as well. "I

think the phrase you're looking for is 'Good job, Charlie. Thanks for doing our work for us.'" She pointed at the book in Dante's hands. "I nearly got killed for that!"

"Because you were reckless and impulsive," Dante said angrily. "Instead of waiting for us, you ran off after Marko yourself. You take a couple self-defense classes and you think you can fight a terrorist?"

"I wouldn't have had to fight him if you'd done your job!" Charlie yelled, louder than she'd expected to. "If it weren't for me, the Furies would have Pandora right now."

"We'd have recovered it," Bendavid said.

"Yeah, right," Charlie muttered. "By the way, there's a sniper in the botanical gardens. And I left Marko unconscious in the bushes. You guys might want to round them up."

Dante was examining the book, noticing what Charlie had found. "The sniper's probably long gone," he said. "And he took care of Marko before he left."

Charlie felt her anger instantly change to fear. "He shot his own man?"

"So he wouldn't talk when we got him," Milana said coldly.

Charlie felt like she would have thrown up again if her stomach hadn't been empty.

Rats came running down the road, flushed and out of breath, sweat soaking through his shirt.

"Where's Alexei?" Bendavid asked him.

Rats could only shrug. "He had too big a head start on me. I lost him in the crowd."

Bendavid frowned in a way that indicated Rats had failed where she wouldn't have. Rats noticed this and simmered in response.

Dante brutally tore the cover off the Holmes anthology. The piece of paper Einstein had concealed there fluttered out.

Milana caught it before it hit the ground. Everyone leaned in to look.

It was a piece of notebook paper, decades old, veined with parallel blue lines. There was a sprawl of numbers on it:

$$\frac{(91-60)^8}{88M} + \left\{ 3 \left(\frac{99c}{49}\right) \times \left[\frac{(192)^5}{5M} + (13 \times 16)(16 \times 15)^2 \right] \right\} -$$

$$\left(\frac{754}{10X}\right)(851) + \left(10X + \frac{78}{92}\right)\left(\frac{10X}{16}\right)^8 \div (15i)\left(\frac{22}{55}\right) = \pi$$

Despite her exhaustion and her nausea, Charlie's heart raced with excitement. She was staring at something Einstein himself had written down and hidden, something that no one else had ever seen except the great man. Something that would change the world.

Her next thought caused her considerably more concern.

"My God," Bendavid whispered. "We found it. We found Pandora."

"No, we haven't," Charlie said.

The others all turned to her, confused.

"What are you talking about?" Rats demanded.

"That isn't an equation," Charlie told him. "It's a clue."

"I could kill them all," Oleg told Alexei.

They stood on the slope of a hill on the opposite side of the canyon, in the botanical garden, under the cover of a grove of eucalyptus trees. Alexei was winded after shaking the CIA agent who had chased him across the campus. The remaining five Furies had gathered here, which had been the plan if anything went wrong. And things had definitely gone wrong.

"They're all behind that building," Oleg went on, pointing to the Department of Theoretical Physics. "I just need to find the right angle, and I can take them all out. It will only take a few minutes."

"We don't have a few minutes," Alexei said. "We need to get out of here before the police arrive. Or worse, the Mossad." He didn't add that he doubted Oleg would be able to pick off *one* of the CIA agents if he was lucky, and that wouldn't solve anything. The CIA would just take cover and fire back, the Mossad would swarm the botanical gardens, and the Furies would be captured while the CIA ended up with Pandora for good.

Alexei started to lead the way up the hill, toward where they had parked their car.

The other Furies followed him, except for Oleg, who stood his ground.

"Your plan is to run?" Oleg asked angrily. "But they have Pandora!"

Alexei paused and turned back to his men. "Running is not my plan at all. We have a contingency."

He quickly explained to his men what he intended to do.

Oleg's anger instantly dissipated. And then he began to laugh. All the Furies joined in.

Those idiots in the CIA, Alexei thought. They had no idea what was about to hit them.

TWENTY

I t sure *looks* like an equation," said Milana Moon.

She was back in the SUV with Charlie, Dante, and Rats, heading through Jerusalem. They had left the campus as quickly as they could, while Agent Bendavid had stayed behind to deal with the police. Rats was driving; Dante had graduated to the passenger seat, while Milana sat in the back with Charlie, looking over the piece of paper they had found in Einstein's book.

Charlie no longer felt like she was going to pass out, but her body still ached from her fight with Marko. She had bruises the size and color of plums all over her. The SUV had an emergency kit, in which she had found ice packs and ibuprofen, but the pain hadn't fully gone away and that was making her grumpy.

"It's not an equation," Charlie told Milana for the second time.

"How do you know? You barely even looked at it."

"For starters, it's way too complex."

Charlie caught Rats looking at her in the rearview mirror. There was derision in his gaze—as if he was thinking that maybe Charlie wasn't as smart as he'd heard she was. It was a look Charlie had received a great deal throughout her life.

Milana was staring at her too, although she seemed intrigued rather than disappointed. "Of course it's complex," she said. "It's the most important equation in history."

"So was special relativity. And look at it." Charlie had a notebook open in her lap. It took her all of three seconds to write out the equation:

$$E = MC^2$$

"Only three variables and no numbers," Charlie explained. "The two doesn't count, because you're really just multiplying C by itself. Or consider the most significant equation in physics before *that*, Newton's law of gravitation." Charlie wrote that down too.

$$F = G\frac{m_1 m_2}{r^2}$$

"Five variables and no numbers. Not very complicated either. The history of physics has been the search for simplicity. Because the laws of the universe, for the most part, *are* simple: Newton's laws of thermodynamics, Kepler's laws of planetary motion, the theory of relativity—you name it. Whenever Einstein—or any physicist—devised an equation they felt was too complex, they were generally sure they didn't have it right."

Milana met Dante's eyes in the rearview mirror. Both seemed impressed by what Charlie was saying—and possibly a bit annoyed with themselves that they hadn't thought of this.

"Now look at this," Charlie said, and pointed to Einstein's scrap of paper:

$$\frac{(91-60)^8}{88M} + \left\{ 3\left(\frac{99c}{49}\right) \times \left[\frac{(192)^5}{5M} + (13 \times 16)(16 \times 15)^2\right] \right\} - \left(\frac{754}{10X}\right)(851) + \left(10X + \frac{78}{92}\right)\left(\frac{10X}{16}\right)^8 \div \left(15i\right)\left(\frac{22}{55}\right) = \pi$$

"Twenty-seven numbers but only seven variables. Plus a dozen separate mathematical functions. It doesn't look like any law of physics I've ever seen."

"That doesn't mean it can't be a real equation," Rats argued.

Dante added, "Physics *is* getting far more complex as we delve to the subatomic level. Quantum physics isn't as easy to describe as gravitation."

"That's true," Charlie agreed. "And yet that was always Einstein's problem with it. He *hated* the randomness and uncertainty of quantum physics. While he admitted it was successful at describing the subatomic world, he always felt it was only a temporary solution. He believed there had to be a more concise formula for explaining every-thing, which put him at odds with virtually everyone in physics. By the end of his life, the general population might have revered Einstein, but in the scientific world, he had become a crotchety old stick-in-the-mud who refused to be open to new ideas."

"Most people get stuck in their ways as they age," Milana said. "Even geniuses, maybe."

"But Einstein wasn't like most people," Charlie argued. "So maybe the reason he was so reluctant to change his mind was because he'd *already found* the equation that proved he was right."

Milana and Dante shared a look. "Makes sense," Milana said.

Rats still wasn't convinced. "That's *your* theory," he said to Charlie. "Here's mine: That equation isn't a clue. It's Pandora. It's just too complicated for you to understand."

Charlie sighed. "There are other things wrong with it besides the complexity. Like the variables. Einstein hasn't left any sort of key as to what they stand for—and with-out knowing that, an equation is useless. If this really *was* Pandora, why would Einstein go through all the trouble to hide it and then not leave a key?"

"Maybe he thought anyone smart enough to find it would know what he meant," Rats said.

"I *do* know what he meant," Charlie snapped. "This is not Pandora. It's a clue to *finding* Pandora."

"So it's a clue," Dante said, before Rats could argue any more. "What's it mean?"

"I have no idea."

Rats snorted with disdain. "Great."

"Look," Charlie said testily. "The man who created this clue had an IQ of 230. Mine's 220 at best, so it's going to take me a little while to figure this thing out."

"Why would Einstein go through all the trouble to just hide a clue?" Rats asked.

"It's what we do at the CIA all the time," Dante said. "It's basic security. Adding layers of protection. Creating firewalls." He pointed to Einstein's clue. "If this *was* Pandora and we'd been five minutes later, the Furies would have it now. But that wouldn't be the case if they faced a code they couldn't crack. So if Charlie says this isn't an equation, it's not an equation."

Rats didn't say anything in response. It looked like he *wanted* to, but he kept it to himself, staring out the window ahead. Charlie noticed that his knuckles had grown white on the steering wheel, meaning he was gripping it hard, probably in anger.

The SUV rounded a corner, and suddenly the ancient walls of the Old City of Jerusalem loomed ahead, the weathered, rough-hewn stone a stark contrast to the shining, modern city around them.

"We're not heading to the airport?" Charlie asked.

"Why would we do that?" Dante replied.

"The Furies are *here*," Charlie said. "Now that we have this clue, I figured we'd want to get as far away from them as possible. . . ."

"We *are* getting away from them. They won't be able to find us where we're heading."

"Where's that?"

"Someplace safe," Dante assured her. "I promise." When Charlie started to repeat her question, he cut her off. "I have this under control. So you handle *that*." He pointed to Einstein's clue. "I need to know where that leads. Immediately."

"Immediately?" Charlie asked. "This isn't a word search on the kids menu at a restaurant. It's a clue devised by the smartest person who ever lived. For all I know, it could take weeks to figure it out. Or months maybe."

"We don't have weeks," Dante told her. "And we certainly don't have months."

"What *do* we have?"

"Hours would be nice. Though I'd prefer minutes."

Charlie shot him a look of astonishment. "I can't promise you that. Heck, there's a chance I'll *never* figure it out."

"That's not acceptable," Dante said coldly. "Our deal wasn't for you to find a clue. It's for you to find Pandora."

"And what if I can't?"

"That wouldn't be in your best interests."

"What are you going to do? Turn me over to the FBI for Barracuda?"

"It's a possibility."

"You'd do that to me?" Charlie asked, stunned. "You might be the worst brother of all time."

"Just solve the clue," Dante said. "And find Pandora."

TWENTY-ONE

The Old City of Jerusalem was a dramatic collision of cultures. Brand-new cars and broken-down pushcarts shared roads that had first been laid five thousand years before. Men in three-piece suits strolled alongside women in traditional burkas. Market stall vendors sold fresh fruit, ancient artifacts, gummy bears, and DVDs of pirated American movies side by side. Newly built pizza parlors and falafel joints stood across from ancient Roman ruins. Walled off from the rest of Jerusalem, the Old City was a labyrinth of well-traveled tourist routes, meandering alleys, and secret passages known only to locals. It had been built and rebuilt so many times that street level had risen fifty feet over the centuries and now sat atop the detritus of a hundred civilizations.

The Old City was only 220 acres, about a quarter the size of Central Park in New York City, and it was divided into four uneven quarters: Muslim, Christian, Armenian, and Jewish. The walls around the city had been built in 1535 by the Turkish sultan Suleiman the Magnificent. And there were only six gates. The CIA's SUV entered the city through the Zion Gate, in the southern wall, passing into the Jewish Quarter. Because the old, narrow roads hadn't been built for cars, they were driving so slowly the pedestrians were moving faster than they were.

Normally, Charlie would have been staring out the window. She was usually fascinated by new places. There were always a million things to see.

Instead, she was forced to stare at Einstein's clue, trying to decipher it.

She probably would have been doing that anyhow, even if her brother hadn't threatened her, because the equation was a puzzle created by Einstein *himself*. How could she possibly resist trying to solve it? But she was irritated by the tactics Dante had used on her. He hadn't even *thought* to ask her nicely or offer encouragement. Instead, he had gone right to the threat, like she was an enemy, rather than family.

She tried to push her anger at Dante aside, not wanting it to cloud her mind, and focused on the clue:

$$\frac{(91-60)^8}{88M} + \left\{ 3\left(\frac{99c}{49}\right) \times \left[\frac{(192)^5}{5M} + (13 \times 16)(16 \times 15)^2 \right] \right\} - \left(\frac{754}{10X}\right)(851) + \left(10X + \frac{78}{92}\right)\left(\frac{10X}{16}\right)^8 \div (15i)\left(\frac{22}{55}\right) = \pi$$

"What do you have so far?" Dante asked.

"Nothing," Charlie said tartly. "You can't make some-one think harder by threatening them, you know. That's not how thinking works."

Dante ignored this. "I'm sure *something* must have grabbed your attention."

Charlie looked back at the clue. "Okay. The last charac-ter doesn't make any sense."

"The pi sign?" Milana asked. "What's wrong with it?"

"Pi is a very specific number," Charlie explained. "3.14159 and so on for another trillion numbers."

Dante said, "Your mother claims you memorized it to two hundred and fifty places when you were seven."

"Three hundred and fifty," Charlie corrected. "And I was six. The presence of pi is another reason I know this isn't an equation. Pi is useful if you need to calculate the area of a circle, but it's an extremely unwieldy result for a complex formula. The chances of this equation being equal to pi has to be a quadrillion to one. . . ."

"Fine," Rats said curtly. "What's your point?"

Charlie said, "The numerical definition of pi probably isn't relevant here. But pi is also the letter P in Greek. And since Pandora was a character in Greek mythology, then pi probably stands for 'Pandora.'"

"Okay," Dante said, sounding pleased. "That's some-thing."

"Not really," Charlie replied. "To Einstein, this would have been obvious. Kiddie stuff. All I've done is determine what I'm solving for. I haven't even scratched the surface of the clue."

"Then let's talk about that," Milana said. "What are you thinking?"

Charlie looked at her. She liked Milana's technique much more than Dante's. Milana seemed concerned about her. Sisterly. Nurturing. Maybe she was just playing good cop to Dante's bad cop in some sort of routine they'd worked out, but it still made Charlie like her more.

And yet . . . There was still something that bothered her about how the CIA was handling Pandora. Personally, she had a better plan to protect the equation, but she didn't want to mention it, because she was sure that Dante and all the others, even Milana, wouldn't agree with her. Instead, she figured it would be best to do what they asked of her, to be a team player for now, while she waited for the opportunity to make her move.

Charlie pointed to Einstein's clue. "I'm going to assume this is a cipher, and your most basic form of cipher is a cryptogram. That's where one character or group of characters stands for another. This would be the simplest version." She quickly sketched out a diagram on the pad:

A	B	C	D	E	F	G
1	2	3	4	5	6	7

"Here, A equals 1, B equals 2, C equals 3, and so on, so the word 'CAB' would be '312.'"

"This is ridiculous," Rats said suddenly, like he'd been biting his tongue and now couldn't stay silent anymore. He spoke to Dante as though Charlie weren't even in the car. "I get that this kid might be some sort of math prodigy, but now you're gonna let her lecture us on codes?"

"I know plenty about codes," Charlie told him coolly.

"How?" Rats challenged. "Has the CIA trained you to be a specialist in it?"

"Puzzle magazines," Charlie said. "Any newsstand has dozens of them. I've been solving cryptograms and other ciphers since I was three."

"And that qualifies you to tell a bunch of CIA agents what to do?"

"Charlie has succeeded at everything we've asked her to do so far," Milana said to Rats sharply. "She located this cipher in the first place—and defeated one of the Furies to get it—while *you* let their leader escape. So I'd really appreciate it if you'd let her speak."

Rats fell silent again, although Charlie could see in the rearview mirror that he was seething.

"Sorry about that," Milana said to Charlie. "Now, if this *was* a cryptogram, how would you solve it?"

Charlie grinned, heartened by her show of support. "I'd start trying to decrypt something by looking for patterns that correspond to the patterns in words. If a pattern showed up with great frequency, I could assume it's a letter that appears frequently, like *E*, *A*, or *S* in English. Or I could look for keystone words, which have distinct letter patterns. For example, the word 'people' has a unique pattern in English, with the *P* and the *E* being repeated in that specific order. So in this basic substitution cipher, it would show up as '16-5-15-16-12-5' or more likely, '1651516125.'" Charlie sketched out what she meant:

P	E	O	P	L	E
16	5	15	16	12	5

"But the problem is," she continued, "I have no idea what language Einstein would have set up this cipher to translate into. The guy spoke German, French, and English fluently—and for all I know, he spoke Portuguese and Esperanto, too. Then again, maybe this doesn't translate into words at all. If Pandora is a formula, then maybe these numbers just translate into more numbers."

Leaning over the back seat, Dante shared a look of frustration with Milana as they both realized that the clue was far more complicated than they'd hoped—and that perhaps Charlie was right that it might take months or more to solve.

Rats turned the SUV off a road choked with cars and tourists onto a surprisingly quiet residential street in the Jewish Quarter. The bustle and noise of the city seemed to disappear, as though they were suddenly a hundred miles away from everything, instead of mere yards. However, Rats still had to drive slowly, as the street had been built hundreds of years before anyone had even imagined a car. It was so narrow at points that the SUV could barely fit between the buildings.

Dante said, "Let's start with the assumption that this clue translates into a language. Do you see any patterns at all?"

"Not really," Charlie replied. "Only four numbers appear more than once: Five and fifteen appear twice, while ten and sixteen appear three times. Then there are two Ms and three Xs. But that's a very low frequency of repetition. For example, in English words, the letter E is so common it appears about once every twelve letters. And I think it has a similar frequency in German. Now, I don't know about other languages, but I'd have to assume that . . ." Charlie trailed off suddenly, struck by something.

"What is it?" Milana asked.

"I'm an idiot," Charlie said. "I've been looking at the numbers instead of the variables. There are only four variables in this clue. Do you see what they stand for?"

Milana shook her head. "They could stand for lots of different things. M could mean meters, milliliters, miles . . ."

"Or mass," Dante added. "Like in E equals MC squared."

"And *C* could be centimeters, centiliters, or the speed of light," Milana said. "Meanwhile, *X* generally represents an unknown variable, while *I* stands for imaginary numbers. That's a strange collection of variables to find in one equation. . . ."

"Exactly," Charlie said. "But if you pull them out of the equation, you get something completely different." She pointed to the variables in order. "MCMXXXI."

Milana's eyes widened in surprise. "Roman numerals."

"1931," said Charlie.

Dante swung around in the front seat, looking impressed. "You think Einstein means the year?"

"I suppose," Charlie said. "I'm not sure what else he *could* mean."

Milana said, "In 1931, Einstein was still living in Germany, teaching at the University of Berlin."

"Maybe that's the year he found Pandora," Dante suggested.

"Maybe," Charlie agreed. "But if so, it still doesn't give us much insight into what the rest of the code means."

Rats suddenly stopped the SUV.

Charlie pulled her attention from the code and looked out the window.

The quiet, twisting street they were in had come to an

end—sort of. Ahead, it narrowed too much for the SUV to fit through, becoming a pedestrian route.

They were in a residential area, surrounded by homes. Each was hundreds of years old, but had been updated for the modern world. All were three stories tall, built of the same Jerusalem stone, and were connected, wall-to-wall, creating a sprawling, misshapen block. From the outside, it was impossible to tell where one house started and the next stopped. Ahead, the room of one home even formed a bridge over the narrow street.

Rats had parked in front of a house with a garage, which Charlie realized was highly unusual in the Old City. Right next to the garage door was a heavily secured entry door with a coded-entry keypad and a camera mounted above it. This struck Charlie as a blatantly obvious security system—the kind of thing that screamed "secret CIA headquarters"—until she noticed that every other residence around her had the same thing. Apparently, people in this section of the Jewish Quarter were very concerned about safety.

"Is this a safe house?" Charlie asked.

"Brilliant deduction," Rats said sarcastically, hopping out of the SUV.

The moment his door was open, the sounds of the city filtered back to Charlie. Ahead, down the narrow section of the road, she could hear the chatter and bustle of what might have been a market street.

Rats typed a code on the keypad by the front door, and the garage door rose. He hopped back into the SUV and drove inside.

The inside of the garage confirmed to Charlie that this wasn't a normal home. Normal homes would have had things stored in the garage, like bicycles and tools and old cans of paint. Especially in a crowded place like the Old City, where space was probably at a premium. This garage had none of that. There were only a few shelves of supplies in bulk: toilet paper, window cleaner, toner cartridges.

Everyone piled out of the SUV as the garage door slid closed behind them, cutting out the sunlight. The only other exit was through a door into the safe house. Rats led the way through it, Milana following him.

In the garage, Charlie turned to Dante and asked, "What's the deal with you and Milana?"

Dante's steps faltered, ever so slightly. "There is no deal with me and Milana."

"You like her, though, don't you?"

Dante's face remained stoic, but Charlie noticed the tips of his ears turn red from embarrassment. "My relationship with Agent Moon is purely professional."

"That's a shame. She likes you too."

"She does?" Dante asked, unable to stop himself—and then immediately regretted it.

Charlie grinned, pleased to have found a chink in her brother's hard exterior. "I *knew* it! You like her!" She began to sing tauntingly. "Dante and Milana sitting in a tree! K-I-S-S-I-N-G . . ."

"Quiet!" Dante hissed, and Charlie fell silent.

They passed through the doorway from the garage into a small foyer. To their right was the door to the street. To their left, a staircase led up to a second security door, which Charlie figured protected the rest of the safe house.

Rats and Milana were already at the top of the stairs, by the second door, waiting for them. Dante waved them on. "Head on in," he said. "We'll be up in a few."

Rats entered a code on the keypad and the upstairs door clicked open. Then he and Milana passed through it—although Milana gave them one last look before entering.

"That's what I'm talking about," Charlie said. "That little glance she gave you? Did you see how she was looking at you?"

"I didn't see anything," Dante said.

"You didn't? Jeez, you might know a whole lot about terrorist cells, but you don't know much about women. That was a full-on 'I wish Dante would say to heck with the regulations and just kiss me' look."

"You're full of crap," Dante said, although he couldn't

hide the fact that he was really hoping that Charlie spoke the truth.

"I am not," Charlie said. "This is how she was looking at you just now."

Dante turned to face her.

Charlie hammered it up, fluttering her eyelashes and puckering her lips. "Oh, Dante," she cooed. "You're soooo dreamy."

"Can it, you little jerk," Dante said, although he was smiling, pleased by the thought of Milana Moon liking him, dropping his guard around Charlie.

Which was exactly what Charlie had been waiting for. The time had come to put her own plan to protect Pandora into action, but she needed to work fast.

She quickly drove her knee into her brother's crotch.

Then, as Dante doubled over in pain, she bolted through the security door into the street and ran as fast as she could.

TWENTY-TWO

While it might have seemed reckless for a twelve-year-old girl to flee from a safe house and head out alone into a foreign city, Charlie had a plan to survive. She had been working it out from the moment she had first arrived in Jerusalem.

The sun was blinding as she emerged from the dark stairwell of the safe house, and her body was still hurting from her fight with Marko, but she didn't stop moving. Her ruse had bought her only a few seconds. She raced into the narrower section of the street, toward the noise and bustle she had heard before. If she could make it to where there were people, she could blend into the crowd.

However, there was something Charlie needed to do even before she had ensured her escape.

She crammed Einstein's clue into her mouth and chewed.

She rounded a corner and found herself in a crowded bazaar. The whole thing was underground, in an arched passageway that appeared to be thousands of years old. Alcoves in the ancient walls were filled with shops. Unlike the other markets Charlie had seen so far, this one wasn't for tourists, selling souvenirs; instead, it was for the residents of the Old City, selling the basics of daily life. Tailors slaved over ancient sewing machines; grocers hawked fruit and vegetables; spice merchants displayed tables full of their wares; butchers hacked apart sheep carcasses with cleavers. As Charlie had hoped, the market was filled with people, most with loaded shopping bags slung over their shoulders. She ducked into the crowd, hoping to quickly disappear.

Something slammed into her from behind.

It was Dante. Either her knee to his crotch hadn't hurt him as much as she'd hoped—or the man had an impressive tolerance for pain. Charlie was thrown several feet by their combined momentum and crashed into a kiosk selling fresh fruit. Dante landed on top of her, crushing the wind from her lungs, while a table full of figs upended on top of them.

Charlie struggled under her brother, but as she had learned when fighting Marko, she was no match against someone who was actually trained to fight. She had caught Dante off guard once; he wasn't going to let it happen again. He shoved her down on the hard stone, then jabbed her in a pressure point at the back of her neck that she'd never even known she had. Pain shot through Charlie's body. She screamed, unable to control it, and Dante snatched Einstein's clue right back out of her mouth.

"You stupid little punk," Dante snarled, and then wrenched Charlie's arm behind her.

"Ow!" Charlie yelled. "You're hurting me!"

"That's the point. And I can make it a lot worse." Dante roughly yanked Charlie to her feet.

The kiosk's owner was shouting at them in Hebrew, angry about the destruction of his property.

"Help me," Charlie said to him in Hebrew. "This man is trying to abduct me!"

"Don't listen to her," Dante said, surprising Charlie by speaking in Hebrew himself. He flashed his badge with his free hand and said, "I'm CIA, working with the Mossad. This girl is connected to an anti-Semitic terrorist cell."

The people surrounding them backed off, now glaring at Charlie hatefully. A few even spit at her. Only the kiosk's owner held his ground, still shouting at them until Dante fished some crumpled bills from his pocket and handed them over. "This ought to cover the damage."

That quieted the vendor. He immediately began cleaning up the mess Charlie and Dante had made.

"You're not the only one in the family who can speak multiple languages," Dante told his sister, keeping her arm twisted behind her back. He checked Einstein's code, confirming that Charlie hadn't destroyed it, then shoved it in his pocket and clamped his hand on her neck.

In that position, Charlie had no choice but to march back toward the safe house.

"Here I was, thinking that I'd been wrong about you all these years," Dante muttered. "Thinking that you weren't just out for yourself. That you actually had some decency in you. And then, even though you know what's on the line here, you still put your own freedom ahead of the safety of millions of people."

"I was *trying* to protect those people," Charlie shot back. "*You're* the one who's putting them in danger."

"Really? You didn't just try to escape with the clue to Pandora's location?"

"No. I tried to *destroy* it. If the point of this mission is simply to keep Pandora from ending up in the hands of our enemies, then solving the clue isn't necessary. All we really have to do is get rid of it."

A flicker of worry flashed in Dante's eyes.

It was a small reaction, but it instantly confirmed Charlie's worst fears. "However," she said, "the point of this mission *isn't* simply to keep Pandora away from our enemies, is it? It's to get Pandora for ourselves."

"Would that be such a bad thing?" Dante demanded. "Pandora could solve all the world's energy problems. . . ."

"Yeah. I'm sure *that's* why the government wants it. It has nothing to do with making weapons at all."

"You don't have the slightest idea what our government plans to do with it."

"I can make a pretty good guess. The weapons budget at the Pentagon is twenty times what the *entire* budget at the Department of Energy is. America's priorities are pretty darn clear: The first thing we do with any major discovery is try to kill people with it."

"That's not true."

"It's what we did with relativity. What did the government build first? Bombs or power plants?"

"That was different. We were at war. Einstein himself pressured President Roosevelt to build weapons."

"And he later regretted it, but the US didn't listen to him then. They kept on making bigger and bigger bombs. So imagine what they'll do when they have Pandora. . . ."

"Our government doesn't want to destroy the world, Charlie. We want to make it safer."

"Then prove me wrong." Charlie nodded toward the clue in Dante's hand. "Destroy that."

"Why? So that no one will be able to find Pandora except *you*?"

Charlie looked at him, surprised.

"I may not be a genius," Dante told her, "but I'm not an idiot, either. I know you've memorized this."

"And you'd rather run the risk of letting Pandora fall into someone else's hands than letting only me have it?"

"No one else is going to get it—as long as you don't try anything stupid again."

"I'm not the one being stupid here, Dante."

"Shut up." They were back at the safe house. Dante shoved Charlie up against the door, then typed in the entry code. When the door clicked open, he yanked her into the foyer.

Charlie tried to hold her ground, grabbing the banister so Dante couldn't get her up the stairs. "You can't make me do this!"

"We'll see about that." Dante wrapped his arms around her from behind, pinioning her arms to her sides, and carried her up the steps while she kicked and writhed.

"You're going to have to drag me back to America and throw me in jail," Charlie threatened. "I don't care! I'm not helping you find Pandora!"

"Of course not. Because you don't do anything that isn't selfish."

"I am not selfish!"

"Really?" Dante set Charlie down on the landing outside the second security door and spun her around so he could look her in the eye. "What's your plan for the rest of your life?"

"I'm just a kid, Dante. I'm not supposed to have a plan."

"All kids have plans. They want to be doctors or firemen or astronauts or spies. But not you. You've got all that incredible intelligence and you're not doing anything with it."

"I got into college!"

"So you could get away from your parents! If you really cared about your education, you'd show up to class once in a while!"

Charlie's jaw dropped slightly in surprise.

"Yeah, I know about that," Dante told her. "I've been keeping tabs on you. So I know everything you've been doing. Or, really, everything you *haven't* been doing. You don't know *everything*, Charlie. There are teachers at that university you could learn from. There are classes that could challenge you. But you're not interested in them. Because all you want to do is goof off until you're old enough to have access to all that money you stole—and then you're just going to goof off even more and waste your life away."

"I *tried* to do something good once," Charlie argued. "I created a code that could have helped protect our financial systems. And it got stolen from me."

"So you decided to never try to do anything ever again?" Dante asked. "You have a gift, damn it! Maybe one person in a generation comes along with the intellect you have. You could cure cancer someday. Or design a rocket that gets us to the stars. Or revolutionize science like Einstein did. You could make the world a better place."

"I don't owe the world anything," Charlie said bitterly. "All Mom and Dad ever tried to do with my talents was get rich from them. And now you and the CIA are using me as well, without any care for my safety at all!"

"We're not . . . ," Dante began, but then caught himself, realizing that perhaps Charlie had a point. He took a breath, calming himself, and his angry gaze became softer and sadder as he tried again. "I *do* care about your safety. And I promise I'll protect you. But I'm not upset that I brought you in. And someday maybe you'll even thank me for doing it."

"Thank you? For kidnapping me, blackmailing me, and putting my life in danger?"

"All the talent in the world doesn't mean a thing if you squander it," Dante said. "But now you can make a difference."

With that he opened the door to the safe house and forced her inside.

The moment they were through the door, someone attacked them. One person grabbed Charlie, slamming the door shut behind her, while two others ambushed Dante. Charlie tried to fight the man holding her, but he was far too strong. Dante tried to come to her aid, but he was outnumbered and had been caught by surprise. Charlie watched in horror as he was overpowered and beaten down. Then she was held tightly from behind and a gun was pressed against her head.

Now that she was subdued, Charlie had a chance to look around the room to see the trap she had stumbled into. Dante was held facedown on the floor by two men, who were stripping him of his weapons and his phone. The third was holding Charlie, while a fourth had Milana Moon pinned to the far wall with a gun to her head. Charlie recognized them all from the photos in the dossier she had seen. The Furies had somehow infiltrated the CIA's safe house.

And their leader, Alexei Kolyenko, stood in the center of it all, smiling cruelly at them.

"Welcome home," he said menacingly. "Now hand over Pandora."

TWENTY-THREE

The scrap of paper with Einstein's clue on it was in Dante's pocket. Instead of handing it over, Dante looked at Alexei and said, "I don't know what you're talking about."

Alexei nodded to Fez, who was holding Dante on the floor with Hans. Fez smiled in a way that made Charlie cringe; she knew from Fez's file that he was a psycho who liked causing pain.

Fez got to his feet and kicked Dante in the stomach so hard it made Dante curl into a ball.

Charlie winced just watching it, knowing it had to have been even more painful than Dante was letting on. Vladimir, the one holding the gun to her head, tightened his grip on her.

"Let's try this again," Alexei said. "Hand over the equation."

"I still don't know what you mean," Dante said.

Alexei grinned, like he had been hoping things might come to this. "You want to be tough? Maybe this will jog your memory." He nodded to Oleg, the terrorist who was holding Milana.

Oleg placed the barrel of his gun in Milana's mouth.

"All right!" Dante shouted. "Don't hurt her! Pandora is in my pocket!"

Alexei signaled Oleg to wait, then nodded to Fez, who knelt by Dante's side and rifled through his pockets.

Charlie was terrified. Everything had gone so wrong so fast. She could feel panic start to grip her, the same way it had back in the parking lot at the university, when one of the Furies had been shooting at her. So she willed herself to remain calm, the same way she had then. She breathed deeply and focused on her surroundings, trying to piece together what had happened, looking for anything that would give her an edge over the Furies.

She cased the room. It had once been a living room, but the CIA had modified it into a workspace. It was sterile and official in design. Where a real home would have had couches and maybe a coffee table, here the walls were ringed with desks, each with a computer perched atop it.

The safe house was narrow. The room they were in took up the entire front of the building, with a large window onto the street. There was only one exit besides the door Charlie had just come through. An open arch led back toward the rear of the house. Charlie could see a hallway beyond Alexei, leading back toward what was probably the kitchen, and a staircase leading upstairs.

Charlie couldn't see any sign of Rats, which she feared was probably bad news for Rats.

Somehow, the Furies had known about the safe house. So they had raced here from the botanical gardens and gotten the jump on the CIA. There had been no sign of forced entry, so they must have known the entry codes. Charlie assumed they hadn't broken in through a back door, because the safe house would have been alarmed; Rats would have certainly been alerted to something like that.

Fez gave a cry of triumph as he discovered Einstein's clue in Dante's pocket. He held it up reverently, as though it were a holy object. The other Furies stared at it with awe. Only Alexei maintained a sense of calm, staring curiously at Charlie.

Charlie did her best to avoid his wolfish gaze, continuing to case the room, seeing what she could use to her advantage. There wasn't much, though. The desks didn't appear to belong to anyone in particular. They were there for whoever was using the safe house at the time. Therefore, the desktops were free from clutter. If there was anything that could be used as a makeshift weapon—scissors, staplers, thumbtacks—it was tucked away in the drawers, inaccessible. There were only computers and keyboards and a single mug full of pens. . . .

But wait . . .

The front window was behind Charlie, facing the street. The blinds were open and the room faced south, so the midday winter sun slanted through them. A slash of light blazed across the desk along the wall farthest from Charlie, slowly edging toward the computer.

The computer wasn't on, but that didn't matter to Charlie. What mattered was the monitor.

The moment Charlie's eyes fell upon it, the numbers came to her.

They flashed through her mind in an instant. Adjusting for certain factors, in three minutes and forty-two seconds Charlie would have a very slight edge over the Furies. An edge she could exploit. It would be risky, but as far as Charlie could tell, it would be the only chance she, Milana, and Dante would have to escape.

Now they just had to stay alive until then.

TWENTY-FOUR

ez handed Einstein's clue to Alexei. To the surprise of his own men, Alexei didn't even look at it. Instead, he kept his gaze locked on Charlie and asked, "Why don't you believe this is Pandora?"

It took a moment for Charlie to realize how Alexei knew this. Then she noticed the security monitor mounted on the wall by the door. Alexei had eavesdropped on everything in the stairwell. Charlie had told Dante she wouldn't help him find Pandora.

Charlie met Alexei's gaze. She was already terrified, and now the predatory look in his eyes unnerved her. She fought to stay calm. According to her watch, she needed to stall him for another three and a half minutes until she could put her plan into action.

She knew from the CIA's dossier that Alexei wasn't that smart, but he was proud. She decided to play to that. "How well do you know physics?" she asked.

"Very well," Alexei replied, in a way that indicated he actually believed it.

Charlie said, "Then it should be obvious to you that what's on that paper isn't an equation."

Alexei looked at Einstein's clue. His brow furrowed in confusion. But he didn't want to admit that what was obvious to a twelve-year-old wasn't obvious to him. "Who are you?" he demanded.

"I'll tell you—if your friends here stop acting like animals." Charlie nodded toward Dante. "Let him up off the floor." Then she nodded toward Milana. "And take the gun out of her mouth."

Alexei acted as if he hadn't even heard the request. "You can't be CIA. You're only a little girl. So what are you doing here with them?"

"Please," Charlie said, doing her best to sound weaker now. The way she thought Alexei would like to hear someone like her speak. "If you just do what I asked, I'll tell you whatever you want to know."

Alexei considered Charlie a second longer, then gave his men orders in German.

The Furies were confused. None spoke English well enough to follow what was going on. But they listened to Alexei's orders. Hans and Fez let Dante get to his feet, but kept their guns trained on him. Oleg took the gun from Milana's mouth—but kept it aimed at her chest.

"Better?" Alexei asked.

"Not much," Charlie replied.

"Now tell us—or we'll kill these pigs. Who are you?"

Charlie considered lying to Alexei, but decided it was too risky. If he realized she wasn't being honest, he might get angry, and that was the last thing she wanted. So she told the truth. "I'm a criminal. A couple years ago, I hacked into some computers and stole a couple million dollars. Unfortunately, I didn't cover my tracks as well as I thought. The CIA found me and blackmailed me into helping them look for Pandora."

"The CIA needs the help of a *girl* to find this?"

"Apparently so."

Alexei broke into laughter. "The CIA must be full of idiots."

"No," Charlie said. "I'm just really freaking smart."

"No girl can be *that* smart." Alexei turned to his men and spoke in German. "The CIA are such fools they need this little girl to help them!"

Now Alexei's men broke into laughter.

"I'm smart enough to speak German as well as you do," Charlie said. In German.

The men stopped laughing and looked at her, surprised.

"I can speak lots of other languages as well," Charlie continued, then shifted into each as she said the name.

"French. Spanish. Chinese. Do you know Chinese?"

Alexei now looked at her, confused. "That's not even a language."

Given their reactions, Charlie was now sure that none of the Furies spoke Chinese. But she knew that Dante did. And so did Milana, according to her file.

So Charlie glanced at her watch and then continued speaking Mandarin Chinese in a casual, conversational tone to disguise the gravity of what she was saying. "In exactly a hundred and eighty-six seconds, be ready to kill these guys." She didn't even glance at Dante or Milana for fear of letting the Furies know she was speaking to them.

"Enough!" Alexei snapped. "We will speak English from now on!" It probably would have made more sense for him to speak in German, so the other Furies could understand, but he seemed to want to prove his intelligence to Charlie. To show that he was multilingual as well.

"All right," Charlie said.

Alexei held up Einstein's code. "If this is not Pandora, then what is it?"

"A clue to finding Pandora."

"And have you solved it?"

Charlie hesitated, pretending as though she wasn't sure what to say. She glanced at the other Furies. They were all confused by what was happening; Alexei was no longer showing disdain for her, but was now actually listening to what she had to say. Their guard was beginning to drop. Although Vladimir was still holding her with an iron grip, keeping his gun to her head.

Charlie looked back to Alexei. "Yes. I know how to solve it."

"What does it say? Where is Pandora?"

"I still need a little time to work that out."

Alexei fixed Charlie with a suspicious stare. "You just said you'd solved it."

"No, I said I know *how* to solve it. This isn't a simple cipher. Figuring it out involves a chain of mathematical processes that I don't think anyone—except maybe Einstein—could do in their head. Now, if you'd like, I can explain it to you."

Alexei looked back at Einstein's clue. He didn't want to admit that he needed Charlie's help, but he obviously had no idea how to decode the message himself. "I'm sure I would figure it out soon enough," he said pompously. "But for the sake of time, I'll let you do it."

"I need some paper and a pen. Can you tell your gorilla here to let me go for a minute?" Charlie nodded backward toward Vladimir.

Alexei frowned at this.

"What? Are you afraid of a little girl?" Charlie asked. In German, so all the Furies could hear her.

Alexei bristled. "Of course not." Then he ordered Vladimir, "Let her go."

"Let her go?" Vladimir repeated, surprised.

"Let her go!" Alexei shouted, angry to have his authority questioned.

Vladimir let go of Charlie.

Charlie quickly stepped away from him, toward the desk with the mug full of pens. "What happened to Agent Ratsimanohatra?" she asked.

"The brown man?" Alexei asked. "He's dead. We tossed him in the bathroom."

Charlie swallowed hard. She had expected this, but it was still unnerving to hear the truth. Especially given the psychopathic lack of remorse in Alexei's voice.

"If I tell you where Pandora is, will you let the rest of us live?" Charlie asked.

"Of course," Alexei said, but it was an obvious lie. So obvious, Charlie couldn't tell if Alexei wanted her to think he was toying with her, or if he was simply a bad liar.

By Charlie's count, she had exactly eighty seconds left to stall.

"To figure out that clue, I had to make a few assumptions," she said. "The first is that this wouldn't be a substitution cipher. It's too difficult to transfer numbers into letters without leaving an easily detectable pattern. . . ."

"I don't care *how* you solved this," Alexei snapped. "I just want to know what it says."

Sixty-five seconds.

"I'm just telling you this clue isn't going to translate into words. It won't say 'Pandora's box is hidden in such and such a place.' It's going to translate into more numbers. That would have made sense to Einstein, because numbers are a universal language. However, what these numbers will *mean* is anybody's guess. Theoretically, they'll be coordinates like latitude and longitude, but I can't guarantee that."

"Fine. Give me them."

"Okay. But I still have to work them out."

"I want to see," Alexei said.

"All right." Charlie stepped to the desk. The only paper was a stack of Post-it notes, but she figured those would do. She wasn't planning on writing much anyhow, and if she started opening drawers, the Furies would probably freak out and shoot her.

She needed to continue to put up a good front for the Furies, to look like she wasn't remotely a threat.

Charlie strained to remain calm, keeping an eye on her watch, praying her math was right. If it wasn't, these could very well be her last moments alive.

Thirty seconds.

Alexei came to the desk by Charlie's side. He was now

close enough for her to smell him. He reeked of sweat and stank like a dead fish.

Charlie picked up the Post-it notes and chanced a final look around the room. Hans and Fez were looking at her, rather than Dante. Oleg was still pinning Milana against the wall, but his focus was on Charlie as well. Vladimir was now a few steps away, too far to grab her.

At the front window, the sun continued slanting through the blinds, the beam of light slowly edging across the room while the earth rotated. . . .

"Let's begin with the first number in this equation," Charlie said. "Ninety-one minus sixty to the eighth is a massive number, so we'll have to represent it in scientific notation. . . ."

She casually reached for the mug full of pens.

One second . . .

Behind Charlie, the ray of sunlight slid a fraction of a millimeter across the desk beneath the window, catching the tilted glass of the computer monitor for the first time. There was a sudden flash as the light glared off the monitor, momentarily blinding Alexei.

Charlie grabbed the mug and smashed it on Alexei's temple, sending him reeling.

Then she threw it at Vladimir, hitting him in the face.

The other Furies wheeled on Charlie with their guns,

but she had positioned herself so that Alexei was directly between her and them.

And while the Furies were distracted by her, Milana and Dante leapt into action.

Milana quickly wrenched Oleg's gun from his grasp and flipped him over her shoulder.

Dante grabbed Fez and flung him into Hans, sending both tumbling to the floor. "Charlie!" he yelled. "Up the stairs!"

Charlie didn't question the order. She was out of her element here. So she ran toward the staircase.

Alexei lunged at her, but he was big and slow and she was quick and lithe. She ducked him easily and hit the stairs running. From behind her came the sounds of fists striking flesh and furniture breaking. Two guns discharged, the explosions ear-shattering inside the house.

Then there were footsteps on the stairs behind her. Terror gripped her, but before Charlie could even pause to see if it was one of the Furies, Milana yelled, "It's me! Keep going! All the way up!"

Charlie obeyed and kept moving.

Another gunshot rang out below her, this one followed by a *thud*.

Charlie reached the third floor and saw what Dante's plan was: The stairs didn't stop there, but continued upward, and there was a door at the top, bright sunlight peeking around the edges. Charlie unlocked it and threw it open, and suddenly she was out on the roof, the city spread out all around her.

The roof wasn't only the roof of the safe house, but of *all* the roofs of the connected houses, an enormous swath of white plaster, blinding in the sun.

Milana was out the door behind her a second later, but Dante stopped on the third floor and reloaded his gun, preparing to make a stand.

"Dante!" Charlie yelled to him. "Come on!"

"Milana! Keep her moving!" Dante yelled in return.

Milana wavered, then started back down the stairs.

"No!" Dante exclaimed. "Keep Charlie safe! They still have the clue! If I don't get it back . . ."

He didn't have time to finish the statement. The Furies were on their way up the stairs; Charlie could hear them. Dante fired down, directly through the floor. There was a scream of pain from below, and then Dante dove away as more bullets tore upward through the floor, splintering the wood and pocking holes in the plaster of the ceiling.

Charlie understood what Dante was about to say, though: If he couldn't get the clue back from the Furies, then the only other copy of it was in her mind.

Milana understood too. She grabbed Charlie by the

arm and raced across the rooftops with her, leaving Dante behind to face the Furies by himself.

Charlie had no idea how many of the Furies were still alive. But it was certainly more than one. Dante might have had the high ground in this battle, but he was definitely outnumbered and outgunned.

He was risking his life to protect Charlie's.

There was a very good chance that Charlie would never see her brother again.

Before she could truly deal with the cold, harsh reality of that, someone else started shooting at them.

TWENTY-FIVE

In parts of the Old City of Jerusalem, the rooftops were as much of a thoroughfare as the streets. The big, amorphous blocks of homes were topped by wide, flat spaces and connected to one another by bridges and arches that spanned the narrow streets. While each house had its own private door, like the one Charlie and Milana had just emerged through, there were also public staircases that led directly down to the streets, allowing any pedestrian in the city access to the area—if they knew how to find it.

Charlie and Milana raced across the rooftops, running for their lives.

The wide expanse of white plaster lay before them. It was uneven and rolling, changing with every home, dotted with satellite dishes, ventilation grates, and the occasional piece of old furniture someone had discarded. None of that provided much cover from the sniper, though.

Several other people were up there as well, commuting via rooftop: Hasidic businessmen in dark suits with tzitzit hanging down from the waist, Muslim women draped in hijabs—a group of schoolboys was even playing soccer. All lay down flat when they heard the gunfire, trying to stay low, although Charlie noticed no one panicked. Jaded by years of living in a dangerous city, the Jerusalem citizens calmly made sure they weren't the targets, then stayed low to ensure they weren't hit by stray bullets.

Charlie and Milana just kept running.

They had no choice. There had been no time to determine where the sniper was. They only knew the general direction the first shot had come from—and since then they had simply been running the other way.

Charlie followed Milana's lead, juking left and right without any pattern to keep the sniper from being able to draw a bead on her. Three steps left, one right, one left, five right . . . They heard more shots ring out, saw the occasional puff of dust as a bullet missed them and hit the roof instead.

Despite Charlie's attempts to focus on her running, other thoughts kept creeping into her mind, things she tried to ignore but that rose to the surface anyhow.

Like the fact that Dante might be dead. The way that Rats already was.

Four steps right, two left, two right . . .

Charlie didn't want to believe it, but she couldn't help seeing the numbers. The probability was that he hadn't survived.

The simple idea was devastating. Charlie had never been close to Dante; for much of their lives, she had believed her half brother hated her. But now she knew that probably wasn't true. Dante had merely been jealous of her and then disappointed in her. And to make matters worse, Charlie realized Dante was right.

Her brother's last words to her still rang in her ears: *All the talent in the world doesn't mean a thing if you squander it.* It was true. Charlie knew she had been barely using her gifts. In fact, she had been perversely proud of that.

But now you can make a difference, Dante had added. Which had a much greater resonance now that he had sacrificed his life to protect hers. The last thing she wanted was for Dante to have died in vain. . . .

A bullet ricocheted off the ground at Charlie's feet, snapping her back to the crisis at hand.

"We have to get off the roof!" Milana shouted.

Charlie brushed the hair from her eyes as she ran and desperately scanned the horizon, looking for a way out. There were many doors leading down into homes, the same as the door they had emerged from, but they were certainly locked, while the closest set of public stairs leading down from the rooftops was a long distance away. . . .

Charlie suddenly caught sight of something ahead to her right. A slash of darkness on the white rooftops.

"Follow me!" she yelled.

Three blocks away, the sniper watched them through the scope of his gun.

He wasn't trained as a sharpshooter. He didn't even have a proper rifle; he only had a .46 Magnum. He shouldn't have even been in this position, trying to shoot these agents. If Alexei had done his job, the women would have been dead down in the safe house and Pandora would be in his hands. But now, somehow, that whole plan—that perfect, foolproof plan—had failed and the CIA agents were still alive and on the run.

As usual, he would have to take care of everything.

The Magnum was powerful enough to kill someone three blocks away, but it was big and heavy and hard to aim. It was difficult enough to hit a stationary target with it, let alone one zigzagging erratically. But the sniper was getting the hang of it. He had stopped trying to freehand the gun and now steadied it atop an air conditioner. His last shots had been closer to their mark. Now he had three bullets left in the clip, and he intended to make them count.

He focused on the girl with Milana Moon. The sniper didn't know who the girl was; he couldn't even tell how old she was from this distance. But he presumed she was important. After Bern, the CIA had been flummoxed, its plans to track down Pandora in shambles. And suddenly they were here in Jerusalem with her. She had ruined everything at the university. Things had fallen apart after her arrival at the safe house. She was nothing but trouble. Therefore, she had to be taken out first. Without her, Agent Moon would be useless.

The sniper pivoted the Magnum slightly on its grip, lining up a point just ahead of his target. Despite the unpredictable path the girl was taking, she was moving in the same general direction. Which meant that no matter which way she zigged or zagged, in just a few seconds she would pass through the point in space the sniper was aiming.

Sure enough, the girl jogged left, away from where the sniper was aiming, but went only a few steps before cutting back in her original direction.

The sniper pulled the trigger three times, emptying the clip.

In the distance, his target dropped.

TWENTY-SIX

It was suddenly quiet in the stairwell at the safe house. Dante was crouched in the hallway on the third floor, ready to make a stand, his heart pounding like a jackhammer in his chest. The Furies were gathered on the floor below him, shouting back and forth to one another in German, plotting the best way to take him out. He and Milana had banged them up, but they were all still alive. Dante figured he had the skills to take out one or two, maybe even three of them, but not all five. His number was certainly up. Still, it would be worth it to protect Charlie, Milana, and Pandora. He would at least give them a fighting chance.

And then the Furies were retreating back down the stairs, racing for the door.

Dante sagged against the wall, relieved—but only for a moment. Then he realized that the Furies hadn't backed off because of *him*. They had fled too quickly for that to be the case.

They had simply changed their plans. Killing him was no longer their priority.

Charlie was.

They weren't heading for the roof anymore because they were hoping to ambush her somewhere else.

Dante leapt to his feet and raced down the stairs.

Charlie and Milana came crashing down into the marketplace.

The dark slash in the rooftops Charlie had spotted was the ten-foot gap between the stone walls. A low arch of green glass spanned it, crusted with dirt and spackled with pigeon droppings, but the glass wasn't thick and it collapsed easily under their weight.

Charlie and Milana both knew there were risks involved, dropping into the market this way. They could have cut themselves on the glass, or broken a bone if they landed wrong, but staying up on the rooftops any longer meant certain death, so this was still better.

As it was, Charlie felt a bullet pass right over her head as she fell; if she had jumped a second later, she would have been dead. She smacked into the awning over a rug shop and tumbled off it. The startled tourists and locals below her scattered as she dropped to the stone street.

She landed on her feet but lost her balance and tumbled into a rack of dried fruits, which upended all over her.

Milana, being bigger, tore through the awning and landed on a pile of rugs.

Charlie instantly snapped to her feet, brushing apricots and figs off her, sweeping her hair from her eyes. The shop's owner screamed at her in Hebrew, pointing at his wares and the shattered glass above.

"I'm very sorry," Charlie replied in Hebrew. "Trust me, I'm more upset about this than you are."

The owner grabbed her arm roughly and raised a hand to strike her in a way that indicated this was a common behavior for him.

Charlie tensed for the blow, but it never came.

Milana had caught the man's hand in midstrike. She was glowering at the shop owner with the same hatred she had shown the terrorists. "That is no way to treat a woman," she said, then wrenched the man's arm so hard that he howled in pain, releasing Charlie. "Not so much fun when you're the one getting hurt, is it?" Milana asked.

The man whimpered and shook his head. Milana shoved him backward, sending him sprawling into the pile of fruit.

"Thanks," Charlie told her.

Another commotion erupted farther along in the market, shoppers squawking in surprise as they were roughly shoved aside.

The Furies. Three of them. Oleg, Fez, and Hans. They had probably split up from Alexei and Vladimir to cover more ground.

Charlie and Milana fled. They had landed in a tourist market, where merchants hawked T-shirts, souvenirs, and ancient artifacts that probably hadn't been acquired legally. The narrow walkways were jammed with people, making it hard to run. The Furies, being bigger and tougher, were able to bulldoze their way through the crowds faster and quickly closed the gap on them.

Milana gave Charlie orders as they ran. "If they catch us, you won't be able to beat them in a fight. So let *me* do the fighting. You use your strength . . ."

"You said I didn't have any!" Charlie protested.

"I said you're a bad fighter. But you still have strengths. Don't use your body against these guys. Use your brain. Figure out what's around you and use it against them, the same way you used the skateboard to take down Marko. Or the computer against Alexei."

"Gotcha." Charlie suddenly felt surprisingly confident, given her circumstances. The Furies no longer seemed like thugs who were going to overwhelm her as much as problems that needed to be solved. Charlie quickly scanned the market ahead, as Milana had suggested, looking for what she could use to help her.

The road angled downward, and ahead it intersected

with the underground market Charlie had come across earlier, which gave her an idea. The Furies were now almost upon them, although the market was too crowded for them to use their guns. Charlie willed herself a final burst of speed, hooked around the corner, and spotted exactly what she was hoping for: a spice merchant. Tables in front of the shop were laden with dozens of bowls piled high with ground seasonings. As Oleg bore down on her, Charlie grabbed a handful of chili powder and flung it into his eyes.

Oleg roared in pain and stumbled forward blindly. Milana spun around and drove a knee into his crotch, folding the man like a hinge. Then she shoved him backward into the path of his fellow Furies.

They nimbly raced around him. Charlie flung a second handful of chili, but Hans and Fez were ready for it, blocking their eyes with their arms, and then they were upon her.

Milana caught Fez and used his momentum against him, whirling him away from Charlie and flinging him into a butcher shop, where he skidded on the blood-slicked floor and face-planted in a pile of innards.

Charlie ducked Hans's attack and the Fury shot past her. By the time he had turned around, Charlie had snatched a samovar filled with boiling water from the front of a tea shop. She popped the lid open and threw the boiling water into Hans's face, scalding him and burning his eyes. Hans fell backward, blinded and screaming.

In the butcher shop, Fez got back to his feet, grabbed a cleaver from a carving block, and charged. Milana lifted an entire sheep's leg off a hook and parried the attack. The cleaver sank into the bone, embedding so deeply that Fez couldn't pull it free. Milana then cracked Fez across the face with the sheep shank. The Fury smashed head-first through a glass display case and went down for good.

Milana stepped out of the butcher shop, took a look at Hans, wailing on the ground, and nodded approval to Charlie. "Now, *that's* how to play to your strengths."

There was no time to celebrate, however. Alexei and Vladimir were still out there. Heavily armed men who wanted them dead.

Milana swiped the guns from the other Furies and then she and Charlie fled into the Old City.

TWENTY-SEVEN

Langley, Virginia

No one was answering the phones in Jerusalem.

Jamilla Carter's staff had been trying to reach someone for the last ten minutes. Finally, Carter had grown annoyed and started placing calls herself, but the result was the same. Nothing but voice mail.

The spy game was different than it used to be. Back before cell phones, you didn't expect to reach anyone whenever you wanted. If someone went deep into Afghanistan or Nicaragua or even parts of Eastern Europe, there might be weeks between communications from them. But now you could pretty much reach anyone, anywhere, at any time.

Of course, you had to expect there would be occasions when an agent couldn't be immediately accessible. But an entire team of agents was a different story. That meant something had gone wrong.

So Carter ordered her chief technology officer to access the mainframe in Jerusalem. There were three dozen security cameras in and around the safe house. Digital records for each were stored for two months and could be accessed by anyone on the CIA system.

"Here we go," the CTO announced. "This should be the live feed from camera one." Carter took a seat behind him in the computer station. There was a lag of a few seconds for the images from Jerusalem to load, seeing as they had to be bounced off a satellite, but then the screen filled with . . .

Static.

The CTO checked the feed from each camera and found the same thing.

"Is that a transmission error?" Carter asked.

"No. The connection's fine. And it looks like the system is still recording. The problem must be with the cameras. . . ."

"Then rewind what you've got."

The CTO typed a few commands. The static on his monitor shifted slightly as the recording rewound at high speed.

Carter's secretary signaled that he needed her attention. A call had finally come in from Jerusalem.

Carter took the phone quickly, expecting it to be Dante Garcia. Instead, it was Leah Bendavid. She apologized breathlessly for not getting back to Carter sooner; she had been down in the vault at the library, talking to the university police, and since the vault was in the basement, the phone reception was crap, so it wasn't until Bendavid had left the library that she even realized anyone had been trying to call her. . . .

Carter interrupted her. "So you haven't been to the safe house?"

"Not since early this morning."

"Have you had any contact with any of the Jerusalem team in the last hour?"

"No. But I wasn't expecting to. Is something wrong?"

On the computer monitor, the static ended and there was suddenly activity on the screen, though it was running so quickly in reverse no one could tell what was happening.

"Hold on," Carter told Bendavid.

By the time the CTO stopped the digital recording, it had rewound two minutes past the point where the static had begun. Now it began to play forward again. The CTO altered the connection so that the monitor was split into eight squares, each representing the feed from a different security camera in the safe house.

Carter and the CTO watched everything unfold.

It all went down fast.

A figure approached the CIA's safe house from the

street, moving quickly, keeping his head down so his face couldn't be seen—although Carter could presume he was a man from his build. He typed the access code at the security door, then raced up the stairs and entered the code for the second door as well.

The CIA's Jerusalem team was small; the Agency's main office was in Tel Aviv. There were only three senior agents, and all were currently deployed on senior operations, so there were only two young agents on duty inside the safe house. They showed no sign of alarm, probably assuming it was Bendavid returning.

The unknown figure came through the second door with his gun drawn. He shot both of the agents before they could even react. Then he swiftly went to each security camera and clipped the feed wire, turning each picture to static.

Carter could guess what had happened after that. But she needed to know for sure.

She returned her attention to the phone. "Agent Bendavid?"

"Yes, ma'am?"

"How long have you been with the Agency?"

"Three years and four months."

"Have you ever been in a situation where you had to use your gun?"

"No, ma'am, but I spend three hours a week at the

shooting range. And I served in the armed services here for two years. I hate to ask again, but . . . is something wrong?"

"The safe house has been compromised. Everyone there was taken out by an assassin who knew the entry codes."

There was a long pause. When Bendavid spoke again, she sounded distant and confused. "I don't understand. How could an assassin know those codes?"

"That's what you need to help us figure out. I have a relationship with a Mossad agent named Isaac Semel. Have you ever met him?"

"Yes, ma'am. Several times."

"I'm calling him. I'll have him contact you. Stay where you are until then. Do not return to the safe house until Semel and his team can accompany you. Do you understand?"

"Yes, ma'am."

Carter hung up and looked back at the computer screen, thinking of the agents she had just seen die and wondering how Dante's team had fared. None of them would have expected the safe house to be compromised. They would have had their guard down when they entered. Had anyone survived? How on earth had the killer learned the safe house access codes? And who was he? A member of the Furies? A rogue agent? Or a new player to the game entirely?

A name suddenly flashed through Carter's mind.

Charlie Thorne.

Things had gone very badly since she had come aboard.

Carter knew Charlie was only twelve, but twelve-year-olds all over the world had been co-opted into doing very bad things: setting off bombs in the Middle East, running militias in the Congo, working for criminal enterprises throughout the United States. And Thorne was smarter than almost anyone else alive. She had hacked the computer system of one of the biggest software companies on earth; maybe she could have hacked the CIA, too, getting the pass codes, the names of agents, or anything else she wanted.

If Charlie had decided to switch to the dark side—or had been aligned with the dark side all along—she would be a very formidable enemy.

An enemy that would have to be dealt with in the strictest way possible.

TWENTY-EIGHT

Jerusalem

Charlie and Milana ran for some time longer, thinking they had shaken the Furies but unwilling to assume it. They turned left and right at random, creating a trail no one could follow until, legs aching and lungs burning, they found themselves at the Church of the Holy Sepulchre.

It was a massive edifice, one of the holiest sites in Christianity, as it was erected atop the Hill of Calvary, where Christ had been crucified. The small plaza in front of it was thronged with pilgrims, and yet, to Charlie's surprise, there were no guards, X-ray machines, or any other security at the church.

Without saying a word, Charlie and Milana both fell into line and funneled inside. Despite their disheveled state, no one regarded them suspiciously; pilgrims often came to the church looking far worse after their long, arduous journeys.

Inside, the church was surprisingly large and unusual in design. Unlike most churches Charlie had been in, there was not one central space; this church had been destroyed and rebuilt repeatedly since its original construction in 325 AD and was now a sprawling labyrinth of chapels, some cramped and some cavernous. To the right of the entrance, a stone staircase led up to the supposed site of Christ's crucifixion, while to the left, a small structure known as the Edicule covered the site where Christ's body had been laid, though it was dwarfed by a soaring rotunda more than two hundred and fifty feet high. The church was dim, lit only by sacramental candles and oil lamps, the ceiling stained by centuries of accumulated smoke.

Charlie and Milana discovered that the crowds thinned greatly beyond the Edicule. Despite the sacredness of the church, many areas were practically ignored. In some spots, construction supplies were piled up for repair projects that appeared to have been either stalled or abandoned. Charlie and Milana found a stone bench tucked deep in the shadows where they could still keep a close eye on the crowd. While some of the pilgrims and tourists were silent in reverence, most talked freely, and the church resounded with their voices. In the cacophony, Milana felt it was finally safe to speak.

"How much of what you told Alexei about Einstein's clue was true? Have you really solved it?"

Charlie gaped at her, upset. "You want to talk shop *now*? My brother could be dead!"

"There's a chance he's not. . . ."

"I can handle the truth. I know the odds aren't promising."

"I'm not just saying this to make you feel better. And I'm not saying that the chances are good. But here's what I *do* know: Our mission is to obtain Pandora, and so far it's been a disaster. We don't have our phones, half of the Jerusalem division is dead, and the Furies have the only clue to Pandora's location. If we want to beat them to it, you're our best hope. So, did you really solve that clue?"

"No. That was a lie. I haven't solved anything. . . ." To Charlie's surprise, she started crying. The weight of everything that had happened suddenly came crashing down on her: the awareness of how close she had come to death, the knowledge that she might be the only thing standing between the Furies and Pandora—and, most of all, the fear that Dante hadn't survived.

Milana's composure softened, and tears welled in her eyes too. She put an arm around Charlie and pulled her close, letting the young girl sob into her shoulder. It occurred to Milana that Charlie was so worldly and composed that it was easy to forget she was only twelve.

There were agents who had been through years of training at the Farm who cracked after their first life-or-death encounter in the field. Charlie had been thrust right into all this with no preparation at all. The CIA had promised to keep her safe and then failed miserably.

"Dante is a top agent," Milana said softly. "If anyone could have survived that situation, it's him."

Charlie wasn't religious; no one in her family had been. And now, here she was, sitting inside one of the most important churches on earth. It occurred to her that maybe she should take that as a sign and pray for Dante.

She pulled away from Milana and stood to go light a votive candle, as many of the other pilgrims were doing.

But Milana caught her arm. "What are you doing?"

"Something for Dante."

"If you *really* want to do something for Dante, help me find Pandora. So that all he did wasn't in vain. If you haven't solved the clue, did you at least memorize it? Or was that a bluff too?"

"No. That was the truth."

"Could you write it down again? We could send it to our cryptographers at Langley, have them take a crack at it."

Charlie shook her head. "That's a terrible idea."

Milana bridled at the insult. "Why?"

"Because we can't trust anyone at Langley," Charlie said. "There's only one good explanation for how the Furies ambushed us at the safe house."

"What's that?"

"Someone in the CIA sold us out."

TWENTY-NINE

You think someone turned on us?" Milana asked angrily. "That's not possible."

"It's the only thing that makes sense," Charlie replied. "Consider the location of the clue in the first place. The only time Einstein ever mentioned it was inside the Sherlock Holmes book was on his deathbed—and the CIA had the only recording of that."

"That tape has been around for almost seventy years. The staffs of a dozen White Houses could have heard it. The FBI, the NSA . . . anyone could have let a copy slip accidentally. . . ."

"Fine. Then how do *you* explain the terrorists inside your own safe house? Who gave them the access codes? How do you explain the fact that they even knew there was a safe house in the first place—not to mention its exact location? That ambush wasn't a last-second backup plan. That was worked out way before we got here. Someone in the Agency is corrupt and working with the Furies."

"No way."

"I'm not saying it was someone on your team," Charlie told Milana. "It was more likely one of the CIA agents stationed in Jerusalem. . . ."

"Who? Rats? Rats is dead. And so is *everyone else* in the Jerusalem office."

"Not Barbie."

Milana shook her head. "I've seen Bendavid's file. She's solid. Jerusalem is one of the toughest beats the CIA has. No one gets sent here unless they've been vetted six ways from Sunday. . . ."

"Well, *someone* is working with the Furies. Because there's one more of them than you realized."

Milana sat back, suddenly grasping what Charlie meant.

Charlie counted them out on her fingers. "Marko got killed by his own people. Alexei, Oleg, Hans, Fez, and Vladimir ambushed us at the safe house. Those are the only six the CIA had in the file. So who was the sniper on the roof?"

"I don't know. Maybe the team missed someone in Bern. . . ."

"After doing reconnaissance on them for months? No way. The Furies picked up this new person *here*. Plus, according to their files, none of the Furies had any serious weapons training. But whoever was shooting at us on the roof *did*. The kind of training Bendavid would have had at the Farm—or in the Israeli army."

Milana shook her head again. "There's no way Bendavid was involved. . . ."

Charlie sighed, exasperated. "The CIA must have defectors all the time. Not everyone's a Goody-Two-shoes like you and my brother. Maybe Bendavid isn't as nice as she seemed. . . ."

"I'm not talking about corruptibility. I'm talking about access. No single agent at the CIA had all the information the terrorists needed to pull this off. No one in the Jerusalem office knew about Pandora or the Einstein tapes until this morning. And no one on my team knew the safe house location or access codes."

"The Furies knew about Pandora. Maybe they reached out to Bendavid months ago, looking for someone they could corrupt."

"And how would they have found her?" Milana demanded sarcastically. "Called the CIA here and asked to speak with any corruptible agents? Bendavid is a covert op. Her own parents don't know what she does for a living. How could the Furies?"

Charlie frowned, realizing the argument made sense. And yet she still didn't see how the Furies could have pulled off their ambush without an insider. "How often are the access codes to the safe houses changed?" she asked.

"Ideally, it ought to happen every day. But it doesn't. Did you see the access panel here? It might as well be as old as this church. Someone would have to update it manually every day and then inform the team, which is a pain in the rear, so it never gets done."

"Never?"

"Well, not nearly as often as it should."

"So maybe the codes hadn't been changed in a few months?"

"I suppose that's possible."

"Is there anyone who worked in the Jerusalem office in the past few months who also worked on Pandora?"

"Not that I know of."

"You're sure?"

"Well, there was one agent," Milana said, annoyed by Charlie's persistence, "but there's no way he could be working for the Furies, because he's dead."

Charlie stiffened, surprised. "The agent who died in Bern had worked in Jerusalem?"

"Yes," Milana said, though her annoyance had already faded, because she was now concerned about the connection herself.

"What happened in Bern?" Charlie asked.

Milana stared off across the church, watching the pilgrims lined up around the Edicule, thinking back to what she'd read in the files on Bern and all that had gone wrong there.

And then she told Charlie the story.

John Russo had been one of the stars of the CIA, a young agent who was fluent in Arabic, Hebrew, German, and Pashto. At just twenty-six, he had already done more undercover work than most veteran spies. His skills were in such demand that every time he came off one mission, another was waiting for him. He had just finished a six-month stint in Jerusalem, nailing a rogue Hamas cell, when the call had come from Bern.

In Switzerland, John had posed as a blue-collar German named Maxim, working as a bartender in a sleazy dive where the Furies drank. The CIA gave him fake German papers and a fake swastika tattoo to match Alexei's. The Furies didn't have much money, so John occasionally slipped them free drinks—and made it clear they shared the same views on race and immigration. The Furies were cautious about recruiting new members, but one drunken night they opened up to John about what they were plotting and John begged to become a part of it. Soon afterward he was joining the Furies on their excursions to search for Pandora.

Everything had been going perfectly—until one fateful night. John had been hanging out with the Furies in their apartment, drinking beer and winning their confidence, when he suddenly botched a simple phrase in German, revealing that he wasn't the man he claimed to be. The Furies, drunk and vengeful, had shown no mercy.

"What did they do to him?" Charlie asked.

Milana turned to her. This was the first time Charlie had spoken since she'd begun talking, an uncharacteristically long silence for the kid. She had just sat there, listening intently, until now.

"You don't need to know the details," Milana said.

"Actually, I think I do."

"It was bad, Charlie."

"How bad? Could you recognize the body afterward?"

"No. The Furies were brutal."

"Did anyone do a DNA test on the remains?"

"Now you're a forensics expert?" Milana asked.

"I've seen plenty of crime shows," Charlie replied. "Was there a test?"

"There wasn't any point to it, from what I understand. John was wearing a wire when they caught him. The CIA overheard everything. By the time they got to the apartment, they found what was left of John's body."

"Not *his* body," Charlie corrected. "Someone else's. John Russo is still alive—and he's working with the Furies."

THIRTY

In the marble shower of his suite at the King David Hotel, John Russo scrubbed two weeks' worth of dirt off his body.

The King David was one of the finest hotels in Jerusalem, where presidents, kings, and sheikhs had stayed for decades. It perched on the edge of a ravine directly across from the Old City, which John had a view of from his balcony.

He had just come from there, after meeting with Alexei in a nondescript falafel shop. That had been part of their plan all along, to reconvene after the ambush at the safe house. What *hadn't* been part of the plan was that three CIA agents would still be alive. They should have all been dead; John had practically gift wrapped them for the Furies, but those idiots had still screwed things up. First, they had somehow allowed the agents to escape the safe house—and then three Furies had gotten their butts kicked by two women in the market, one of whom was only a child.

And yet the operation had been a success. John still had plans in place to neutralize the CIA—and more important, he now had what Einstein had hidden in the book. Alexei, aware that he was too stupid to comprehend it, had handed it right over to John.

The Furies had no idea he was in this hotel, splurging on this high-end room. They thought he had merely gone somewhere quiet to study Einstein's code. Alexei certainly would have been upset to know he was here. He would have considered checking into such a decadent place simply for a decent shower and some air-conditioning to be an unnecessary luxury. But John had spent enough of his life paying his dues, living in roach-infested hovels while he did his undercover work; he deserved a little luxury.

Originally, John hadn't minded the hardship. He had always wanted to be an undercover agent, and hardship was part of the package. So he was prepared for the rigors of pretending to be someone else for months at a time. But what had surprised him was that sometimes after the mission was over it was hard to go back to being himself. Every time John returned from an operation, he felt as though he had lost a piece of who he was. Undercover agents were supposed to have long gaps between assignments to recover and build themselves back up emotionally—but because the CIA was strapped for agents with his skill set, John kept rotating back into play. He had told his superiors he could handle it, that it wasn't taking a toll on him, but it was, slowly and surely. So slowly he didn't notice it was happening himself.

Then, one day in Bern, after more than a month undercover, he had realized he felt more comfortable as Maxim than he did as John. He could remember his fake background more readily than his real one: fake birth date, fake parents, fake memories. Even worse, he began to fear returning to life as John. This didn't mean he agreed with the Furies; on the contrary, he still considered them fanatical morons. But he no longer wanted to bring the Furies down the CIA's way, because once he did, his mission would be over and he would have to go back to being himself. Which meant he would soon have to pretend to be yet another person, and another after that, and another, and so on—a prospect John wanted to avoid at all costs.

He had kept all this to himself, knowing that if he spoke a word of it to the CIA, the Agency would pull the plug on the whole operation and he would have to return to real life again that much faster. So he kept grinding away, acting like a good soldier, looking for a way out.

And then, one day, he found it. The key to everything.

The discovery that would solve his problems and provide him with the means to never have to work again.

There was a trove of Einstein's papers in Bern: Thousands of pages were stored in the archives at the city's historic museum, as well as at the museum in Einstein's old home. The public had access to many of them, so long as they were handled with extreme care. The Furies were combing through it all, pretending to be graduate students, hunting for the book Alexei suspected contained Pandora—or any clue to its location.

Most of the papers were useless. It sometimes seemed as if every single thing Einstein had ever written down had been preserved, no matter how mundane. The archives held his journals from elementary school, textbooks he had never opened, even shopping lists from the early years of his marriage. To make matters worse, John was sure that over the past decades, the CIA, MI6, and various other covert organizations had swiped anything of value anyhow, so all he was left with were the meaningless scraps. But he helped sift through it all, because everyone—the CIA *and* the Furies—wanted him to.

One day, he had been idly flipping through one of Einstein's high school texts when he noticed something was hidden inside the back cover. A single piece of paper, tucked into a hairline slit. John carefully removed and examined it. At first it merely appeared to be a jumble of numbers; John would have dismissed it as idle doodling had it not been so carefully concealed. Upon closer examination he realized what it was: Teenage Einstein, probably sitting bored in the back of a classroom, was devising a secret code. And John held the key to it in his hands.

What Einstein wanted to say at the time wasn't particularly important. The future scientist's mind wasn't on mass, energy, or the space-time continuum. Instead, he was concerned with what any teenage boy generally was: girls. The greatest genius of the twentieth century was passing notes in class. Only, he had created a cipher to do it.

John pounced on a pile of journals from Einstein's college years that he had already examined. Every now and then he had seen a notation in Einstein's writing on the pages, something which he and decades of snoops before him had dismissed as mere scribbling. Armed with the key, however, John could now see the notations were much more.

Einstein was writing notes to himself.

There was rarely much to them, but they were always about something that Einstein wanted to keep private: new thought experiments, ideas on wave-particle theory and Brownian motion, the genesis of special relativity.

But while Einstein's fields of interest changed often throughout his life, his coding system remained exactly the same.

John suddenly felt as if destiny had smiled upon him. He alone had stumbled upon the secret to Einstein's innermost thoughts. John couldn't guarantee that Pandora would be encoded, but given the great lengths Einstein had taken to hide it, he guessed it would be—and he was now the only person alive who would know how to read it.

Meanwhile, the Furies had a very good idea where Pandora was hidden. The KGB agent who had first tipped them off had also suggested the archives in Jerusalem. Since Israel was harder to get to, they Furies had targeted Bern first. But now that Bern had turned out to be a bust, they were laying plans to move on.

The CIA didn't have John wired constantly. Doing so was far too risky for an undercover man. Therefore, it wasn't hard for John to abuse their trust and find a time to come clean to Alexei. Of course, Alexei had been livid at the betrayal, threatening to kill him, but once John explained his plan, Alexei had quickly seen the light. Soon afterward the rest of the Furies were let in on it as well.

As far as the CIA could tell, nothing had changed. John still appeared to be a dutiful undercover agent, meeting with the Furies more and more often, until the time came to put his plans into action.

Late one night Fez found a homeless man the same size and build as John, killed him, and dragged him into the Furies' apartment. The next morning, the Furies dressed the still-warm body in John's clothes. Knowing the CIA was listening in, John faked his linguistic screwup. The Furies pretended to realize he was a spy and then obliterated anything that could be used to ID the corpse.

While the CIA was dealing with the loss of an undercover agent, John was slipping out of Switzerland with the Furies. He had amassed enough passports over the years, courtesy of the Agency, so that getting into Israel wasn't a problem. If an agent died, that didn't mean his alter egos did; it wouldn't have occurred to anyone at the CIA to declare someone dead who hadn't existed in the first place.

John had spent the last two weeks working his way to Jerusalem with the Furies, keeping off the grid, sleeping on buses and ferries, avoiding phone calls and ATM withdrawals, scrounging for scraps of food. It had been an ordeal, but they had finally made it into Israel and headed directly for Einstein's archives.

And then Dante Garcia had shown up with a young girl in tow and ruined everything. John knew who Dante was. Dante had been two years ahead of him at the academy. And he knew Milana Moon via her reputation. But the girl was a curveball. According to Alexei, her name was Charlie, and she was even younger than she looked.

More important, she had unusual mental abilities. John wasn't sure whether to believe that, but the fact remained that with Charlie along, the CIA had certainly caused him a great deal of trouble.

However, John still had Einstein's clue. And the CIA didn't.

John stepped from the shower, toweled himself off, and slipped into a plush bathrobe. It felt wonderful against his skin, and he wanted nothing more than to lie down on the bed in it and take a nap.

But there was no time for that. The few minutes he had spent in the shower and the new clothes he had bought for himself were all the luxury he could afford.

When John had reserved the hotel room that morning, he had expected his day to go far differently. He had assumed the CIA had no idea where Einstein's book was hidden and that he could recover it easily. John had imagined he would have plenty of time to celebrate—to eat a gourmet meal and sleep in a nice, soft bed for the first time in months. But so much had gone wrong. He could no longer stay here tonight. He had to get to work right away.

John unfolded Einstein's clue on the desk in his hotel room. It was amazing to think that the great genius himself had written this and that it had been hidden for decades, protected from the world until just this morning.

The once pristine paper was now crumpled and torn. But the numbers on it were still legible.

John laid out a fresh sheet of hotel stationery and began translating. In the months since he had learned Einstein's cipher, he no longer needed the key and was able to quickly convert the numbers to words.

Only, the results threw him.

It wasn't only Charlie Thorne who was tossing a wrench into the works today. Now Einstein himself had done it. The code hadn't revealed Pandora. It had simply revealed another clue.

John considered it carefully. He was an intelligent man and he had studied Einstein's life in detail over the last few months. After a few minutes of thought, everything began to make sense. A smile spread across his face.

In addition to renting the hotel room, John had splurged on brand-new clothes. His old ones reeked and were crusted with two weeks' worth of dirt and grime. John tossed the old clothes into the garbage and dressed quickly in the new ones. It was time to move again.

He was now the only man on earth who knew precisely where Pandora was hidden.

THIRTY-ONE

saac Semel called Jamilla Carter from the Jerusalem safe house.

Semel was an agent with Mossad, the national intelligence agency of Israel. He had served for forty years, ever since joining directly from the Israeli army, and he had seen more than his fair share of adventure. At the age of sixty-one, he was as fit and trim as a twenty-year-old, although years in the Middle Eastern sun had baked his skin into leather. He had known Jamilla Carter for a long time, but they were business associates, not friends. Semel didn't bother with pleasantries.

"You have a real bad situation here," he said.

"How many dead?" Carter asked.

"Your whole Jerusalem team, except for Agent Bendavid."

Carter didn't ask how Semel knew who the people

on her Jerusalem team were, even though their identities were supposed to be secret. He had simply known. The same way he had known exactly where the CIA safe house was, even though that was supposed to be a secret too. The Mossad had probably had the place under surveillance for years.

Carter asked, "Where is Agent Bendavid right now?"

"In the bathroom. Throwing up. She's awfully upset about this whole thing."

Carter considered keeping the presence of Agents Garcia and Moon in Israel a secret, then decided there was no point. The Mossad had probably known they were there from the moment their plane touched down. "I had two other agents in Jerusalem today. . . ."

"Don't you mean three?"

"Only two were agents. The third was an asset. A young girl. Are any of them . . . ?" Carter couldn't bring herself to finish the sentence.

"No," Semel answered. "None of them are here. The only bodies are those of the agents on your Jerusalem team."

"What do you think happened?"

"Your safe house was compromised. Looks like a double agent was involved. There's no sign of forced entry. Whoever came in knew the access codes. And they knew exactly where all your security cameras were."

"Do you think Bendavid could be the turncoat?"

"That's doubtful. She seems genuinely surprised by what happened here."

"She could be faking."

"I've seen people fake being upset plenty of times. It doesn't look like this. My guess is the mole is one of your agents who showed up here today. Quite likely both. Otherwise, one of them would probably be dead here too."

Carter lapsed into silence, thinking this through. The idea that Dante Garcia or Milana Moon could be a double agent seemed impossible—but then, that was generally the case with all double agents. The CIA carefully vetted every employee, submitting them to batteries of psychological tests to determine who was the most trustworthy—and yet people still turned. All the time.

Garcia had come to Carter with the proposal to go after Pandora—and he had asked for Moon specifically. Had the two of them been plotting this all along? And if so, how did Charlie Thorne fit into everything? Was the kid involved—or was she just a pawn Garcia had suggested playing so he could get into the game? Either scenario seemed plausible. The kid was already a proven criminal, so maybe she had cooked the whole plan up herself. And she wouldn't have had trouble tracking Dante down; after all, she was his half sister.

Pandora would be worth millions on the black

market. Enough money to turn even the most stalwart agents. Garcia and Moon—and perhaps Thorne—must have made a play for it, and the Jerusalem office got wise. So they took the whole team out and fled. Which would explain why she hadn't heard from any of them yet.

It occurred to her that Semel was speaking to her.

"I'm sorry," she said. "What was that again?"

"I asked what this new team was doing here in Jerusalem. Were they investigating anything I ought to be concerned about?"

"No," Carter lied. "It was merely a training mission."

"Training?" Semel repeated, obviously suspicious.

Carter spent the next few minutes spinning a tale of what the training mission had been. It was a total fabrication, but she sold it well enough. She knew she couldn't tell Semel the truth about Pandora, because then Semel would want to obtain Pandora for Israel. But with her Jerusalem team dead, Carter needed Semel's help.

"All right," Semel said finally, sounding convinced. "I'm guessing you want to track down these rogue agents right away?"

"Yes," Carter admitted. "Agent Bendavid has all the information you need on them. It was sent to her team this morning."

"I've already seen it."

Carter's secretary suddenly spoke over the intercom.

"Ma'am, I know you told me not to interrupt you, but Agent Moon is calling from Jerusalem."

Carter sat up, surprised. "On her cellular?"

"No, ma'am. Someone else's. I don't know whose."

"Well, find out where she is."

"Already done." This was an easy task nowadays. Cellular phones constantly marked their exact location. People might as well have been carrying homing beacons on their backs. Most CIA agents had phones that blocked these signals, but if Moon was on a regular person's cell—for whatever reason—they could triangulate her position within seconds. "She's at the Church of the Holy Sepulchre in the Old City."

"Good work." Carter got back on the phone with Semel. "Moon is at the Church of the Holy Sepulchre. Do you have any men close to there?"

"I have men everywhere," the Mossad agent replied. "We'll bring her in."

THIRTY-TWO

Charlie visualized Einstein's clue in her mind.

The moment she had first laid her eyes on the clue, she had willed herself to commit it to memory—and then reviewed it again and again. She hadn't expected the Furies to ambush the CIA in their own safe house, but she had still feared *something* might go wrong. Anything as dangerous and powerful as Pandora was bound to be trouble.

Milana had gone off to call the CIA, so she could report what they had figured out about John Russo. Charlie could see her in the crowd, using a phone borrowed from a tourist.

In the meantime, the sooner Charlie could figure out what Einstein's clue meant, the better.

Another tourist had been kind enough to lend her a pen and some scratch paper. Now she wrote Einstein's clue down so she could look at it:

$$\frac{(91-60)^8}{88M} + \left\{ 3 \left(\frac{99c}{49}\right) \times \left[\frac{(192)^5}{5M} + (13 \times 16)(16 \times 15)^2\right]\right\} -$$

$$\left(\frac{754}{10X}\right)(851) + \left(10X + \frac{78}{92}\right)\left(\frac{10X}{16}\right)^8 \div \left(15i\right)\left(\frac{22}{55}\right) = \pi$$

She considered what she had already deduced:

$$\pi = \text{Pandora}$$

$$\text{MCMXXXI} = 1931$$

Then she set about solving the rest of it.

Only, she couldn't.

She stared at the clue for a long time, searching for patterns she might have missed, manipulating the numbers in her mind, waiting for inspiration to strike. But it didn't.

She was stuck.

This was an unusual experience for Charlie. She had been stymied by problems before, of course, but it didn't happen often. Like when she was teaching herself calculus at age five. She had eventually figured it out, but it had taken time and patience, two things she didn't have much of now.

Charlie realized it had been a long time since she had challenged herself. She had been goofing off all through school, doing the least amount of work necessary to get by. Now it seemed as if her brain had gotten rusty. As she futilely scanned the clue over and over, she wondered if she had slipped a bit. Perhaps, by not pushing her limits, she had let her mind grow fallow.

Then again, she *was* matching wits with Einstein.

Frustrated, Charlie tore her attention from the paper. She wasn't sure how long she had been staring at it, but her eyes were getting bleary in the dim light of the church. She shifted her gaze toward the main doors, where bright sunlight flooded through.

Milana was over there, where cellular reception was stronger, silhouetted by the light.

Her back was to Charlie.

Which meant Charlie could slip away.

The thought just sprang into Charlie's mind. Escape would take only a few seconds. There was an emergency exit close by. Charlie could slip out it and melt into the crowds. Milana, on her own, would never be able to find Charlie again. It was a rare lapse of judgment on her part, dropping her guard like this, although Charlie figured Milana wasn't quite herself today. The fact that she was functioning at all after everything that had happened was a testament to her strength.

Still, Milana would realize her mistake soon enough. She would check to make sure Charlie was still there. If Charlie was going to go, she had to go now. . . .

Only, things had changed.

When Charlie had tried to escape from the safe house just a few hours before, all she needed to do was destroy Einstein's clue and Pandora would have stayed hidden forever. Now the Furies had the clue. What if they—or John Russo—already knew how to solve it?

Charlie considered the possibility of leaving the clue behind for Milana if she ran, but she doubted that would work out. The clue would probably be whisked back to CIA headquarters for analysis. How long would that take? Days? Weeks? Whereas the Furies could be moving quickly toward Pandora. By the time the CIA even figured out which end was up, the enemy could have Einstein's equation in their hands.

Therefore, Charlie was the only one who could stop them.

You have a chance to make a difference, Dante had told her.

Maybe Dante had been wrong to drag Charlie into this business by pointing a gun at her, but he had been right to bring her in. The worst-case scenario had unfolded. Now Charlie needed to meet the challenge. She had to solve Einstein's clue. She had to make sure her brother hadn't risked everything in vain.

Only . . . She was still drawing a blank. Einstein had her stumped.

She frowned at the clue in frustration, feeling overwhelmed.

"Any progress?" Milana asked.

Charlie looked up, surprised she hadn't noticed the

agent approaching. She had been too focused on the stupid clue. "What's happening with the CIA?"

Milana held up the phone she had borrowed. "I'm on hold. Waiting for the head of my division. They're pulling her out of a meeting." She nodded to the clue. "How's it going?"

"Lousy."

"Why's that?"

"*Why?* Oh, I'm just trying to decipher a code created by the greatest genius of all time that no one else has been able to crack for nearly seventy years. And there's incredible pressure on me because the fate of millions of people lies in the balance and the bad guys got away and I'm only a twelve-year-old girl. . . ."

"Don't talk like that," Milana said sternly.

"What? You don't like my attitude?"

"I don't like you saying 'girl' like it's a character flaw."

Charlie considered that, then frowned. "Sorry. I'm just frustrated."

Milana sat on the bench next to Charlie. "I've seen your IQ tests. You're just as smart as Einstein was. . . ."

"I don't *feel* as smart as him."

"And he probably didn't feel like a genius when he was your age either. The guy barely spoke until he was five. But he was still scary smart. And you are too." Milana sat back and took in the church around her. "Think about the most famous geniuses in history: Einstein, Newton, Galileo, Darwin, da Vinci, Mozart. What do they have in common?"

Charlie reflected on that for a moment. "They're all men."

"Exactly. But that's not because men are smarter than women. It's because men have had advantages that women haven't. Throughout history, women have been denied education, prevented from having jobs, or simply been ignored. Families sent their sons to school and married off their daughters. Being a genius doesn't mean much if no one will give you a chance to do anything with it. There are probably hundreds of thousands of geniuses who never got the chance to make their mark on the world because they were the wrong gender. Or the wrong color. Or from the wrong rung of the social ladder.

"But that's not the case anymore. You have chances that other people like you didn't, Charlie. The only thing preventing you from changing the world is *you*. So far you haven't been doing much with that incredible brain of yours, but there's still time to do great things. I believe in you. If anyone can figure out what Einstein meant, it's you."

A voice suddenly came through the phone in Milana's hand. "Agent Moon? Are you still there?"

Milana put the phone to her ear. "I'm here," she said, then snapped to her feet and walked away, leaving Charlie alone with the clue once more.

Charlie looked down at it again. It was still the same complicated code, but now she didn't feel as daunted by it. Milana's words had struck a chord in her.

If she wanted to solve this thing, she needed to stop telling herself that she wasn't smart enough to solve it. She had to relax and let it all come to her, the same way the numbers came to her when she was skiing or skateboarding. She had to think the way Einstein would have, to see the patterns he would have.

Charlie took a deep, calming breath and closed her eyes, envisioning the code in her mind.

Chanting echoed through the church.

Charlie's eyes snapped open once again. Several priests were filing past her on their way to the site of the crucifixion, dressed in ornate robes, swinging smoking pots of incense. The tourists stepped aside to let them pass—or to take selfies with them in the background. Charlie watched the priests go, clutching their rosaries and prayer books.

Books.

Charlie sat up, struck by a flash of insight. For the first time, she had an idea as to what Einstein might have been thinking. And if she was right, maybe she could actually solve his code and find Pandora once and for all.

THIRTY-THREE

What if there was more to the clue than just the equation? Charlie wondered. Of all the thousands of books in his possession, why had Einstein chosen a Sherlock Holmes anthology to hide the clue in? In fact, why hide it in a book at all? True, it could have been a random decision—the clue needed to be hidden *somewhere*—but Einstein had never been a fan of randomness. After all, this was the man who had famously declared that he didn't believe God played dice with the universe. Why should he do so himself?

At first Einstein's decision to hide his clue in a Sherlock Holmes anthology hadn't seemed extraordinary. Charlie knew lots of people who had collections of Holmes mysteries. She had one herself, and had read all the stories multiple times. But now that she thought about it, the choice of book seemed odd. While Holmes's devotion to solving crimes through the application of logic might have appealed to Einstein, Charlie guessed that Einstein wouldn't have been a big fan of Holmes's creator. By the time Einstein had developed Pandora, Sir Arthur Conan Doyle had made headlines by turning his back on Holmesian logic and becoming a vocal supporter of spiritualism, proclaiming that an occult influence connected the physical world to an invisible one. Even worse, Doyle's devotion to these beliefs had made him ignore blatant physical evidence and give credence to an infamous hoax:

In 1917, two girls in Cottingley, England, had taken a picture of what appeared to be fairies. Although there had been ample evidence the fairies were merely paper dolls, Doyle had not only been duped by the photos, but had also written an article in a prominent magazine attesting to their authenticity. People who might have otherwise dismissed the photos had been drawn in by Doyle's involvement, and when the fairies were ultimately revealed to be a fraud, Doyle had stubbornly refused to believe the evidence. His reputation quickly changed from that of a brilliant author to a man who wasn't nearly as intelligent as his own creation—if not a downright idiot. The whole event had been quite a scandal back in its day.

So why had Einstein picked Doyle's work, rather than that of a more respected author? Why had Einstein chosen a work of fiction at all, rather than one of the thousands of scientific texts he owned by fellow geniuses like Niels Bohr, Werner Heisenberg, Max Planck, or Ernest Rutherford? The choice of the book couldn't have just been a spur-of-the-moment decision. Einstein had taken great pains to hide Pandora; he wouldn't have left *anything* to chance. As Charlie looked around the church, another of Einstein's thoughts about God crept into her mind. Einstein had been a religious man, but he had claimed the God he favored was that of Baruch Spinoza, who had declared, "God is in the details, the beauty, the math of the world."

God was in the details.

Charlie sat on her bench and watched the candles flicker throughout the church, trying to put herself in Einstein's mind. Back when the great man had hidden Pandora, he must have still held a glimmer of hope for humanity. If this was indeed in 1931, the Nazis had yet to take over Germany. The concentration camps still lay in the future—as did the nuclear bombs the Allies would build, using Einstein's own theory, and the horrors of Hiroshima and Nagasaki. Einstein knew there was good in Pandora, the tiny bit of hope, the promise that, if used properly, it could benefit every person in the world. Therefore, he didn't want to make it impossible to find. So he had taken great pains to construct his clues to its location, hoping that whoever was clever enough to find Pandora would also be intelligent enough to use it wisely.

He had later changed his mind about this, of course, but originally, he had wanted *someone* to find the equation. Otherwise, why leave clues to its location at all? Every piece of the puzzle Einstein had constructed was designed to communicate something to the solver—and that included the book he had concealed the clue inside.

Charlie had been thinking about the clue mathematically, assuming that a legend of physics like Einstein would obviously construct a mathematical puzzle to hide his tracks. But Einstein wasn't merely a scientist. He was a lover of words as well, the rare intellectual who could write for the masses, a linguist who could toss off clever bon mots such as "Two things are infinite, the universe and human stupidity; and I'm not sure about the universe." In addition, Einstein, more than most other scientists, was notable for his sense of humor. This was a man who let his hair grow into a fright wig, regaled friends with jokes, and stuck his tongue out for photographers. Einstein had loved science and math, but he had revered love and laughter. Perhaps, in Einstein's mind, being good at math wouldn't have been enough to qualify you to find Pandora. You would need to be better rounded, someone who thought outside the box.

Charlie considered the Sherlock Holmes mysteries again, trying to discern what would have been attractive about them to Einstein. There were Holmes's staggering powers of observation, his outsider status, the fact that

Holmes, like Einstein, was a student of the violin. Was there a place something had been hidden in one of the stories that Einstein could have mimicked? Was there something about Holmes himself that was important: his wit, his trademark dress, the way in which he solved problems?

Charlie held that thought. What if Einstein had merely wanted whoever found the clue to think like Holmes? How would Holmes have gone about it? Holmes was always keen on all details, able to see the forest for the trees, encyclopedic in knowledge—and willing to draw conclusions only once he had eliminated all other possibilities. He was the first great fictitious practitioner of the idea that the simplest solution generally tended to be the best. "It's elementary," he had famously told Watson, although technically Doyle hadn't even written that phrase. It had come from a stage adaptation of the books. . . .

"Oh," Charlie said, struck by an epiphany.

She looked at Einstein's clue once again and considered it in a new light.

Suddenly, it all made sense.

In her mind's eye, the numbers vanished and were replaced by what they truly stood for. She had solved the code.

Charlie leapt to her feet, heading toward Milana, but then stopped herself. This time there was no point in risking that the clue might fall into enemy hands. She knew what the message said—and she had committed it to memory. It had translated perfectly. All other possibilities had been eliminated; there was no other solution.

She crossed to an altar and laid the scrap of paper on which she had written Einstein's clue atop one of the candles. It caught fire instantly, curled up on itself, and dissolved into ash and smoke.

Then Charlie hurried back to Milana, who was by the entrance, returning the phone to the tourist she had borrowed it from. Charlie hooked a hand under Milana's elbow and steered her out the door, weaving through a crowd of pilgrims pouring into the church. "I know where Pandora is," she said. "We need to get back to the airport right away."

Milana turned to her, astonished. "You're sure?"

"Yes."

Milana beamed proudly. "I knew you could do it! What does it . . . ?"

Suddenly, three of the pilgrims pounced on her, knocking her to the ground. Charlie quickly realized they weren't pilgrims at all, but young, athletic men who had merely used the swarm of tourists as cover—and then she, too, was hit from behind. Her legs were swept out from under her, her face was slammed into the cobblestones, and a gun was pressed against the back of her head.

"Charlotte Thorne," someone snarled, "you're under arrest."

THIRTY-FOUR

John Russo eavesdropped on the Mossad's transmissions as he drove out of Jerusalem, headed for Ben Gurion Airport in Tel Aviv. To do this John needed a specially encrypted radio, but there had been one at the CIA's safe house and he had stolen it after the rest of the Furies had fled. He knew the proper settings and channels from his undercover days in Israel. Now he listened gleefully as everything came together, as the Mossad closed in on Milana Moon and Charlie Thorne, drew the net, and then . . .

Arrested them.

The smile faded from John's face. Cursing, he swerved away from the entrance of the highway that would have taken him west toward Tel Aviv and veered onto a different road.

The Mossad didn't arrest traitors. They killed them.

Sure, they might go through the motions of arresting them in front of tourists, but the moment they were out of sight, they would exact the ultimate price for treason.

There was only one reason Charlie and Milana were still alive. The Mossad knew about Pandora and suspected the women had information about it.

John checked his watch. There was still time to initiate a new plan.

He pulled over in an alleyway and called Alexei. Originally, John had planned to leave Israel without even telling the Furies, to simply abandon those idiots. By the time they realized he had betrayed them, he would have been long gone, never to be seen again, and they would have had no way to ever track him down. But now he would need their help one last time.

Alexei answered after the first ring, sounding impatient. "Where have you been? We've been waiting for more than an hour!"

"I've been deciphering the clue. Where are you now?"

"Right where you left us. Waiting for you. What did the clue say?"

"Pandora is in London," John lied.

"London!" Alexei exclaimed, concerned. "How are we supposed to get there?"

"Leave that to me. I'm working on it. In the meantime, there is something else you need to take care of. The Mossad has captured Agent Moon and the girl."

"Oh."

"There's a chance that girl knows where Pandora is, Alexei. We can't let her live."

There was a pause on the other end of the line. Then Alexei asked, "What do you expect us to do? We are only five men. The Mossad has thousands."

"But they don't know we can eavesdrop on them." John stepped from his rental car into the heat of the alley. There was a dumpster against the side of a building. John slipped the encrypted radio underneath it, then gave Alexei very specific instructions as to where to find it. "How far are you from here?"

"Maybe five minutes."

"Once you get the radio, monitor the channel I have left it on. Find out where the Mossad is taking Thorne and what they plan to do with her. If you get a chance to take Thorne out—do it."

"You aren't going to help us?"

"I'm working on getting us to London as fast as I can. But I'll stay in touch. Keep me apprised of what's going on." John hung up, not giving Alexei the chance to question him, letting him know who was in charge here.

He got back in the car, made a U-turn, and headed

for the airport, expecting that he would never speak to Alexei again.

The Furies were useful foils to send after Thorne, but John didn't need them to help him find Pandora anymore.

He had a plane to catch.

THIRTY-FIVE

he Old City of Jerusalem was deceptive. It looked as though it was built upon solid ground, but it really sat on top of the remnants of dozens of civilizations. They were piled like the layers of a cake beneath the streets. Sometimes the original bedrock was a hundred feet beneath the surface. In some parts of the city these places had been excavated. You could see the exposed remnants of ancient walls in the Jewish Quarter, or Roman baths in the Muslim Quarter. But more often than not the past remained hidden far underfoot.

Such was the case with the tunnel the Mossad was using to spirit Charlie and Milana out of the Old City. The descent into it had taken them far below street level, down a long shaft that had been chiseled through the layers of civilization. They had accessed it through the site of an archaeological dig only two blocks from the Church of the

Holy Sepulchre. Security guards from the Israeli Depart-ment of Antiquities were posted around the dig, but they deferentially stepped aside when the Mossad arrived, as if it was common for the Mossad to use this route.

The walls of the tunnel were built from massive stone blocks. Despite being in the desert, it was damp down here. Moss grew so thick on the stones that it seemed as though they were padded. The tunnel was six feet tall but extremely narrow; portions were barely wide enough for Charlie to walk through without scraping the walls. Given the quality of the masonry, Charlie suspected it had been built by the Romans, probably as flood control, to shunt water out of the city during the rare big rains. The tunnel was gradually leading downhill, following the gentle slope of the mountain, most likely heading toward an ancient reservoir. Electric lighting had been run along the ceiling, and the moist dirt of the floor had hundreds of footprints heading both ways, indicating that this route was still used on a regular basis.

Two Mossad agents were in the lead, then Milana, two more Mossad, Charlie, and yet two more Mossad. Charlie and Milana had their wrists cinched with zip ties behind their backs.

Charlie had to give the Mossad credit for using this route to get them out of the city. For one thing, it kept them out of sight. They were away from view of the crowds, hidden from any spy satellites the CIA might have trained on Jerusalem, and too far underground to get a homing signal. Furthermore, it was easy to keep prisoners under control in the tunnel. It was too narrow for Milana or Charlie to start a fight—and it would have been futile as well, as the Mossad had them surrounded.

The agent in the lead was a man named Isaac Semel. Semel hadn't been part of the team that had taken Charlie and Milana at the church, but he had met them at the archaeological site, right before they descended into the tunnel. He looked to be at least twice as old as any of the other agents, but he also seemed twice as tough as any of them, and they showed him great respect.

The Mossad hadn't told them Semel's name. Charlie had picked it up from their conversations. She hadn't let on that she spoke Hebrew, and the Mossad had mistakenly assumed that she couldn't, given her young age and the fact that she was American. They hadn't said much, but it was enough. She had learned that cars would meet them outside the city walls to take them to Mossad headquarters, which she figured was a bad sign.

"The CIA is going to be livid when they learn what you're doing here," Milana warned Semel.

"The CIA asked us to apprehend you in the first place," Semel replied. "They think you're traitors. They won't care what we do to you."

Charlie was surprised and concerned by this announcement, but Milana reacted as though she didn't believe it. "If you were working with the CIA, you'd be taking us right to the US embassy and turning us over to them."

Semel looked back at Milana and smiled. "That may happen in time. But there are some things I'd like to discuss with you first."

"We are only here on a training exercise."

Semel suddenly stopped in the tunnel, took his gun from his shoulder holster, and pointed it at Milana. "Where is Pandora?"

Due to the narrowness of the tunnel, everyone else had to come to a halt behind Semel.

"How long have you known about Pandora?" Milana asked.

Charlie was surprised by the agent's calm. Her own stomach was tying itself in knots.

"Not until today," Semel replied. "But then you showed up this morning, obviously here for something Director Carter didn't trust the regular Jerusalem team to handle. You went directly to the university library of all places, and next thing I know there's gunplay and a dead European tourist with doctored papers. It's enough to make a man ask questions. The Mossad is an organization that respects its elders. We still have men around who *knew* Einstein. Men who'd heard of Pandora. Of course, they all believed it was just a rumor. . . ."

"Turns out it was," Milana said. "This was a wild-goose chase."

"Don't lie to me," Semel said angrily. "My men are all wired. I heard your friend here say she knew where Pandora was back at the church." Semel shifted his gaze to Charlie. "So maybe I should be talking to *you*, Ms. Thorne. If you don't tell me Pandora's location, I'll kill Agent Moon."

Charlie looked to Milana, but the agent was still turned away from her, facing Semel.

"You're bluffing," Charlie said. "You're not like the terrorists."

"True. But we are just like the United States: We'll do whatever it takes to protect ourselves."

"The United States has always been a friend to Israel," said Milana. "If we find Pandora, we'll happily share it with you. . . ."

"You weren't even going to tell us about it!" Semel snapped. "And now, because of your failures, the terrorists have the advantage. Tell me, if they acquire Pandora, do you really think they'll attack *America*? Or might they instead attack the country the entire world wants to get rid of? The country small enough that one nuclear weapon could wipe it from the earth entirely? The

Eastern Europeans have always hated my people. They might use Pandora to bargain with the United States—but they'll use it to *destroy* Israel."

Milana lowered her eyes, chastened, then nodded agreement. "You're right. Playing this alone was a mistake on our part. We should work together from now on."

Semel sighed, annoyed, as if this statement were even worse than a lie. "Don't condescend to me. Your government will never share Pandora. They'd kill us before they let us get our hands on it."

"That's not true."

"It is," Charlie said.

Everyone in the tunnel turned to her, surprised.

Milana locked eyes with her. "Keep your mouth shut, Charlie. You don't know what you're talking about."

"Yes, I do. Pandora is the stirrup all over again."

Everyone stared at her blankly. "What do you mean?" Semel asked.

"Do you mind if we keep walking?" Charlie asked. "I'm starting to feel like the walls are closing in on me." That wasn't a lie. Between the tight quarters and the desperation to figure out what to do, Charlie could feel the beginnings of a panic attack coming on. The best plan of action, she figured, was to keep moving ahead. If there were cars waiting for them, the tunnel had to end somewhere.

Semel stared back at her through the dim tunnel, then simply turned around and started walking again. Everyone else followed him. "What's this about the stirrup?" Semel asked.

"The stirrup was one of the greatest military innovations of all time," Charlie explained. "It changed the course of history. Up until then people had domesticated horses, but they were useless in battle, because it was almost impossible to use a weapon and stay on the horse. You'd try to hack someone with your sword or stab them with a spear and fall right out of the saddle—and then your enemies would kill you. But then some unknown genius somewhere in central Mongolia invented the stirrup. It was simple, but brilliant. It gave horsemen greater stability, which allowed them to use weapons, and a horseman with a weapon had a major advantage over any schmo without a horse. Suddenly, tiny nations could build cavalries, and cavalries won wars. Any civilization that had the stirrup easily conquered those that didn't. The Mongols defeated China. Genghis Khan took most of Asia. Attila the Hun brought the Roman Empire to its knees."

"Your point being . . . ?" Semel asked.

"Throughout history, whenever a civilization has gained a military advantage, their first instinct has *never* been to share it. Instead, they've used it to try to wipe out everyone else. It happened with the longbow, the machine gun, the tank, the nuclear bomb. Whoever invents the next great military advance becomes the most powerful nation on earth. But there has never been anything so simple, so inexpensive—and so available to anyone—as the stirrup. Until now."

They rounded a curve in the tunnel, and Charlie saw a bright slash of light ahead. The sun, pouring into the darkness. An exit.

"So Pandora is Einstein's stirrup," Semel said.

"Exactly," Charlie agreed. "It could allow men with little training or resources to become great warriors. It could allow small civilizations to instantly become powerful ones. Any nation without it will be at the mercy of any nation that has it. And so *every* nation—even the United States—will kill for it if they have to. And they'll kill to ensure that only they have it. I doubt the United States would have let me live a day once I gave it to them."

"That's not true . . . ," Milana argued.

"Of course it is," Semel said dismissively, then looked to Charlie. "So your participation in this endeavor is unwilling?"

"That's right," Charlie said. "I have no loyalty to the United States. Or the CIA. However, I *am* loyal to Agent Moon. If you let her go, I'll take you right to Pandora. But I'm the only person alive besides John Russo who knows where it is—and if you hurt Moon, so help me, I'd rather let the terrorists blow your country off the map than lift one finger to help you."

They arrived at the spot in the tunnel where the sun shone in. The wall of the tunnel had collapsed here, creating a hole large enough for a man to walk through. The hole was now blocked by a locked iron gate, which was guarded on the other side by an Israeli soldier.

Through the gate, Charlie could see that another archaeological excavation was underway. A pit two stories deep and as wide as a basketball court had been gouged out of the mountainside and was shored up with metal beams. The gate opened into the bottom of the pit, where the ruins of ancient walls could be seen poking out of the ground. It looked to Charlie as though the excavation had accidentally broken into the tunnel, creating the gaping hole she was looking through.

Ahead of them, the tunnel was impassible, filled with rocks and debris. Between the blockage and the locked gate, the Mossad had Charlie and Milana boxed into a dead end.

Semel looked Charlie squarely in the eye and said, "Now it is *you* who is bluffing, Ms. Thorne. I suspect you've worked far too hard to find Pandora to let the Furies have it over something as petty as chivalry." He placed the barrel of his gun against Milana's temple.

"Now, you're not going to make me do anything as child-ish as count to three, are you?"

Milana tried her best to remain stoic, but Charlie saw fear in her eyes.

Charlie said, "Let her go and I'll tell you everything you need to know."

"One . . ."

"I'm serious. Shoot her, and you don't get so much as a peep out of me."

"Two . . ."

Sweat beaded on Milana's brow.

"Three . . ."

"Okay! It's in Denmark!" Charlie shouted.

Semel turned to Charlie, pleased, although he didn't lower the gun. "Very good. But I need a little more detail than that."

"It's in Copenhagen. Einstein left it with Niels Bohr in 1933 just before he fled to the United States. Bohr hid it in his home there, which is a museum. It's in the basement, in a safe under the floor, but I know the combination."

It was all a lie, but Charlie was good at lying to adults. She had done it to her parents all her life. Semel studied her for a few long seconds, then lowered the gun. "Now, that wasn't so hard, was it?" he asked.

Charlie glared at him, then looked to Milana, who sighed with relief.

Semel signaled the soldier outside the tunnel, and the soldier unlocked the gate. Semel led the Mossad and their captives through it into the bottom of the excavation pit. It was a maze of wooden beams, bales of chicken wire, spools of electrical cable. A temporary wooden staircase led up to the surface. Two stories above them, homes were perched right on the edge of the pit—it had been dug smack in the middle of a neighborhood.

It was now late in the afternoon. The archaeologists who had been working at the site had all gone home, but the late-day sunshine was still blinding after so much time in the darkness.

Everyone paused to let their eyes adjust to the light.

Which was why no one was prepared for the attack.

THIRTY-SIX

The first shot caught Semel in the shoulder, spinning him and dropping him to the ground.

The other Mossad agents snapped out their guns and searched desperately for where the bullet had come from.

"Drop your weapons!" a voice called out. "I could have killed Semel if I wanted to. If you don't comply, the next shot takes him out for good."

Charlie broke into a huge grin. She recognized the voice.

Dante Garcia was alive—and he'd come to save her.

The Mossad looked far less pleased. They all turned to Semel for instruction.

Semel struggled back to his feet, clutching his wounded arm, doing his best not to give in to the pain. Dante's shot had been perfect. He had hit Semel in the muscle, which would heal, rather than shattering a bone, which wouldn't. It still hurt like heck, though. Although Semel had experienced worse.

He nodded to his agents, who obediently dropped their weapons.

Dante's voice echoed through the excavation site again. "Now cut Charlie's and Milana's hands loose."

Charlie, like the others, was searching the site, wondering where Dante had positioned himself, but she was unable to tell. He was hidden somewhere up in the mess of girders and wooden beams above, and his voice was echoing off the cavern's sides. Not that Charlie *needed* to know exactly where Dante was. He was here. He was alive.

Semel nodded to his men once again. Two of them withdrew knives from their belts and sliced through the zip ties that had bound Milana's and Charlie's wrists.

Semel shouted back to Dante, "You're making a mistake, Garcia! There's nowhere to run. You'll never get out of Jerusalem, let alone Israel."

"Now let them go!" Dante yelled. "If any of you so much as even *thinks* about grabbing a weapon, I open fire. Got it?"

The Mossad agents all nodded, simmering with anger over being in their position.

Milana and Charlie dashed through the site and up

the wooden stairs. At the top was a small, hastily constructed area with lockboxes to store equipment. A second iron gate led to the street.

A Mossad Humvee sat just outside the gate. It was outfitted for war, with bulletproof plates on the roof, doors, and undercarriage.

Two more Mossad agents lay unconscious on the ground beside it.

Dante came racing down from the hill above, clutching one of the agent's guns in his hands.

Charlie ran to meet him and grasped him tightly in a hug. "You're alive!" she exclaimed.

Dante was caught off guard by her sudden display of emotion. He was relieved to see that she was all right, but he was also worried about the Mossad. So he gave her a quick, perfunctory hug in return, then said, "We have to get out of here. I'm going to need you to drive."

"*Me?*" Charlie asked, startled.

"I trust you more to drive than to shoot," Dante said. "And we're going to need to shoot. They'll be coming for us." He slapped the keys into her hand and ran for the Humvee.

Charlie didn't ask any more questions. She could already hear Semel and the Mossad on the move in the excavation pit, aware that Dante was no longer aiming a gun at them. Semel was shouting in Hebrew, probably on the phone or a radio with other agents. "I need the backup team at the pit now! The Americans are escaping!"

Dante shot a quick glance at Milana as they ran for the Humvee.

"It's good to see you're alive," she said.

"It's good to see you too," he replied.

Charlie leapt into the front seat, brushed the hair back from her eyes, and started the Humvee. Dante climbed into the passenger seat while Milana got in the back. There was another gun waiting for her there, from one of the unconscious Mossad agents, Charlie figured.

"This isn't going to be pretty," she warned her brother, then floored the gas. The big car took a moment to respond, and then it leapt forward faster than she'd expected. Charlie flattened a road sign and two bicycles parked beside it before getting the Humvee under control.

Behind them, two more Humvees swerved onto the street and took up the chase. More Mossad agents coming after them.

The part of Jerusalem they were in now was quite different from the part Charlie had seen before. The area between the university and the Old City had been upscale and cosmopolitan, with wide streets and new buildings and fancy restaurants. This area was much poorer, with ramshackle houses piled on top of one another. The narrow, twisting streets were clogged with cheap secondhand cars, stray dogs, and young boys playing barefoot.

Charlie would have had a hard time driving a regular car in such a place, but the Humvee was more like a tank: big, heavy, and too wide for the roads. Charlie knocked the driver's side mirrors off three cars and shaved the bumpers off two more before she had even gone a block.

The pursuing Humvees paused outside the excavation site just long enough for Semel and some of his agents to leap inside and then took up the chase again.

At that very moment, the Muslim call to prayer began playing over loudspeakers throughout the community, echoing off the hills. The locals instantly stopped what they were doing and responded to the call, prostrating themselves on the sidewalks to pray.

"What happened to you?" Milana asked Dante. "We thought you were . . . well . . ."

"Dead?" Dante asked. "I thought so too. Back at the safe house. But the Furies pulled back and went after you. I tried to follow them, but I lost them—and you."

A hail of bullets ricocheted off the rear fender. Milana fired back as Charlie slewed around a hairpin turn. The next street had cars parked on both sides; there wasn't quite enough room for the Humvee to fit between them. Charlie had no choice but to gun the engine and force her way through. The Humvee knocked the cars aside like they were toys, smashing them into the houses built beside the road.

"So how'd you find us?" Charlie yelled over the sound of rending metal.

"I came back to the safe house and kept an eye on it," Dante explained. "It wasn't long before the Mossad showed up. Then they left in a big hurry, so I followed them. I figured there was a decent chance they were heading to you. I just didn't expect them to arrest you."

Charlie sent the last car on the street skidding into a storefront. The Mossad was gaining on them, as Charlie had cleared the road for them.

Dante leaned out the window and fired a few shots their way. "When they took you down into that tunnel, there was no way I could follow, but it wasn't hard to figure out which way it went. Downhill. Out of the city. So I followed the line, came across those two Mossad guys with this Humvee, and guessed they were waiting for you."

"Lucky guess," Milana observed.

"Looks like I was right though . . . Charlie!" Dante screamed as the Humvee swerved around a corner into an open-air market.

The market was small, crammed into a narrow plaza, and the Muslim stall owners and shoppers were prone on the ground, answering the call to prayer. They scattered as the Humvee barreled through, smashing the stalls into splinters and upending tables laden with figs, cucumbers, and sacks of grain. A crate full of chickens burst apart and the birds scattered away, leaving a cloud of feathers in their wake.

"Would you watch where you're going?" Dante demanded.

"I'm doing my best!" Charlie yelled back. "This is my first car chase! And this thing handles like a cinder block!"

Another line of bullets stitched the rear gate of the Humvee. Milana responded, firing back out the window.

The right front tire of the first Mossad Humvee blew out and the vehicle lost control, smashing through a vegetable stall and embedding itself in the front wall of a restaurant.

The second Humvee sped past it and dropped in right behind Charlie. In her rearview mirror, she could see Semel behind the wheel, glaring at her, seemingly immune to the pain from his gunshot wound.

Charlie blasted out of the market and onto yet another narrow road, leaving a horde of angry people yelling after her.

"Were you telling the truth this time?" Milana asked her. "About Denmark?"

"No."

"Then where is Pandora?"

"Mind if I concentrate on not crashing for right now?" Charlie veered around a corner and found herself on a slightly wider street. Unfortunately, there was a camel standing in the midst of it. To Charlie's astonishment, it was wearing a sombrero. Hand-lettered signs dangled on both sides of its hump, making it a living message board for a local restaurant.

"A freaking camel???" Charlie exclaimed. "Are you kidding me?" She pounded on her horn. "Move, you stupid ungulate!"

Despite the Humvees bearing down on it, the camel remained unfazed. It stayed rooted right in the middle of the street, staring blankly at the oncoming cars.

Charlie considered plowing right over it, but she didn't want to kill an innocent animal—and she worried that a camel that weighed half a ton might do some serious damage if it came flying through the windshield. So she yanked as hard as she could on the steering wheel. The Humvee skidded around the camel, which didn't so much as blink, then clipped the side of a flatbed truck bearing a load of enormous cement pipes, each one several feet in diameter. The side of the truck tore off, releasing the pipes, which clattered into the road.

Between the pipes and the camel, Semel had nowhere to go. He tried to thread the gap between them, but a pipe slammed into the side of his Humvee so hard it knocked the car sideways. It crashed straight through the corner of a store and flipped over into a ditch.

Dante turned to Charlie, trying to remain stoic but unable to hide the respect in his eyes.

"You can say you're impressed," Charlie told him. "I bet they don't teach defensive driving against camels in the CIA."

"More Mossad will be coming soon," Dante warned. "And they certainly have this Humvee tagged on GPS. We need to ditch it and move by foot."

"Right," Charlie said. "Let me just put a little more mileage between us and Semel." Having finally got the hang of driving the Humvee, she gunned the engine and raced through the narrow streets. Upon spotting a sign for the highway to Tel Aviv, she turned that way.

"We can't go all the way to Tel Aviv," Milana cautioned. "We need to find a place to lie low before the Mossad finds us."

"No way," Charlie argued. "We have to get out of the country. We have to get to Pandora before Russo can."

"Russo?" Dante repeated. "John Russo?"

"Oh yeah. He's still alive and he's working for the bad guys," Charlie told him. "You missed out on a whole lot while we thought you were dead."

"That's our theory about Russo, at least," Milana corrected, then added, "The Mossad controls this entire country. We won't be able to get out via the airport. We'll have to slip over the border."

"That will take way too long," Charlie said. "I know a much faster way. I just need to get to a phone."

"Who are you calling?" Dante asked skeptically. "The president? Because we're going to need someone awfully powerful to get us out of here."

"Oh, we need someone more powerful than the president," Charlie said. "I'm calling my banker."

THIRTY-SEVEN

Tel Aviv

B uying an airline ticket only an hour before the flight was expensive, but John Russo wasn't concerned about money.

In the months before he faked his death, he had slowly shifted most of his assets out of his true bank account into a subsidiary, doing it in a way that wouldn't set off alarms at the CIA. In addition, he had also been carrying several thousand dollars in a money belt for the last week.

All the fake passports that the CIA had issued John over the years were hidden in the money belt as well. John selected one for an alias he had never even used—one the CIA had probably forgotten they had ever created—as he climbed out of the rent-a-car shuttle at Ben Gurion International Airport.

In his new clothes, showered, and shaved, John

looked enough like a diplomat to avoid much scrutiny. Even so, he had stopped at a thrift store and purchased a properly aged suitcase and enough clothing to make it appear as though he would be traveling for a few days. Buying a one-way ticket in cash slightly before flight time would raise eyebrows, especially in a suspicious country like Israel. However, if you bought a round-trip ticket and acted as though you were leaving on a sudden diplomatic mission, those concerns faded. And while Israel was infamous for being excessively cautious at customs, that tended to be primarily for people entering the country rather than leaving it.

John had no trouble convincing the ticket saleswoman at Ben Gurion that he was an average, everyday American diplomat, stationed in Jerusalem but hurrying back to the States for a meeting that somebody, somewhere had decided he absolutely needed to attend just before it took place. In fact, he was convincing enough—not to mention charming enough—to get the saleswoman to bump him up to business class for free, seeing as it was a fourteen-hour flight and all.

It still took a while to get through customs. By the time John did, he had to rush to make his flight. He was hurrying through the airport when his phone rang. Alexei. He answered expectantly, hoping for good news.

But it wasn't.

"The CIA and the girl escaped from the Mossad," Alexei reported.

John grimaced, then asked, "How is that even possible?"

"I don't know. We just heard it on their radio. The Mossad doesn't even know where they are. They're combing the entire country for them."

John was so distracted he almost ran into a stupid tourist who had left her bags right in the middle of the walkway. He couldn't believe what he was hearing. The Mossad was one of the most elite spy agencies in the world. He had never heard of anyone escaping from them. Not when the Mossad had them completely outnumbered. What on earth had happened? Who was this Charlie Thorne, and how did she keep weaseling out of every trap he had set for her?

His gate was just ahead. Business class was already boarding. For a brief moment he considered not getting on the plane. He could stay in Israel and take care of Charlie Thorne himself.

But that was crazy. He was so close to Pandora. There was no sense in turning back now. Even if Charlie managed to elude the Mossad and his men, there was no way she could possibly crack Einstein's code *and* beat him to Pandora.

Still, he couldn't just let her go. "I know where she's

heading," he said. "You need to get there first and kill her."

"Kill her?" Alexei echoed. "But she's just a girl."

"I don't care!" John shouted, so loud that other passengers turned to him in surprise. He lowered his voice and said, "She's the only thing that can stop us. So we need to get rid of her. Do you understand?"

"Yes," Alexei said.

"Good," John replied. Then he told Alexei where to go and boarded his plane.

THIRTY-EIGHT

Jerusalem

I t took only one call.

Charlie made it from a pay phone at the back of a pizza parlor, one of the last remaining pay phones in Israel, it seemed. She had the phone number committed to memory. There was no need for a credit card or any form of ID that could be traced; any calls to this number were collect.

Before she had robbed Lightning, Charlie had done a lot of research on banks. Up until that point, she had assumed that most banks were like the one on the corner near her house, where people went in, set up accounts, deposited their paychecks, and got money from the ATM on occasion. Her mother had helped her set up a bank account there when she was six so she could save her allowance. The problem was, a young girl couldn't just go to a bank like that with millions of dollars and open an account. The government tended to notice things like that.

But it turned out there were other kinds of banks, far more covert ones that catered to people with large amounts of money that they wanted to keep secret. Banks that asked no questions about who was starting the account—or how they had obtained the money. These banks tended to be located in countries with lax financial laws like the Bahamas, Grand Cayman, and Macau, though Switzerland was the most famous place for them. So Charlie had gone with Switzerland.

It hadn't been too difficult to set up an account. She had simply called a telephone number and spoken with a person who was very eager to help take care of her money. No one had ever asked her age. (Swiss policy was to keep the owners of all accounts a secret, even to the banks themselves.) Once the account was established, Charlie funneled her money into it and let it accrue interest. She had never touched it since. In fact, she had never even called the bank again until now.

The woman who answered at the bank was very discreet. She didn't ask questions about what Charlie requested, no matter how unusual it might have been. She simply checked Charlie's account to make sure there was enough money to cover the cost, then assured her everything would be taken care of immediately.

While Charlie was doing that, Dante was swiping a car for them. Dante wasn't proud of himself for doing it; as a CIA agent, he was supposed to uphold the law. But they were in desperate straits. They had to get out of Jerusalem fast, and they couldn't take a cab or use any ride-hailing services. The Mossad would doubtlessly be monitoring those. But Dante couldn't just smash the window of a car and hotwire it either. That might attract the police.

So he had watched the valet service of an upscale restaurant next to the pizza place. A person sitting down to a fancy meal probably wouldn't notice their car was gone for a good two hours, by which time Dante, Milana, and Charlie would hopefully be out of the country.

The valets hadn't been paying close attention to the keys in the key box. Dante watched a wealthy jerk drive up in a new SUV and mouth off to the valet, who obsequiously took the insult and parked the car in a lot on the corner. When the poor valet came back, Dante nicked the keys, walked down to the lot, and easily swiped the jerk's car.

Minutes later he, Charlie, and Milana were heading down the highway to Tel Aviv. Dante and Milana sat in the front seats, while Charlie was in the back. Like they were a normal family rather than three fugitives from justice.

Night had settled by now and the desert sky was full of stars.

"So, care to enlighten me about this brilliant plan of yours?" Dante asked Charlie. "Where are we heading?"

"Ben Gurion Airport."

Milana looked at Charlie like she was an idiot. "The Mossad's going to be crawling all over that place."

"Maybe at the main terminal. But we're heading to the one for private jets."

Milana's gaze remained disdainful. "They won't let us get back on our CIA jet. They've probably impounded it."

"We're not taking that jet. I ordered us a different one."

Dante's eyes met Charlie's in the rearview mirror. "You ordered a private jet? From your *bank*?"

"Yes."

"Exactly what kind of bank is this?" Milana asked.

"The kind that likes to keep its clients happy."

"Are a lot of those clients criminals?"

"I wouldn't know." That was the truth, although Charlie could make an educated guess. There were a lot of incredibly wealthy people in the world who had gotten rich through illegal means. Like her. And, like her, they needed a discreet place to park their money.

"All I ever got from my bank was a toaster," Dante observed. "They gave it to me for opening an account and it was such a piece of junk it caught fire after two days. You're only twelve and you can get a freaking jet delivered whenever you want?"

"The jet is only for emergencies," Charlie said. "And it's not a freebie. I paid for it."

"How much?" Dante asked.

Charlie didn't answer. Instead, she said, "It's coming from Ankara. It should be here by the time we get to the airport."

"How much did you pay for this?" Dante repeated.

Once again Charlie ignored the question. "The way I figure it, the private terminal is the last place the Mossad will expect us to go. They're probably not expecting us to head to the airport, period, because that's the most obvious way out of the country. But they'll still post agents there to cover their butts. Around the commercial terminal, at least. But the private terminal? You need big bucks or high diplomatic status to go in and out of there, and as far as they know we don't have either of those things right now. So why waste agents there when they could be better used looking elsewhere for us?"

"Semel still might take that chance," Milana warned. "He must have hundreds of agents at his disposal."

"Then I guess we need to stack the odds in our favor," Charlie said. "I need another phone."

THIRTY-NINE

Mossad headquarters was a heavily fortified but unmarked building in central Jerusalem. Isaac Semel was now running the show from there. The bullet wound in his arm had been padded and wrapped in gauze, but he had refused medication, wanting to keep his mind sharp. He was working through the pain, doing his penance for allowing himself to be bested.

He had already placed every available agent into the field. Israel wasn't an easy country to get in and out of—its borders were fenced, walled, strung with barbed wire, and seeded with land mines—but no system was perfect. The only land routes out of Israel led to countries that were increasingly hostile to Americans, but good CIA agents would have contacts and be able to navigate their way. Plus, even a small country like Israel had several hundred miles of border. And now it was night. It wouldn't be easy to police it all.

Semel had agents fanning out to the ferry terminals and every airfield in the country. He had men posted at Ben Gurion, too, although he couldn't imagine that Dante Garcia would even *try* to book a flight.

The private terminal was still an issue, though. Because the private terminal catered to the rich and powerful. It didn't really matter if you inconvenienced thousands of tourists in the name of a manhunt—but if you aggravated one billionaire, heads could roll.

As Milana Moon had suspected, Semel had already ordered the CIA's jet impounded. He had done it hours before, as a precaution, shortly after learning that the CIA was after Pandora. Semel had also filed a request for the private terminal to enact security procedures, but he had no idea if that had been done. It was possible that his orders hadn't filtered through the extra layer of political bureaucracy. To be on the safe side, he had sent an agent to Ben Gurion to liaise with security. It might take an hour, but in Semel's estimation, there was no way his targets could line up a jet any faster than that. They were CIA agents, not billionaires.

An aide came racing across the room. "We've got the girl!"

"How?"

"She went into a convenience store five minutes ago. The security cameras got a match on her face. She bought a phone. Dumb kid probably thinks it's a burner that we can't trace, but we've got it. We're locked in on her right now."

"Where is she?"

"Twenty-two kilometers southwest of us and moving."

"Was she with Garcia and Moon?"

"We don't know. They didn't go into the store. But still . . ."

"Bring her in."

"We already have teams moving in, sir."

Semel suppressed a smile, not wanting to assume any success yet.

For the hundredth time, he wondered who this girl was. She was smart, no doubt. But she was also almost a teenager. Semel had children of his own. He had faced some of the most dangerous people on earth in his job—and none of them were as frightening as a preteen on a bad day. Even the smartest ones made bad judgment calls all the time. So maybe Charlie Thorne had grabbed a phone while the others were gassing up the car, thinking it couldn't be traced, that it couldn't hurt to call her boyfriend or her best friend back home or maybe even her parents to tell them that she was all right.

Whatever the case, she had made a mistake.

Semel was under a great deal of pressure to find Pandora. His orders had come from high up the chain of command. Perhaps from the prime minister himself. Whatever country controlled Pandora would instantly become a superpower. The United States already had the leverage to intimidate its enemies; Israel didn't, but they could certainly use it.

Besides, if Einstein had wanted *any* country to have Pandora, it was Israel. The country might not have even existed if not for Einstein. After the great scientist had become an international celebrity, he had used his clout to support Zionism, making speeches and pressuring leaders all over the world to establish Israel. He had helped found the university. He had even left the clue to Pandora in the university's own vault—only everyone there had carelessly overlooked it for decades.

Another aide hurried over to Semel. One of his teams had spotted the SUV and was closing in.

Semel finally allowed himself a smile. Perhaps Israel would end up with Pandora after all.

The Furies sped along the highway from Jerusalem in a stolen van. The driver lay unconscious in the back. Merely taking the car from him would have been risky; he would have immediately called the police, who would have put out an APB for the car.

Alexei was going well above the speed limit. Oleg held the Mossad radio, listening to the agents closing in on Charlie Thorne. Fez, Hans, and Vladimir sat in the back, clutching their guns, ready for battle.

Alexei floored the gas and prayed to God that he would get to Charlie Thorne before the Mossad.

FORTY

Thirty miles from Tel Aviv

O n a country road outside of Beit Shemesh, the Mossad agents closed in on the SUV. They stayed several car lengths behind it for half a mile, far enough so as to not raise suspicion, waiting for a team coming east on the highway to move into position. It was late enough for traffic to have thinned out; there was plenty of open road around the SUV.

At a signal from the team leader, the eastbound team suddenly veered across the median. The SUV swerved to avoid them, skidding off the side of the road and slamming into an embankment. The Mossad boxed it with their Humvees, then leapt out with their guns raised, screaming for everyone inside to get their hands up.

Only the driver complied. The Mossad yanked the rear doors open.

There was no one else inside.

• • •

Semel grew angrier and angrier at himself as his agent explained what had happened:

The car hadn't been driven by anyone at the CIA. Instead, there was a teenager from Jerusalem at the wheel. He had pulled into a gas station off the highway fifteen minutes before and a cute girl had come over to ask for directions. When the Mossad had shown the teen a photo of Charlie Thorne, he had immediately recognized her.

What the teen *hadn't* known was that Charlie Thorne had duct-taped the burner phone to the rear bumper of his car. It was dialed to a technical support line in America; the call was still on hold, creating a false signal for the Mossad to home in on.

Semel screamed in rage. The ruse had distracted his men for less than fifteen minutes, but still, that might have been enough. The highway to Bet Shemesh cut south of the route to Tel Aviv. Semel had pulled teams off that road to pursue the false target, leaving a hole in the net.

Now more precious time had slipped by.

"Get back to the exit points!" he ordered his men over the radio. "Cover the airport and the ports. I don't want another plane or boat leaving this country until we have Charlie Thorne!"

• • •

Alexei listened to Semel yelling over the radio as he swerved into the drop-off lane at Ben Gurion Airport. He had made the right choice, trusting John Russo and coming here rather than following the Mossad. However, he now had a new challenge. John had said Charlie Thorne would be coming to the airport, but they still had to find her.

Ben Gurion wasn't an extremely large airport, but it was still busy at this time of night. The Furies abandoned their car outside the main terminal and split up, Alexei staying outside to observe the arriving passengers, the others going in to scan the security lines.

Alexei hurried back and forth, searching desperately, every second feeling like a lost opportunity. Doubt was just beginning to gnaw at him—wondering whether John had made a mistake, just like the Mossad—when God smiled on him again.

He wasn't sure why he had turned away from the terminal; he simply had. And in that moment he saw an SUV speed past him, driven by Dante Garcia. Charlie Thorne was in the back.

Alexei watched it pass the main terminal, heading toward the smaller private terminal nearby, then called his men and hailed a cab.

Charlie, Dante, and Milana were the only passengers in the small private terminal. There were no other private planes leaving at that time. Halfway through the terminal was a security screening area, and beyond that were three gates for boarding. The boarding areas were much fancier than those in the regular passenger terminals Charlie had seen, with leather couches and plasma-screen TVs.

There were only two security agents on duty, and despite the menacing guns they carried, they seemed happy to see people, excited to have something to do. They didn't seem concerned that Charlie, Dante, and Milana had no luggage; that wasn't unusual for chartered flights. The CIA agents had reluctantly left the guns they had taken from the Mossad back in the car, not wanting to cause alarm.

The far end of the terminal was a wall of glass. Charlie could see the jet she had ordered on the tarmac, fueling up for the long flight they had ahead.

Charlie struggled to remain calm as the security agents scrutinized their passports, doing her best not to show any nerves, to act like this was routine for her, like she flew private jets all the time. The agents asked them all a few questions, then nodded happily at their answers.

"Have a nice flight," one told them.

And then a red phone at the security station started ringing. Both security agents looked at it curiously, as though they had forgotten the phone even existed. It appeared neither had ever heard it ring before.

Charlie looked to Dante, worried. Dante mouthed, *Run*.

Then Dante looked at Milana and nodded.

One of the security agents answered the phone.

Charlie bolted for the end of the terminal.

The security agents turned toward her, taking their eyes off Dante and Milana, who immediately leapt into action. The CIA agents caught the poor security agents by surprise, rendering them unconscious within seconds.

The phone clattered to the floor. Dante could hear someone on the other end, speaking in Hebrew, saying the Mossad wanted the terminal shut down.

Charlie glanced back their way as she ran. Behind Dante and Milana, at the other end of the terminal, she saw the doors slide open.

The Furies raced through them, guns in their hands.

FORTY-ONE

ante!" Charlie yelled. "The Furies!"

Dante and Milana dove behind the X-ray scanners as the Furies opened fire. Charlie leapt over a couch in the waiting area and took cover behind it.

Both CIA agents grabbed the guns from the unconscious security agents and returned fire, forcing the Furies to take cover themselves.

They were now in a standoff, neither the CIA nor the Furies able to move without placing themselves in the line of fire.

Crouched behind the couch, quivering with fear, Charlie looked back out the window at the jet she had ordered. She was much closer to the gate than the CIA, far enough from the Furies that she could probably make it out the door without getting shot. If she could get to the jet, she could escape. She was the one who had paid for it, after all. She could track down Pandora for herself—and then disappear, if she wanted to.

But she couldn't abandon Dante and Milana. If she left them behind, even if they did survive against the Furies, they would still be at the mercy of the Mossad.

A large industrial fire extinguisher was strapped to a support column close by. Charlie scurried from the cover of the couch to the column, yanked the extinguisher free, and rolled it back the way she had come. It moved slowly along the floor until it bumped up against the large floor-to-ceiling windows close to the security area.

Charlie whistled for Dante's attention.

Dante looked back at her, seeming annoyed that his little sister was interrupting him in the middle of a gunfight.

Charlie pointed at the extinguisher. Dante immediately understood what she wanted him to do.

He took his gun and fired at the extinguisher. The first two bullets ricocheted harmlessly off the metal canister, but the third pierced it. The contents inside were under intense pressure, and when the casing was ruptured, it exploded in a cloud of white foam. The floor-to-ceiling window shattered, creating an instant escape route.

Under the cover of the cloud, Dante and Milana ran for the hole in the window.

The Furies came after them, firing wildly, unable to see their targets but hoping to get lucky.

Charlie, concealed by the cloud as well, ran through the exit nearest her, the one she would have taken anyhow to get to the jet. As she emerged onto the tarmac, the noise of the busy runway was overwhelming. The scream of jet engines from the passenger terminal and the stench of jet fuel filled the air.

A man was still pumping fuel into the private jet from a tanker. Like everyone else on the tarmac, he had plugs jammed into his ears so he wouldn't go deaf from all the noise.

Charlie waved wildly for the pilots' attention. She also shouted, even though there was almost no way they could hear her, because it couldn't hurt to at least *try.* "We need to go! Now!"

Behind Charlie, Dante and Milana had made it through the hole in the glass and were sprinting across the tarmac.

Inside the cockpit, the pilots spotted Charlie. Their orders were to do whatever she asked. So despite the fact that fuel was still pumping in from the tanker truck, they fired up the engines and began to turn toward the runway.

The hose dropped from the tanker, spraying fuel across the tarmac.

The tanker's operator started toward the truck to shut the gas off, but retreated when he saw the Furies emerge from the terminal, shooting at the CIA.

Dante and Milana fired back as they ran.

The jet was designed for speed in the air, not the ground. As it slowly rotated away from the terminal, airplane fuel pooled beneath it. Charlie skidded in it as she scrambled for the door.

The pilots opened the jet door automatically. A set of stairs descended with a railing attached. Charlie snagged the rail, hauled herself up, and dove inside.

But she still wasn't safe. The Furies didn't have to shoot her to kill her; they just had to shoot the fuel tanker.

The tanker was only twenty feet away, easily holding enough fuel to reduce the jet to scrap metal.

Plus, it was an easy target.

Dante and Milana realized this too. Both spun and dropped to the tarmac. In the darkness, they were hard to see, whereas the Furies were out in the open with the well-lit terminal behind them, making them far better targets. The CIA agents emptied their guns.

One after the other the Furies screamed in pain and dropped. Alexei was the last to go. He was hit three times before he finally collapsed.

The CIA agents leapt to their feet and ran after the jet again.

The jet was now moving faster. Charlie leaned back out the door.

Behind Dante and Milana, more people began

streaming out of the hole in the terminal. Mossad agents most likely. They started shooting too.

Milana reached the jet first. Charlie stuck out her hand and Milana grabbed on. Charlie hauled her to the steps and through the door. Milana collapsed on the floor inside, exhausted.

However, Dante was still a few feet away and the jet was picking up speed. Bullets pinged off the tarmac around him.

"Get inside!" the pilots yelled to Charlie. "We need to close the door so we can take off!"

Charlie didn't move from the stairs. She wrapped one arm around the railing and leaned toward Dante, extending the other arm. "Come on!" she yelled.

Dante used the last of his strength to lunge the final few steps, diving for the plane.

On the tarmac, Fez was badly wounded but still alive. He rolled over with his gun and made a last-ditch attempt to stop the plane. He aimed at the fuel tanker and emptied his clip.

Bullets sparked off the metal.

Charlie caught Dante's arm. His weight nearly yanked Charlie off the jet, but she held on tight.

The tanker exploded. A ball of fire raced toward the plane. The pool of fuel on the ground ignited.

The concussion of the blast threw Dante forward, onto Charlie, and both tumbled into the cabin of the jet.

The jet raced toward the runway, pulling clear of the fireball as the flames licked its tail and the tarmac burst into flame behind it.

Fez fell back to the ground, his body searing with pain, and screamed in frustration.

The Mossad agents swept toward the fallen Furies.

Lying on the tarmac, Alexei was dialing his phone, calling John Russo.

To his surprise, the call went right to voice mail. Even though John had said he would remain available.

Through the flickering heat of the blaze on the tarmac, Alexei saw the private jet speed down the runway and lift into the air.

"The girl is still alive," Alexei gasped. "And she's on a plane."

Then the Mossad was upon him.

On the jet, Charlie, Dante, and Milana were so exhausted they could barely buckle themselves into their seats. Charlie looked out the window as Israel dropped away beneath them, a curve of bright lights along the inky blackness of the Mediterranean Sea.

The copilot emerged from the cockpit, looking shaken from the takeoff. "Is everyone okay back here?" he asked.

"We've been better," Charlie replied. "Thanks for your help back there."

The copilot nodded. "I know the standard contract says that you're entitled to discretion, but I have to ask: Who on earth are you guys?"

"Bible salesmen," Charlie said. "Unfortunately, there were some misprints in the new versions we were selling. They said you should respect the Lord your Dog. That was a sect of rabid fundamentalists you just saved us from."

The copilot shook his head and smiled. "All right. I'll let you be." He ducked back into the cockpit and closed the door behind him.

Dante turned to Charlie and said, "Where are we going, kid?"

Charlie replied, "Get me a pencil and paper and I'll explain it."

At Mossad headquarters, Semel answered the call from Ben Gurion.

"Commander. This is Agent Avakian. The CIA and the girl escaped."

Semel furiously kicked over a trash can. "How did that happen?!"

Avakian quickly explained. He also told Semel about the five other men who had been shooting at the CIA. Three had died from gunshot wounds, while the two who survived were being interrogated. They had coughed up plenty of interesting information, but seemed to truly have no idea where the CIA jet was heading.

"Where did the pilots file a flight plan for?" Semel asked.

"Copenhagen."

Semel sighed. "So Copenhagen is the one place in the world we know they're *not* going. Did anyone get the plane's ID number?"

"NC177806."

There was a good chance that was fake too, but Semel didn't have many other leads. "Did the tower keep track of the plane once it took off?"

"They know it headed toward Europe, but most flights from here take off in that direction. And the ground crew had nearly filled the tanks while it was here, so it has enough fuel to go all the way to America."

Or anywhere else on the planet, thought Semel. He asked, "Can you get the exact coordinates of its angle of departure?"

"I'll try."

It took Agent Avakian a few minutes. The jet had, in fact, locked coordinates for a northeastern route and maintained them until they had left the range of Ben Gurion's radar, fifty miles out. The jet wouldn't *have* to keep the exact coordinates it had started off for, of course, but Semel guessed it wouldn't alter them too much. And if it didn't, there was a way he might be able to find it.

It was a long shot, but he would have to bet on it.

PART THREE

THE BEGINNING OF THE UNIVERSE

You never fail until you stop trying.

—ALBERT EINSTEIN

FORTY-TWO

Somewhere above the Mediterranean Sea

The hired jet was much nicer than the one Charlie, Dante, and Milana had come to Israel on. There was a fully stocked kitchenette and bar—not to mention a bedroom, a small screening room, and a bathroom with a working shower. No one had eaten the entire time they were in Israel and they were all starving, so Dante and Milana made sandwiches while Charlie, seated on the couch, sketched Einstein's clue from memory again:

$$\frac{(91-60)^8}{88M} + \left\{ 3\left(\frac{99c}{49}\right) \times \left[\frac{(192)^5}{5M} + (13 \times 16)(16 \times 15)^2 \right] \right\} - \left(\frac{754}{10X}\right)(851) + \left(10X + \frac{78}{92}\right)\left(\frac{10X}{16}\right)^8 \div (15i)\left(\frac{22}{55}\right) = \pi$$

When Dante and Milana brought the sandwiches over, Charlie presented her work and said, "It's elementary."

"Meaning it's easy?" Milana asked, incredulous.

"Because it's not."

"No, it's *elementary*," Charlie corrected. "That's Einstein's clue to solving the problem. Sherlock Holmes's most famous quote. This cipher is *literally* elementary: The numbers are all atomic numbers for the elements. It's not math: It's science. Einstein's greatest love."

There was a small library on the jet—a few shelves of books to divert passengers on long flights. Charlie found a dictionary and opened it to "element," where, as she had expected, there was a periodic table. She handed it to Milana, who instantly recognized the lopsided grid she had spent hours studying in chemistry class:

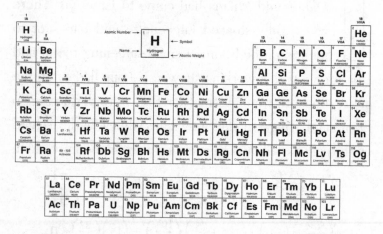

"Each element has a different number of protons," Charlie continued. "That's where we get its atomic number. And each element has an international symbol, which is the same, no matter what language you speak."

Charlie laid Einstein's cipher beside the periodic

table. "So the first number, ninety-one, is the atomic number for protactinium, atomic symbol 'Pa.' Sixty stands for neodymium, or 'Nd.' Then you've got oxygen and radium. . . ."

"Pandora," Dante said.

"Exactly." Charlie handed her brother the pen so he could decipher the rest. "Ignore the actual letters in the formula. I'll explain those in a moment."

Dante quickly went to work, converting Einstein's message with the help of the table. Milana hovered by his shoulder, watching. Charlie noticed that the two of them were standing much closer together than they had at the start of the day.

In just over a minute, Dante had translated:

Pa/Nd/O/Ra Li/Es In H/U/B/B/Al/S S/P/He/Re

Be/Ne/At/H Ne/Pt/U/Ne/S O/P/Ti/Cs

Dante turned to Charlie, excited by the discovery but confused by the message. "'Hubbal's sphere?' I assume he's referring to Edwin Hubble . . . ?"

"Yes. The misspelling is unavoidable, I think. The cipher is pretty limited by the letter combinations in the periodic table."

Milana asked, "Hubble was the astronomer who determined the size of the universe, right?"

"Correct again."

"Well, then, wouldn't 'Hubble's sphere' be the entire

universe?" Dante asked. "That's a pretty big place to hide something."

"True," Charlie admitted. "But that's a metaphoric translation. I think Einstein was being a bit more literal, meaning 'sphere' as in 'the place in which someone has influence.' Like your sphere would be the CIA."

Milana asked, "So you think Einstein left Pandora where Hubble worked?"

"I can almost guarantee it," Charlie answered. "Because Einstein left another clue. Remember, the letters in the formula are simply Roman numerals, which, taken together, give us the year 1931."

Dante looked at the clue to confirm this, then back at Charlie. "What happened in 1931?"

"First, you have to understand that Einstein was a big fan of Hubble. He thought Hubble's discoveries were as amazing on the cosmic scale as his were on the atomic. At the beginning of the twenty-first century, everyone— even Einstein himself—believed that our galaxy was the only one in the universe. That our galaxy *was* the universe. And then Hubble comes along and discovers that was totally wrong. In fact, Hubble found dozens of other galaxies, each with billions of stars. Suddenly, the universe was an infinitely larger place than everyone had thought. That blew a lot of people's minds."

Charlie took a bite of her sandwich, then continued.

"But Hubble wasn't satisfied with just that. He noticed that all these galaxies he'd found were significantly different from one another. There were spirals and ovals and pinwheels and clouds. So Hubble began to catalog all of them, documenting all the variations . . . and in doing this, he noticed something *really* surprising: All the galaxies were moving away from one another. And they were doing it at a rate constant to the distance between them."

"Hubble discovered the universe was expanding," Milana said.

"Exactly!" Charlie agreed. "This blew everyone away again—except for Einstein, who was thrilled by Hubble's discovery. Because back in 1917, when Einstein had produced his general theory of relativity, he had developed a model of space based on it that said space was curved by gravity—and therefore it ought to be able to expand or contract. But even Einstein thought this sounded crazy. After all, the current wisdom at the time said the universe was static. So Einstein assumed he had made a mistake. Then Hubble comes along and proves Einstein was right all along. General relativity makes sense. Einstein is vindicated. He was so psyched, he took a trip to meet Hubble and thank him personally . . . in January of 1931."

Dante and Milana shared a look of excitement. "Where was that?" Milana asked.

"The Mount Wilson Observatory," Charlie answered. "In the San Gabriel Mountains."

Dante's eyes widened in surprise. "That's right by Los Angeles. You think Pandora's there?"

"Absolutely," Charlie said. "It makes perfect sense. Back in 1931, Los Angeles wasn't much of a city yet. It was just a little podunk town where they made movies. That's why the observatory was built there; it was on the edge of civilization. There was hardly any light pollution. No one ever expected that the city would grow to be the second largest in the country."

Milana asked, "So you think Einstein's trip to visit Hubble was just a cover for his looking for a place to hide Pandora?"

"That's my bet." Charlie wolfed down the last of her sandwich. "Nazi Germany was on the rise in 1931 and Einstein was worried about it; only two years later, he moved to America to escape it for good. If he wanted to hide Pandora as far from the Nazis as possible, Mount Wilson was a good place. At the same time, it was a research facility, meaning it would remain under government care, which was an added bonus. An awful lot of treasure in the world has been lost because people buried it out in the wilderness. The wilderness changes. Rivers alter course. Mountains collapse. Fields erode. But a government facility is forever."

Dante considered that carefully, then nodded. "I guess that makes sense."

"But that only takes care of 'Hubble's sphere,'" Milana said. "What does 'Neptune's optics' mean?"

Charlie said, "Hubble's telescope, I assume. Telescope lenses are optics, and in 1931, the biggest telescope in the world was the Hooker at Mount Wilson. Its lens was a hundred inches across—and the bigger the lens, the farther you can see into space. A lot of scientists consider the Hooker the most important scientific instrument of the twentieth century, given all the discoveries that were made with it. It allowed scientists to see all sorts of cosmic objects for the first time: comets, asteroids, nebulas . . . and even Neptune and Uranus."

"No one had ever seen those planets until then?" Milana asked, surprised.

"Nope," Charlie replied. "Neptune's existence was mathematically determined in 1845, but it was so far away no one ever got a decent look at it until the Hooker was built. Einstein saw it for the first time when he visited Hubble. The Hooker's still in operation at Mount Wilson."

Dante asked, "So you're assuming Pandora is hidden somewhere beneath the telescope?"

"Yes."

"Where?" Milana asked.

"We'll have to figure that out when we get there."

Despite this final bit of uncertainty, Charlie grinned, proud of herself.

Dante couldn't help but smile back. The day hadn't gone nearly the way he had hoped, and there were still plenty of problems to contend with, but for now, at least, it appeared that his hunch to bring Charlie aboard had paid off. They didn't know *exactly* where Pandora was, but they were much closer than anyone had been in more than half a century. And while John Russo had a head start on them, they were making up time. Perhaps they were even ahead of him.

Milana yawned suddenly, then seemed embarrassed she had done it. "Sorry."

"Why?" Dante asked. "We've had an incredibly long day. We're all cruising on fumes, and we have a long flight ahead of us. You should get some sleep." He pointed to the bedroom.

Milana nodded agreement, then stood up, yawning again.

"That goes for you, too, kiddo," Dante told Charlie. "Share the bed with Milana. I'll sleep here on the couch."

Charlie watched Milana shuffle toward the small bedroom, then asked Dante quietly, "You're sure you wouldn't rather be in there with her? You could do a little smooching before bed."

Dante flushed red, then glanced to see if Milana had

overheard this, but she was already in the bedroom. He turned back to Charlie. "Can it with that, will you? It's unprofessional."

"I'm *twelve*, Dante. Of course I'm unprofessional. Eight years ago I was still picking my nose and eating it."

"Then I guess I need to be the adult here." Dante stood and pointed to the bedroom. "Bedtime. Now."

Charlie stood and shrugged. "Okay. But I think she'd like a little smooching too."

"Go to sleep," Dante ordered.

"Fine." Charlie teasingly made a kissy face as she headed into the bedroom.

The room was at the rear of the jet and thus was quite narrow. The bed was only a twin size, so there was barely enough room for two people. Milana was already lying on one side, on top of the covers, facing the wall, the only way to give Charlie any privacy. She was still wearing her clothes from that day, even though they were dirty and sweaty and had some spots of what Charlie suspected was other people's blood on them. They had nothing else to change into.

Charlie lay down beside her, looking up at the ceiling. "You like Dante, don't you?" she asked.

"Of course I like him. He's an excellent agent."

"That's not what I meant. I mean, you *like* him. Right?"

"How much did you pay for this jet?" Milana asked.

"You're avoiding the subject."

"Because I don't want to talk about it. How much?"

"Half a million dollars. Plus a ten percent charge to the bank for arranging everything."

Charlie felt Milana stiffen in surprise next to her. "That's a lot of money for one flight."

"The expense seemed worth it, given that the fate of the world was at stake."

"Still . . ."

"What else was I going to do with it? Buy half a million dollars' worth of candy?"

Milana said, "You should know, when Dante first came to me with this plan, I thought he was insane. I didn't think there was any way that some girl your age could possibly be of use to us. But you have—and under far more dire circumstances than we imagined. You've done good, kid."

Milana expected a cocky response to this, but none came. Charlie didn't say anything at all.

Because she was asleep.

"You've done good, kid," Milana repeated, and then closed her eyes and hoped that Charlie was right about Pandora, and that they'd left all the trouble behind them.

In the main cabin Dante waited to make sure that Charlie was asleep, then tried to use the jet's Internet so he could call Jamilla Carter. He wanted to alert her as to where he was heading, maybe have a team get to

Mount Wilson right away. Only, the Internet was down.

He knocked on the door to the cockpit and informed the pilots about this.

"Sorry about that," the copilot answered through the door. "I'm afraid the Internet won't be operational for the entire trip."

Dante was sure that was a lie. "I really need to make a call. It's a life-or-death situation."

"I'm sorry," the copilot responded. "That won't be possible."

"Could you make an emergency landing so that I can get to a phone?"

"Our orders are to fly directly to Los Angeles without making any stops."

Dante frowned. "And who are those orders from?"

"Miss Thorne. She's the one who hired the plane. And she was very specific about this."

"Miss Thorne is only twelve. . . ."

"Nevertheless, she's in charge. If you would like to change the plans, I'd suggest you talk to her."

Dante sighed and returned to the couch. He considered waking Charlie and telling her why he needed to talk to the CIA, but he knew she wouldn't listen. She obviously didn't trust the Agency.

For the time being, she was calling the shots. They were on their own.

FORTY-THREE

At any given moment there were more than four thousand working satellites orbiting the earth. A startling number of them were for espionage. Most were owned by various countries, although some corporations had them as well.

Of that staggering amount of technology floating in space, only five of the satellites were owned by Israel. Four were for spying, and the fifth was a telecommunications satellite that still had some espionage capabilities. The satellites didn't cover the entire world—but they could take in a sizable piece of the northern hemisphere. One was locked in geosynchronous orbit above Israel, constantly scanning the Middle East for signs of trouble, while the others circled the globe at eighteen thousand miles per hour. The one Isaac Semel was using was currently orbiting over the North Atlantic.

Semel had learned the type of jet Charlie Thorne was on and the top speed it was capable of with the gas tanks loaded. He knew the current wind conditions. And he knew the coordinates it had locked in for the first fifty miles of flight. He had some of his specialists run the numbers to give him an idea of where it might be if it wasn't heading to Denmark.

If it was going to Europe, he was in trouble, because it would be there by now, grounded on one of a thousand airstrips. But Semel assumed it wasn't heading to Europe. There would have been no need to top off the tanks unless they were going farther than that.

So he had to consider two other things: the direction the plane had taken off—and where Einstein had been in his life.

The answers pointed to the United States.

Einstein had visited many countries, but he had spent the last half of his life in America. It was a country he loved, a country he knew well, a country he felt safe in.

So Charlie Thorne and the CIA were probably headed there. Now all Semel had to do was find them.

All planes that headed from Israel to America passed over the arctic. The paths were known as great circle routes, and the nice thing about them was very little moved in them except airplanes.

Although thousands of people went from Europe to

North America and back every day, that didn't translate into very many planes—only about two hundred, and those weren't all in the air at the same time. Furthermore, most of those planes were quite large: commercial jumbo jets and military transports. Only a few thousand corporations and a few hundred individuals had private jets capable of making the flight—and those jets were significantly smaller than the other planes.

So all you had to do was calculate where the jet holding Charlie would be, given the plane's weight, speed, and the prevailing winds—and then look for it. It was dark over the North Atlantic now, but jets had lights and—more important—heat trails. Over the cold, inky darkness of the arctic, they were easy to locate. Finding the right one wasn't like looking for a needle in a haystack; it was more like looking for a specific needle in a pincushion. There were only a few dozen possibilities. You simply had to examine each closely to see if it was your target.

Semel ordered the satellite facility to put their best recon men on it.

They nailed the jet on their fourth try.

It was exactly where it should have been, crossing over Ellesmere Island above the arctic circle. It was moving at the right speed. And while it was hard to tell from so high above at night, the plane appeared to have the proper shape and heat signature. And nothing else in the sky matched it.

They had the plane.

Now they just had to see where it was going.

FORTY-FOUR

Los Angeles International Airport

John Russo couldn't believe his ears.

He had checked his phone messages the moment the plane landed, expecting news from Alexei. He hadn't necessarily expected it to be good news; with their greater numbers, the odds were that the Mossad would have captured Charlie Thorne before the Furies could kill her. But according to Alexei, Charlie hadn't just stayed alive; she had somehow gotten on a plane.

How had she done it? Who on earth was Charlie Thorne? And more important, was she heading to Mount Wilson?

John wanted to believe she wasn't. She couldn't be. Charlie didn't even have a copy of Einstein's clue, let alone the key for decoding it. And she was only a kid. And yet by now John's experience told him to take nothing for granted where Charlie Thorne was concerned. He would have to keep his guard up.

The moment his plane reached the gate, John leapt to his feet. From his business-class seat, he was almost the first off the plane.

It was ten minutes after six a.m.. It was still night, although day would be breaking soon.

While Alexei's phone call had been upsetting, there was one bit of good news. According to John's phone, the call had been made at forty-six minutes after midnight in Israel. John's flight had taken off at midnight on the nose. So, if nothing else, he had a forty-six-minute head start.

He still needed to get his luggage, but his suitcase was also the first off the plane. Alexei would have said that was God smiling upon them, proof that their mission was divinely inspired. Alexei had seen the hand of God everywhere.

John merely assumed it was a perk of business class.

John didn't believe in God. He considered Alexei's constant interpretation of events as God's will to be mere rationalization for bad behavior. As for his own bad behavior, he knew exactly what the root of that was: He no longer wanted to be John Russo.

But to become someone else, he needed money. And Pandora was worth millions.

Countries would pay handsomely for the power Pandora offered. And they would pay to make sure other countries *didn't* have it. Which country ended up with it would simply be a matter of price.

Once John had his hands on Pandora, he would ransom it. He would contact the security agencies of the twenty most powerful countries in the world and convince them he had Einstein's last equation. He would give them the facts first. And if they didn't believe him, then he would prove it.

He would blow something up.

Nothing in a city, of course. John wasn't a mass murderer. He had no interest in causing death, destruction, and despair simply to make a point. No, he would set off a bomb somewhere remote. A desert. Or an island in the South Pacific. The same way governments had let the world know they had nuclear weapons back in the 1940s. Sure, a few people might get poisoned by the radiation, and he might decimate the local wildlife and bake the sand into glass, but you couldn't make an omelet without breaking a few eggs. After that everyone would know he truly had Pandora. Then he'd begin taking offers.

He would have the highest bidder wire the money to a Swiss bank account, and then he would be free to be whomever he wanted. The last trace of John Russo would vanish from existence, and a very wealthy and satisfied man would take his place. With the money, he could go anywhere he wanted and become anyone he wished.

John needed only one thing from the suitcase. The clothes were mere window dressing, to make it look as though he were a normal traveler. Tucked among them was his gun.

Rather than wait for the shuttle to the rental car company lot, John took a cab there, then picked up an SUV with four-wheel drive. Even though it was sunny at the airport, which sat by the beach, it was winter where John was going.

According to the SUV's GPS system, it was fifty-six miles to the Mount Wilson Observatory.

It had been thirty-five minutes since John's plane had landed. If Charlie Thorne *was* heading to Los Angeles, her plane wouldn't have even landed yet.

John still had a big head start—and Pandora was less than an hour away.

FORTY-FIVE

Dante woke to the smell of frying bacon.

He snapped upright on the couch, startled to find Charlie was cooking breakfast. Dante couldn't believe he had slept through it; he couldn't remember another time he had slept so hard.

Milana was still asleep as well. The bedroom door was open a tiny bit, and Dante could see her on the bed.

"Good morning!" Charlie said cheerfully. "Sorry to disturb you, but I was starving. In my defense, though, I *did* tell you to take the bedroom."

Dante had set his watch for Pacific Standard Time before going to bed. He checked it now to see that it was six fifteen in the morning. They were getting close. He lifted the window shade and saw it was still dark outside. There were few lights in the land below, indicating they were over a sparsely populated area. Central Utah or

Nevada, or the Mojave Desert in California.

Every muscle in Dante's body ached. He had taken a beating the day before, and his muscles had all tensed up while he had slept on the couch. "Any chance you could make some breakfast for me while you're at it?"

"Already done." Charlie slid bacon and eggs onto plates. "You like yours scrambled with chilies and blue cheese, right?"

"Right," Dante said, surprised the kid had remembered that. They had eaten breakfast together only once, and that had been years ago. But then, the kid didn't forget *anything*.

"Well, I didn't make them that way," Charlie replied. "There's no chilies or blue cheese on this plane, and besides, that combination is disgusting." She laid out bacon and eggs for herself.

Dante was surprised that Charlie didn't seem to be in the tiniest bit of pain, even though she had been banged around as much as he had. But then he remembered that back when he was twelve, his own body had been far more resilient. There were advantages to being young.

Charlie sat at the table and dug into her breakfast. "There's been a slight change of plans," she said.

Dante took the seat beside her. "What's up?"

"We lost a little time in the air. Nasty headwinds over the arctic. They wouldn't have slowed a jumbo jet much, but they were rough on us, so we're trying to cut some corners. According to the pilots, there's a small airport in a town called El Monte. It's a lot closer to Mount Wilson than LAX."

"I assume there's no customs or immigration at El Monte, either."

"As it happens, no."

"So we're breaking the law."

"It's for a good cause."

"The FAA might notice."

"They probably won't." Charlie placed a flight map of Southern California that she had gotten from the pilots on the table. "Turns out, the Los Angeles Basin has the largest concentration of small airports in the country. Twenty-four in all. The FAA can barely keep tabs on them—and if they do, Homeland Security and the DEA probably prefer them to concentrate on planes coming north from Central and South America."

"Still, if they tag us, we could have a real mess on our hands."

"That's why we're going to move fast on the ground. Deplane, grab the car, and get moving."

"What car?"

"My friends at the bank are having a rental delivered."

"What's that costing you?"

"They threw it in for free. I've been a good client." Charlie grinned.

Dante took another bite of his breakfast. Outside, the sky was beginning to brighten. Dante could see the dark shapes of mountains looming in the distance. The San Gabriel Mountains to the north of Los Angeles. The home of Mount Wilson—and Pandora. They were so close—and yet still so far away.

"I tried to call the CIA last night," Dante said.

"I know," Charlie replied. "The pilots told me."

"You're making a mistake. We need to contact the Agency. . . ."

"The same Agency that assumed we were traitors and sent the Mossad after us?"

"That was understandable, given the circumstances. We need support now. There's an office in LA. They can have a team at Mount Wilson before we land."

"No way."

"Don't be stupid, kid. . . ."

"If there's one thing I'm not, Dante, it's stupid."

"You don't know what we're going to come up against today."

"John Russo is the only one left—and odds are he's not even here. Maybe he hasn't solved Einstein's clue yet. Or maybe he got it wrong. . . ."

"And if he didn't? What if he finds Pandora before us? Do you realize how bad that would be?"

"Yes. Almost as bad as the US government finding it before us."

Dante grew angry, just as Charlie had expected. "You're aware that I work for the US government, right?"

"So did John Russo."

"He's the exception, not the rule. Most government employees are like me. They're good people, trying to do the right thing. To help others, keep them safe, make their lives better. With Pandora, we could solve all our energy problems. *The world's* energy problems. Climate change could become a thing of the past."

"If you could guarantee that would happen, I'd be happy to hand Pandora right over. But you can't. And you know it. No matter how well you try to protect Pandora, sooner or later some jerk like John Russo or Alexei Kolyenko is going to get ahold of it. And then we're screwed."

"The kid has a point," Milana said.

Charlie and Dante turned to see her standing in the doorway of the bedroom. She was wide-awake and ready for action.

"Right now our priority is beating John Russo to Pandora," Milana continued. "Once we have it and we're safe, then we can discuss what to do with it."

Dante grimaced at this statement, as though Milana had betrayed him. But Charlie was pleased. "So you agree turning Pandora over to our government could be a mistake?" she asked.

"Maybe," Milana said. "You've been right about everything else so far. All I know for sure is if John Russo ends up with Pandora, we have a serious problem."

Despite the heaviness of the statement, Charlie found herself smiling anyhow, pleased that at least one of the CIA agents was starting to see things her way. "Then let's get to Pandora first," she said.

FORTY-SIX

Beverly Hills, California

enny West's phone had rung at five a.m.

Benny West wasn't his real name. In his previous life, he had served twelve years in the Mossad under Isaac Semel. He would have still been active, but he had ended up on Hezbollah's hit list and then an informant had blown his cover. So Benny had been sent on the lam. The Mossad had helped his whole family—his wife and two little girls—slip out of Israel in the middle of the night and set up in Los Angeles. There were a couple of ex-Mossad guys out there, brothers who had made a lot of money running weapons, then started a film production company and made even more money. Half their employees were Mossad agents who'd had to flee the country. Benny had changed his name, gotten a job in the accounting department, and formed friendships with all the other families who worked there. It was a good life, but they all still stayed in shape and went to the firing range every week, because even though they were out of Israel, they weren't out of the Mossad. You were never out of the Mossad.

Isaac Semel gave Benny his orders personally. By this point, he had been tracking Charlie's jet for hours and now could tell it was headed toward LA. As the plane got closer, he would get a better idea of which airport it would land at. In the meantime, the Mossad was going to hedge its bets and cover as many as possible.

Benny didn't question anything and didn't complain that he'd been out of the game for a long time. Instead, he got right to work. He called his office and told them he wasn't coming in for the day. Then he called six other Mossad agents one by one and explained the situation. Meanwhile, Semel was activating other teams all over LA. Within half an hour, they were all fanning out across the city.

So when the private jet touched down in El Monte, a Mossad agent named Leo Kolodny was there. He was fifty-five, but still built like a linebacker, one of Benny's crew. Leo watched Charlie, Dante, and Milana deplane, then called Semel and described them. Semel confirmed Leo had the right people and gave his next orders: Tail the targets to wherever they were going, then take whatever they found by force.

Then Semel called Benny and told him to coordinate with Leo. Wherever Charlie Thorne ended up, he wanted the whole team there.

FORTY-SEVEN

San Gabriel Mountains, just north of Los Angeles

The Mount Wilson Observatory had been founded in 1904. At the time, the San Gabriel Mountains were regarded as one of the best sites for viewing the heavens in the United States. The desert skies were dry and clear. Light pollution was nonexistent. No one could imagine that in less than a century, the tiny city of Los Angeles at the mountains' base would balloon to more than eighteen million people, or that the newly invented automobile would clog the roads in numbers so great that the sky would turn brown from their exhaust.

Even with the massive metropolis sprawling below it, the modern observatory still remained useful, due to the height of the mountains. While the San Gabriels weren't the tallest range in the United States, they were the steepest. They rose almost straight out of the desert floor, thrust upward in the blink of an eye in geological time due to the action of the San Andreas Fault. In fact, the mountains were still growing; during the Northridge earthquake of 1994, parts of the range had lifted as much as fifteen inches.

The peak of Mount Wilson was nearly five thousand feet above Los Angeles, high enough to have a radically different climate. While the city below was parched for much of the year, with summer temperatures that could hit 110 degrees, the upper flanks of the San Gabriels were covered with forests of towering pines, firs, and redwoods. They could receive several feet of snow in the winter— and in the spring this would melt and churn through dozens of precipitous ravines, some so steep and inaccessible they had still never been explored. The observatory was the only occupied spot in a large, untamed wilderness; black bears, bighorn sheep, and mountain lions commonly roamed the grounds.

When the observatory had been built, it was as close to the frontier as was left in the United States. The only way to reach it was up a harrowing miner's trail, nine miles of dirt track hacked into the edges of sheer mountainsides. The components of the original telescopes all had to be hauled up by mules, several of which turned gray from the effort. The observatory had been serviced this way for more than thirty years; in 1931, Einstein himself had arrived by mule for his visit.

In 1935, the Angeles Crest Highway was completed, allowing automobiles access to the observatory via a sinuous two-lane road, but even decades later, getting there wasn't always easy. Winter snows often closed the highway for days, and the rumblings of the San Andreas fault regularly caused landslides or fractured the road itself. The observatory staff was always prepared to be cut off from civilization for at least a week.

It had been an unusually wet winter for Los Angeles, and the snowpack was heavy as Charlie, Dante, and Milana wound their way up the Angeles Crest in their rented SUV. Signs at the base of the mountain had warned of treacherous conditions. Much of the road was slick with ice, whereas other portions had crumbled into the ravines, leaving deadly gaps that had merely been marked with strands of plastic yellow police tape.

Thankfully, Charlie had thought to prepare for bad weather. Along with the SUV, she had asked her bank for winter clothes for herself, Dante, and Milana, seeing as their old ski clothes had been left back in Israel. They were wearing the new clothes now.

However, Charlie hadn't thought to request extra ammunition for their guns, and there was no time to wait for the sporting goods stores to open. She could only hope they would have no need for weapons.

Surprisingly, they weren't alone on the road. The

mountains' proximity to such a large city guaranteed there would always be people visiting them, even that early in the day; families with saucer sleds, cross-country skiers, and teenagers with snowboards were heading up to the snow. Since there was only one road, there was no way to tell if any of the other cars were following them or merely heading into the mountains. Therefore, Leo Kolodny's SUV didn't stand out as it tailed them, five cars back.

The turnoff to Mount Wilson was a narrow road, poorly marked with a small, rusted sign. They followed it until a mile from the observatory, where they encountered a substantial roadblock. A cliff had partially collapsed, spilling boulders the size of armchairs across the road. Charlie, Dante, and Milana had no choice but to park and continue on foot. There was no place to hide their SUV. If anyone else arrived looking for Pandora, they would know someone was ahead of them.

At this altitude, they were as high as the clouds, and it was misty and cool. The road beyond the landslide was covered with five feet of snow. Charlie, Dante, and Milana trudged through it, bundled up against the cold, until they arrived at the observatory complex.

With the paved roads hidden beneath the snow, the complex didn't look much different than it would have when Einstein had visited. Gleaming white telescope domes were interspersed through the woods, as were a few support buildings: employee housing, maintenance sheds, and a small museum. The structures were scattered randomly on the steep slopes, built wherever there was suitably flat space. As clouds scuttled across the peak, buildings materialized out of the fog and then vanished back into it again: a solar telescope perched atop a 150-foot tower, several prefab buildings, and the CHARA Array—the Center for High Angular Resolution Astronomy—a series of six domed telescopes spread out over a quarter mile, linked by computers to create the same image that a single, enormous telescope would. Each of the six domes was the size of a small house, with a large propane tank that provided power and heat. Beyond everything, at the far end of the complex, the biggest dome of all loomed above the trees, six stories tall, home of the Hooker telescope itself.

"The house of Hubble," Charlie said, with awe in her voice. "I've always wanted to come here."

"To use the telescope?" Milana asked.

"No," Charlie replied. "For the same reason Einstein visited. To pay my respects. Almost everything we know about the universe—like astrophysics and the big bang theory—we know because of this observatory. It makes more and more sense that this is where Einstein hid Pandora. A big idea like that would be in good company up here."

Dante peered uneasily through the shifting haze of clouds. "Speaking of company, where is everyone? Is this place closed for the winter?"

"No. It runs year-round," Charlie replied. "But since the stars are only out at night, most telescope operators sleep during the day. Only the guys working the solar scopes would be up. And even then, they're probably not at their posts today. No one's going to see anything through this." Charlie waved at the clouds around them.

The most direct path to the Hooker dome was a narrow footbridge, which crossed a shallow, snow-choked gully. As Charlie, Dante, and Milana crossed over it, they passed a small reservoir and pump house.

"What's this for?" Milana asked.

"Firefighting, I'll bet," Dante observed. "In the summer, after a dry winter, this whole place is probably a tinderbox."

Halfway across the bridge was a commemorative plaque with a faded photograph of Einstein and Hubble standing in that very spot in 1931.

"Looks like we're in the right place," Dante said.

As they stepped off the bridge, Milana came along Charlie's side. "I have something for you," she said, then opened her hand to reveal a small, black elastic ring.

"A hair band?" Charlie asked.

"I've noticed your hair keeps getting in your eyes,"

Milana said. "Hopefully, we're not going to end up in danger here, but if we do, this might be helpful. And even if we don't . . . being able to see the world clearly is generally a good thing."

Charlie knew the hair band had cost maybe three cents, but she was surprised to find how touched she was that Milana was looking out for her. "Thanks," she said, then pulled her hair back into a ponytail and wrapped the band around it.

"It's one of the tools of the trade they never teach you about in the academy," Milana said. "Probably because most of the instructors there are men."

"What are you two talking about?" Dante asked suspiciously.

"Girl stuff," Charlie told him, then shared a smile with Milana. Dante sighed and rolled his eyes.

The Hooker dome was locked, and no one answered when they knocked. But the CHARA control center sat close by, and when Dante banged on the door, a woman answered. She wore lots of flannel and an expression that said it had been a long time since she had encountered strangers up here. When Dante flashed his CIA badge and requested access to the Hooker dome for reasons of national security, the woman's confusion didn't lessen much. But she radioed the head of operations on the mountain, who agreed to come quickly.

A few minutes later Tim Ralston hustled across the footbridge. He was dressed haphazardly, as he had just been roused from sleep, but was an otherwise hale and athletic man. He was in his early sixties and, despite having been woken, was in good spirits. An ebullient golden retriever, whom he introduced as Quark, followed at his heels.

Upon seeing the CIA badges, Tim quickly agreed to help in any way he could. At Dante's request, he unlocked the doors to the Hooker dome and led them inside.

As he started up the Angeles Crest Highway, Benny West called Leo Kolodny. Benny had met up with three other Mossad agents at the base and now they were all piled into one SUV. He gave Leo their location and asked what the situation was.

Leo told them he was keeping an eye on the targets, who had no idea he had followed them. They were inside a big white dome. He had just started to describe how to get there from where he had parked when he gave sudden a gasp.

And then Leo wasn't there anymore.

Benny called his name a few times but got no answer.

Three seconds later, the line went dead.

Benny turned to the guy who was driving and said, "Step on it. We've got trouble."

John Russo could tell the man he had killed was Mossad. He had worked with enough of those guys in Israel to know the look. This guy had been out of action for a while—he was doughy in the middle and he had been caught unprepared for the weather—and yet he probably could have killed John in a fair fight. Even retired Mossad agents were tough as nails—and now more were coming.

Charlie Thorne had led them here.

The whole thing seemed impossible to John. The girl hadn't merely memorized Einstein's clue; she had figured it out as well—on her own, without the aid of Einstein's notes. And then, not only had Charlie managed to get out of Israel; she had somehow managed to beat John here. With Dante and Milana in tow.

John had planned this all so carefully. He had prepared for every eventuality. And yet Charlie Thorne was like a cockroach. You just couldn't get rid of her. She escaped every trap he had laid. She solved every problem she faced. . . .

But maybe there was a way John could use that to his advantage.

The Mount Wilson complex was much larger than John had expected. He had assumed there would be only one telescope; instead, there were at least ten, along with dozens of other buildings. It could take days—or even weeks—to search the whole area. So why not let the girl genius do the hard work? If she was so smart, why not let her find the equation . . . ?

And then John could simply take it.

Yes, John thought, as he dragged Leo's body into the bushes. That would work. In fact, maybe it was a blessing that Charlie Thorne was here after all.

FORTY-EIGHT

The dark sphere of the Hooker dome was dominated by the telescope, a fifty-foot-tall shaft of gleaming blue steel mounted on a massive rotating pedestal. It was the same telescope Edwin Hubble had used to unlock the secrets of the universe, the same one Einstein had gazed at the cosmos through, although it had been upgraded over the years and was now surrounded by banks of relatively new computers.

Except for a few lights down on the operating floor, the rest of the dome was dark. For Charlie, it was easy to imagine that she was actually out in space, the Hooker looking like an interplanetary capsule and the twinkling lights of the computer consoles like stars.

The building was huge, much bigger than Charlie had anticipated; there were thousands of places Einstein could have hidden the equation. Charlie's mind raced, trying to narrow her search. She pointed to all the equipment and asked Tim Ralston, "How much of this was here in 1931?"

"1931?" Tim repeated. "That's awfully specific."

"Thereabouts, then."

Tim scratched Quark behind the ears as he thought. "Not too much, I'd bet. The scope is the same, but everything else has been modernized so many times I'd doubt any of this is original. This entire apparatus used to be controlled with weights and pulleys. And the computers are all post-1931, of course."

Charlie nodded, understanding. The first computer, ENIAC, hadn't been completed until 1946, and it had taken up an entire room—even though it had less computing power than Charlie's phone, or the electronic key for the SUV she had come here in.

Charlie struck the metal floor of the dome with her foot. It echoed. "There's a room underneath us?"

"To hold all the operating machinery for the telescope," Tim answered. "I hate to pry, but it'd be a lot easier if you just told me what you're looking for."

Charlie turned to Dante, who shook his head. Charlie leaned in close to him and whispered, "The guy has a point. He must know this place backward and forward. Without him, it could take a lot of time to find Pandora— and we don't have much of that right now."

Dante sighed, then turned to Tim and quickly explained Pandora.

The astronomer was skeptical at first, but he grew more and more intrigued as the story went on. "And you believe Einstein hid this equation *here*?" he asked.

"We have very good reason to believe so," Charlie replied.

"What?"

"A clue Einstein left."

"And he said Pandora's in this dome?" Tim asked. "Because I've spent an awful lot of time in here over the years. I know every nook and cranny of this place, and I've never seen anything like that."

"Well, he didn't say it was in the dome, per se," Charlie said. "He says it's 'under Neptune's optics.' And since Hubble used this telescope to see Neptune . . ."

"He did. But that was the least of what Hubble accomplished here. This telescope was really built to look way the heck beyond Neptune."

"We know. But I figured Einstein was taking a bit of poetic license. . . ." Charlie trailed off, realizing Tim had a point. Now, standing in the shadow of the Hooker, her conclusions suddenly seemed wrong. There would have been many other ways to refer to the telescope. Einstein's code was limited in what words could be formed, but still, why would he choose Neptune? In 1931, the planet would have been old news astronomically; its existence had been known of since 1846. The real sensation would have been Pluto, which had been discovered only the year before.

"Were any of the other telescopes at Mount Wilson ever used for planetary studies?" Charlie asked.

"Not really," Tim said. "This was primarily designed to be a solar and stellar observatory. I know people have looked at Neptune on occasion, but that was usually more for fun than research. The truth is, Neptune's not a very interesting planet. It looks like a little blue ball. Jupiter and Saturn are far more dynamic. . . ."

Charlie's eyes suddenly lit up with inspiration. "Oh," she said.

Then she ran to the door. The others followed her.

"What are you thinking?" Milana asked.

Charlie said, "I don't think Einstein meant the *planet* Neptune. He meant the God the planet was named after: Neptune, who ruled the water." She exited the telescope dome and headed toward the snow-covered reservoir.

"You think it's in *there*?" Dante asked.

"Maybe," Charlie said. "Think about it: Einstein said the equation was beneath 'Neptune's optics.' Telescopes aren't optics. They *hold* optics. The optics are the pieces that manipulate the light: the lenses and reflectors. And the biggest reflector at this observatory is that." Charlie pointed dramatically at the reservoir, then turned to Tim. "Was that here in 1931?"

"It was just being built when Einstein visited," Tim replied. "In fact, they even had a little ceremony where Einstein laid the cornerstone for the pump house."

Charlie's heart rate suddenly sped up with excitement. She shifted her attention downhill to the pump house. Einstein had said Pandora was beneath Neptune's optics—and the cinder-block hut was certainly below the reservoir.

Charlie ran toward it. The others were right behind her.

"Einstein laid the cornerstone?" Charlie repeated.

"I think the whole event was done in jest," Tim explained. "From what I've heard, the pump house was under construction and Hubble suggested that since Einstein had come all the way from Europe, he might as well do some work. So Einstein set the first block. There's even a little plaque for it."

They slid down into the gully below the reservoir, furrowing trenches in the snow.

Charlie reached the pump house first. She dug into the snow at the base of the tiny building, revealing a small bronze plaque bolted to the lowest cinder block. It was haphazardly engraved, as though a couple of renowned scientists had made it on a lark: ON THIS SPOT

IN JANUARY 1931, ALBERT EINSTEIN DID HEREBY LAY THIS CORNERSTONE.

"Is there a sledgehammer nearby?" Dante asked.

"In the maintenance shack," Tim said. He ran to get it, Quark loping along beside him, and was back within two minutes, brimming with excitement. "I can't believe it," he said. "I must have passed this pump house a million times and the equation might have been here all along."

"We're about to find out." Dante took aim at the cornerstone and swung the sledge like a golf club. His first shot shattered the concrete, revealing the inner hollow of the cinder block.

Milana reached inside and gasped with excitement. Then she withdrew a small metal case the size a watch would have come in.

"Pandora's box," Charlie said reverently.

Einstein had obviously paid a great deal of attention to its construction. It was made of metal, small and light enough to carry around while waiting for the perfect hiding place to present itself, yet strong enough to protect its contents for decades. There wasn't a trace of rust or corrosion. It still looked as though it were brand-new.

There was no latch. Instead, ten code wheels were set into the lid, each with the numbers 0–9. Above them, a message had been etched into the metal:

Perhaps you have come looking for this—but perhaps chance has brought you here. Thus I offer a final challenge: A vial of pure cesium rests in this box. If you enter the wrong number or try to force the box open, the vial will crack. Once the cesium is exposed to air, it will ignite, destroying the treasure within.

"You have to be kidding." Dante sighed. "Another code to crack?"

A hundred yards away, in the direction of the access road, a flock of birds suddenly took to the air, as though they'd been startled. Dante and Milana both tensed, their hands moving to their guns.

"What's wrong?" Tim asked.

"Probably nothing," Dante said. "But I'm going to make sure. You guys figure this out." He climbed out of the gully and headed off to see what had startled the birds.

Milana returned her attention to the box. "'Figure this out,' he says. How? There must be a billion possible combinations for this."

"Several billion, actually," Tim corrected.

"Well, why not?" Charlie asked. "As perfect as this hiding place was, Einstein still couldn't guarantee some random person wouldn't stumble upon it. Therefore, he would want to make sure that only someone *he'd* sent knew how to open the box."

Milana stared at Charlie a moment, then smiled. "You little jerk. You already know the combination, don't you?"

"Of course. Einstein gave it to us."

Milana considered that a moment and then understood. "The clue. It's also an equation after all."

Charlie nodded. She had already done the math in her head. If she counted the variables as the Roman numerals they represented, then:

$$\frac{(91-60)^8}{88M} + \left\{ 3\left(\frac{99c}{49}\right) \times \left[\frac{(192)^5}{5M} + (13 \times 16)(16 \times 15)^2\right]\right\} -$$

$$\left(\frac{754}{10X}\right)(851) + \left(10X + \frac{78}{92}\right)\left(\frac{10X}{16}\right)^8 \div (15i)\left(\frac{22}{55}\right) =$$

$$\frac{(91-60)^8}{88.000} + \left\{ 3\left(\frac{9.900}{49}\right) \times \left[\frac{(192)^5}{5.000} + (13 \times 16)(16 \times 15)^2\right]\right\} -$$

$$\left(\frac{754}{100}\right)(851) + \left(100 + \frac{78}{92}\right)\left(\frac{100}{16}\right)^8 \div (15)\left(\frac{22}{55}\right) =$$

$$5{,}413{,}216{,}482$$

Ten digits long.

"You're positive you know the right answer?" Milana asked.

"Yes."

"So why aren't you opening the box?"

Charlie took a deep breath and said, "When Pandora opened the box in the myth, a lot of bad things happened to the world. Maybe it's better to just enter the wrong code and destroy this."

"Maybe, but I know you won't."

Charlie gave Milana a challenging stare. "How do you know what I'll do? You barely know me at all."

"I know you enough. You chose the code name 'Prometheus' for yourself. Dante thought it was because you imagined yourself an honorable thief, like Prometheus was, but I think there was another reason."

Charlie's stare softened and became something more like respect.

"Prometheus was punished for stealing fire from the gods by having an eagle tear out his liver every day," Milana explained, "but Jupiter decided that still wasn't bad enough. So he came up with a really cruel way to make Prometheus suffer: He created women. Pandora was the first, and Jupiter assigned Prometheus to watch over her. To keep her safe. You imagined yourself as Pandora's protector, Charlie. And you can still be. It doesn't have to be the Furies that come out of that box. Hope can emerge as well."

Charlie smiled. Milana had been right about her. She couldn't bring herself to destroy something Einstein had created. She wanted to see it. To protect it. Besides, hope *was* in the box. She simply had to be careful with the contents.

Charlie slowly rotated the code wheels into position, mentally checking and rechecking the solution to Einstein's equation in her mind.

As the last wheel locked, she felt an almost imperceptible shift inside the box, as though something had just clicked into place.

Charlie lifted the lid.

The vial of cesium rose with it, intact.

Beneath it lay a small envelope. The metal box had been so well constructed the paper had suffered no exposure to the elements. It looked as though it had been placed inside only the day before.

Charlie gingerly removed the envelope, realizing with awe that the last person who had touched it was Einstein himself.

Before Charlie could open it, however, a voice broke the silence.

"Give it to me."

Charlie looked up and found herself staring down the barrel of a gun.

Agent Milana Moon had it pointed right between her eyes.

FORTY-NINE

Charlie's mind was racing. She wondered what enemy faction Milana was working for and how she could have possibly switched sides, but then she realized that was wrong.

Milana was still CIA.

That morning, when she had claimed that it might be a mistake to turn Pandora over to the government, it had merely been a ruse to win Charlie's trust. Maybe Milana and Dante had schemed to play good cop/bad cop long before that. Or maybe she was acting on her own. Whatever the case, Charlie had taken the bait.

"The CIA turned its back on you," Charlie said angrily. "They turned you over to the Mossad because they thought you were a traitor."

"That doesn't mean I should stop trying to be a good

agent. I have orders straight from the director of the CIA herself. Now hand over the envelope."

A few feet away, Tim Ralston watched Milana and Charlie's face-off, frozen in fear. Quark still sat by his side, tail wagging, blissfully unaware of the tension.

Charlie slowly held the envelope out.

Milana reached for it.

Charlie dropped Pandora's box.

It struck the ground at Milana's feet and the glass vial shattered, allowing the cesium to contact the air.

As Einstein had warned, cesium was a highly combustible element.

The explosion was strong enough to knock everyone off their feet. Milana and Charlie were thrown backward into the gully.

Just as John Russo opened fire on them.

John had been aiming for Milana. Even though Charlie was the one who had caused him so much trouble, Milana had the gun and knew how to use it. Once he had taken care of her, he could pick off Charlie and the old man with ease.

But the explosion had saved Milana's life. She had been thrown out of the path of the bullets—and the sudden flash of light had flared so brightly it left John momentarily blinded. By the time he regained his vision, Milana and Charlie were no longer within his line of sight;

both had fallen into the snow at the bottom of the gully.

John bolted from his hiding place, moving to better ground.

And then he saw the Israelis.

At first Benny West had assumed it was the CIA that had killed Leo, but when he reached the landslide on the road to the observatory and found three cars parked there, he realized someone else was in the mix too. Now Benny's unit had two missions: retrieve the equation Isaac Semel wanted—and avenge Leo's death. His small army was coming in locked and loaded, ready for battle.

The six men moved through the observatory complex in a line, making sure no one slipped past. They had cut off access to the road, leaving no way out.

The clouds were thick, but the air was still; the Mossad agents had heard Charlie and Milana long before they saw them. Then there was the flash of the explosion, and as the Mossad closed in, they spotted John, who opened fire on them and ran.

Dante, slinking through the telescope complex, had seen the Mossad. But he hadn't taken a shot at them for a few reasons: They outnumbered him, he had little ammunition, and it went against his code to shoot anyone who hadn't proved to be his enemy.

But somehow John Russo had gotten past him in the fog.

Dante had been trying to formulate a plan when the cesium exploded. And then John had started shooting.

Dante forgot all about the Mossad and started running back toward where he had left Charlie, knowing that one way or another she was in serious danger.

In doing so he exposed himself to the Mossad, but that was no longer his concern. All he could think about was saving Charlie.

When the Mossad spotted him, they didn't give him the same respect he had shown them. They just started shooting.

The explosion had been larger than Charlie had expected. She found herself sprawled in the snow uphill from Milana. Tim Ralston was still upright, having been thrown against the pump house. Quark was unharmed, but whimpering in fear.

The blast had snapped Einstein's envelope from Milana's hand and tossed it into the air. It wafted through the mist now, slowly floating back to earth.

As Charlie sat up, she heard the woods erupt with gunfire. Muzzle flashes flared in the fog.

Charlie turned back toward the envelope.

Tim Ralston was clambering out of the gully with it in his hand.

Charlie went after him.

Milana came to, seeing stars. She had hit her head on a rock and lost consciousness for a few seconds.

Above her, Charlie was scrambling over the lip of the gully.

Milana rolled over and dug her gun from the snow. But before she could do anything, gunfire peppered the ground around her, forcing her to duck behind the pump house for cover.

She spotted John Russo, running and shooting at the same time—and then the Mossad materializing out of the fog, firing indiscriminately at both of them.

Bullets rattled the opposite side of the pump house. Milana wanted to go after Charlie, to get to her before John, but she had no safe route. She would have to loop around the Hooker dome instead.

Just below the pump house, the gully narrowed, tilting steeply toward the astronomer housing. Milana launched herself onto the slope and slid through the snow. Bullets stitched the earth around her, and she felt a sting as one caught her thigh. She tumbled into the cover of the gully, rolled to her feet, and checked her leg. The bullet had only nicked her, although it still hurt like heck. It certainly needed to be tended to, but there was no time for that now.

Milana raced around the homes and into the woods, circling the peak topped by the Hooker dome, hoping to cut Charlie off before the kid got her hands on Pandora.

Charlie knew Tim Ralston was running the wrong way. He was heading toward the Hooker dome, probably thinking he could lock himself inside and be safe, but a locked door wouldn't mean diddly-squat to a bunch of men with guns.

The door to the dome still hung open. Just before Tim reached it, Charlie barreled into him, dragging him around the curve of the building, out of the line of gunfire.

"Leave me alone!" Tim cried. "Those people are after *you*!"

"They're after Pandora," Charlie said. "And if they catch you with it, they'll kill *you*."

On the far side of the dome were the control centers for CHARA Array, two long, low-slung buildings. Charlie hustled Tim into the small space between them. "I need the equation," she said.

Tim regarded her suspiciously.

"Please," Charlie said. "I'm the good guy here."

"How do I know that?"

"Because I'm the only one besides you up here without a gun."

Tim reluctantly took the envelope from his pocket.

"Lock yourself and Quark inside," Charlie instructed. "If anyone breaks in and aims a gun at you, don't try to protect me. Tell them I have this—and then show them the way I've gone." Charlie took Einstein's envelope and raced into the woods in the opposite direction of the gunfire.

Tim did exactly as Charlie had instructed. It was only after he was cowering under a desk with Quark that he realized Charlie was heading straight toward a cliff.

FIFTY

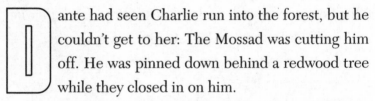ante had seen Charlie run into the forest, but he couldn't get to her: The Mossad was cutting him off. He was pinned down behind a redwood tree while they closed in on him.

"You're making a mistake!" he yelled to them. "We're on the same side here!"

"I doubt it," Benny West replied.

So Dante did the only thing he could think of. "I'm dropping my weapon!" he announced, and threw his gun into the snow, where Benny could see it. Then he came around the tree with his arms raised above his head, hoping the Mossad wouldn't shoot him.

Benny West held him at gunpoint from fifty feet away.

"If you want Pandora, I'll let you have it," Dante said. "Just help me save the girl." He wasn't sure until the moment he said it, but he wasn't lying. Little more than a day earlier, when he had first dragged Charlie into all this, he had been thinking about Pandora, not her. But things had changed. Dante had come to care for his half sister in a way that surprised him. He realized he would do anything to protect Charlie, even if it meant sacrificing his career.

Benny didn't lower his gun. He kept it trained on Dante, deciding what to do.

John Russo was running full tilt. He had left the Mossad behind for now, but that was only because they were moving slowly to ensure no one escaped. They would keep coming and they would do whatever it took to get Pandora.

John swore. How had it come to this? He had prepared so carefully. He had done everything right. Pandora should have been his. And yet everything was coming apart at the seams because of . . .

Charlie Thorne dashed through the woods ahead, an envelope in her hand.

Pandora.

John charged after her.

They were leaving the central complex behind now, heading deeper into the woods. Charlie's tracks were the only ones in the snow. John followed her easily, catching an occasional glimpse of his quarry ahead. The Mossad had stopped shooting for now, and the peak was eerily quiet in the aftermath. The crunch of Charlie's footsteps rang out in the thin air.

Charlie's tracks led toward the final dome in the CHARA Array, a short distance ahead through the trees. Beyond that there was nothing but blue sky.

John grinned cruelly. Charlie was running out of room.

Milana scrambled up a snowy slope to the top of the ridge behind the Hooker dome and found Charlie's and John's footprints leading into the woods to the east, away from the observatory complex. To the west, she could hear the men with guns steadily approaching.

Milana followed the footprints.

Charlie raced past the last dome of the CHARA Array and the world ended.

The dome sat on a thin peninsula of rock, fifty feet wide with sheer cliffs on either side. Charlie skidded to a stop and cautiously peered over the edge. The earth dropped away below her vertiginously, a granite wall plummeting ninety feet into a snow-choked ravine.

Charlie crossed to the opposite side of the peninsula to examine the cliff there. It was even steeper, disappearing into a cloud bank hundreds of feet below.

There was no place to go and almost no time to act. Through the woods, Charlie could see John Russo closing in on her—and she knew he would kill her the moment he had a clear shot.

There was only one thing to do.

John rounded the final dome a second later and saw her. She was only twenty feet away, right in plain sight. She was holding on to the branch of a pine tree and leaning out over the edge of a cliff, teetering above certain death.

In her free hand, stretched out over the void, she held the envelope with Pandora. It was pinched between her fingers.

"You see what the situation is here, don't you?" Charlie asked. "If you shoot me, I fall—and Pandora goes with me."

John considered his options, then reluctantly lowered his gun.

"Drop it," Charlie said.

"Or else what? You'll let go?"

"Just drop it. You'll need both hands to pull me back up."

John slid the gun back in his holster instead; Charlie was in no position to quibble. Then John came to the edge of the cliff, grabbed Charlie with both hands, and pulled her to safety.

When he glanced back toward the envelope, Charlie's hand was now a fist. And it was racing toward his face.

FIFTY-ONE

Charlie hit John with everything she had. By now she knew she wasn't a good fighter, but she was out of options. All she had was the element of surprise.

Unfortunately, John was well trained in hand-to-hand combat. The punch caught him off guard, but he rolled with it and then came in low. He drove his fist into Charlie's solar plexus, then caught her with another blow that floored her.

Charlie landed heavily on the rocky ground. It was like getting punched all over her body at once. Still, she knew she had to fight. She searched the ground for anything she could use as a weapon.

Forty yards behind them, Milana emerged from the woods and saw John standing over Charlie. She was too late and too far to do anything but yell. "John! No!"

John ignored her. Instead, he snapped the gun from his holster.

Charlie grabbed a rock, rolled over, and flung it as hard as she could, striking John in the head just as he was about to shoot her.

John staggered backward as he pulled the trigger. The shot went well above Charlie and struck the propane tank by the telescope dome, piercing its shell.

All five hundred gallons of propane ignited at once.

Charlie rolled over and hugged the ground.

The explosion roared over her and blasted John off his feet, slamming him into a tree with such force that his bones snapped.

Charlie stayed prone until the heat dissipated. When she finally raised her head, she found the world had changed. Seconds before it had been snow-capped and frigid. Now it was an inferno.

All around her was smoke and fire. Only half the telescope dome remained, a charred and groaning hulk. Fragments of it rained from the sky. Charlie hurt everywhere, but she had more pressing problems. A curtain of flame now crossed the peninsula, cutting her off from the rest of the world.

Milana was on the other side of the fire. Charlie could

barely make out her silhouette through the flickering, heat-warped air. While Charlie was stuck on this side with nothing but John Russo and . . .

Pandora.

To her horror Charlie realized she no longer had the equation. At some point during the fight, she had lost it. She spun around, searching wildly. . . .

And there it was. Buffeted by the waves of heat, tumbling toward the edge of the cliff.

Charlie struggled to her feet and staggered after it.

Behind her, there was a bone-rattling screech of metal. The twenty-foot-tall telescope toppled, taking the rest of the dome with it. A smoking piece of steel cartwheeled over Charlie's head and embedded itself in a tree.

The collapse created a gust of wind that caught the envelope and whipped it toward the void.

Charlie lunged for it.

Dante was running now, Benny West and the other Mossad following. They had found Tim Ralston and Tim had done just as Charlie had instructed, pointing the way she had gone and saying she had Pandora. Then they had all heard the explosion, and they knew that couldn't be good.

So Dante raced down the narrow peninsula toward the flame and the smoke, the Mossad on his heels. They found Milana staring helplessly into the wall of fire. She turned to them, her hands in the air, showing that she had laid her gun down, that she had no intention of turning this into a fight.

"Where's Charlie?" Dante asked, unable to keep the fear out of his voice.

Milana pointed through the flames.

Dante felt his breath catch in his throat. Before he even knew what he was doing, he was running straight toward the fire, intending to dive right through it.

But Milana blocked his path and locked him in a bear hug, stopping him. "Are you crazy?" she yelled over the roar of the fire. "You'll die in there!"

Dante struggled against her, but as he did, he realized she was right. The fire was raging. He was still several yards away from it, and it was so hot that it was scalding his skin. He couldn't save Charlie; she would have to save herself.

Benny West kept his gun aimed at the agents. "Where's Pandora?" he demanded.

Milana pointed through the flames once again. "Over there," she said. "Feel free to go get it if you want."

Benny considered the blaze, then sighed heavily. There were times when it was worth risking one's life for one's country, but this wasn't one of them. If Pandora was gone, it was gone. Everyone came out even.

He would need to frisk Milana, of course, make sure

she wasn't lying to him and holding on to the equation somewhere.

But right now they all needed to get to safety, away from the fire, before it consumed them.

They retreated from the flames. The Mossad moved quickly, while Dante was reluctant, staring back into the fire, tears in his eyes.

Milana stayed by his side. She took his hand in hers and held it tightly. "She's a smart kid," she said. "If anyone can figure out a way to survive this, it's her."

Dante could only watch the flames helplessly and hope she was right.

John Russo lay in a crumpled heap, battered, but still alive.

His spine had broken when he had been thrown into the tree. The only part of his body he could move was his neck. He rolled his head slightly and saw Charlie Thorne through the haze of smoke. Charlie had Pandora again; John had watched her grab it a second before it blew over the edge of the cliff. For all John's hard work, for all his intricate planning, he had lost. And to a girl, no less.

John felt a sudden rush of heat and smelled something burning close by. He rolled his head back and saw that the fire had surged closer, igniting the carpet of dead leaves under the tree where he lay. Within seconds, the flames leapt up all around him.

John screamed, but no one heard.

Fire closed in on Charlie from all sides.

The air was filled with the crackle of burning wood and the roar of the blaze. Charlie needed to find a way out, and every second counted.

But there was something she had to do first.

If she was going to die because of Pandora, she wasn't going to die curious.

Einstein's envelope was now crumpled, bloodied, and damp, but it was still sealed tightly. Charlie tore it open.

There was a single piece of paper inside.

On the paper was an equation. Pandora.

It was like a lightning bolt in Charlie's brain. Vintage Einstein. The way special relativity must have seemed to his fellow scientists when he had first unveiled it. Perfection. Genius. A feat of divine inspiration—and yet the moment Charlie laid eyes on it, she couldn't believe she had never thought of it before.

With a gunshot crack, a flaming tree toppled toward Charlie. She dove away, barely escaping the branches, but was showered with burning embers. The heat was now almost unbearable. It was difficult to breathe, the fire sucking all the oxygen from the air. The world was orange and black all around Charlie, save for one spot of blue sky to the north—and that was where the cliff was.

Wait.

A section of the telescope dome lay before Charlie, a sheet of metal five feet long with a slight curve to it. Not a perfect snowboard by any means, but just maybe it could work. The northern side of the peninsula was a ninety-foot drop into the ravine—thirty feet higher than Deadman's Gap at Snowmass. . . .

Charlie grabbed the sheet of metal—and Pandora slipped from her grasp again. The piece of paper Einstein had taken such pains to hide, to protect until the world was ready for it, was whipped away by an updraft. The flames caught it, and in an instant it was gone.

Now the only copy left in existence was in Charlie's mind.

And the chances of that surviving much longer were very small.

Charlie looked toward the small spot of blue sky through the fire. She would have to time her leap perfectly to avoid the flames, then drop nine stories onto a steep slope and nail the landing on a makeshift snowboard. God only knew what would await her in the ravine after that.

But there were no other options. The fire was closing in. Charlie had only a few seconds left.

She focused on the sky.

And the numbers came to her.

EPILOGUE

Mount Wilson Observatory, San Gabriel Mountains

By four o'clock that afternoon, the slopes were crawling with CIA agents.

They would have been there earlier, but they'd had to wait for the forest service to douse the fire.

They had managed to save most of the observatory complex, but everything on the peninsula was reduced to charcoal, scorched metal, and ash. The forensics specialists picked through it all anyhow, hoping to miraculously find a trace of Pandora.

Jamila Carter oversaw them, having flown in directly on her own jet, a frown etched on her face. None of this had gone the way she had hoped, partly due to her own mistakes.

Dante Garcia emerged from astronomer housing. His fellow agents had been grilling him all day, trying to learn every last detail about what had happened. He had told them everything, from Snowmass to Greenland to Jerusalem to here, right up to when the Mossad agents had frisked him and Milana down to their underwear to make sure neither of them was hiding Pandora on them and then headed back to their lives in Los Angeles without another word.

Dante saw Milana standing on the top of a cliff on the opposite side of the ravine from the charred peninsula, far from the other CIA agents. She seemed to sense his presence, turned his way, and beckoned him toward her.

When he got close, she could see that his eyes were rimmed with red, as though he'd been crying.

"Did the techs find anything?" he asked.

"No," she replied. "But they weren't expecting to. A hot enough fire can reduce even human bone to ash."

Dante warily looked over the edge of the cliff into the ravine. "Any chance she could have jumped?"

"The techs don't think so. They say that if she had, they'd have found her remains on the rocks below. As far as they're concerned, she died in the fire."

Dante noticed there was a curious lilt to Milana's voice as she spoke, like she wasn't saddened by this news. He looked at her curiously.

Milana nodded subtly toward the bottom of the ravine in the distance. Like she didn't want to say anything out loud, because there were other CIA agents around, and any one of them could be listening.

At the bottom of the ravine, there was a gouge in the snow. At first there didn't appear to be anything unusual about it to Dante. It looked like a natural indentation, as though a rock had tumbled off the cliff and rolled along.

But when Dante thought about it, he realized that it looked vaguely like the track of a snowboard. Or something that a very talented athlete was using as a snowboard.

The track led down the steep ravine until it disappeared into a stand of trees. And beyond the trees, not so far in the distance, was the sprawl of Los Angeles, where there were probably a billion places for a clever young genius to hide.

Milana turned to him and, not wanting to make a sound, mouthed the words:

She's alive.

And for the first time that day, Dante smiled.

ACKNOWLEDGMENTS

Sometimes it takes quite a while for an idea for a book to come to fruition. In this case, it was more than a decade. I actually had the idea for this book well before I wrote *Belly Up*, the first book I got published. At the time, I had imagined that this would be a book for adults. In the first imagining, Charlie Thorne was older—and a man. But things change. I had success writing for young readers and realized that the story might work well with a younger protagonist. And by that time, I had created many young male heroes, so I thought it would be nice to make the smartest person on earth a girl.

My wife, Suzanne, rooted this project on from the very beginning. As I have noted in the acknowledgments of other books, she passed away very suddenly in 2018, right while I was in the midst of writing this, so she never got to see the final version. I wish she could have. I am so thankful for all the support she gave this story (and me) through the entire long process of creating it.

I also have to thank lots of people at Simon & Schuster for their help with this book. I originally pitched the idea to Kristen Ostby Hoyle, who left the company before I could write it (for the best of reasons: She wanted to spend more time with her kids). The amazing Liz Kossnar oversaw the project after that.

In addition, I am indebted to everyone else on my incredible team at Simon & Schuster: Justin Chanda, Anne Zafian, Lucy Cummins, Milena Giunco, Sarah Woodruff, Michelle Leo, Audrey Gibbons, Lisa Moraleda, Jenica Nasworthy, Chrissy Noh, Anna Jarzab, Devin MacDonald, Christina Pecorale, Victor Iannone, Emily Hutton, Caitlin Nalven, and Theresa Pang. Also, thanks are due to Kelly Heinzerling for keeping my life running smoothly while I wrote this book. And this book—as well as my entire writing career—would never have happened without my amazing agent, Jennifer Joel.

And now, a funny story about quirks of fate. Just before I was about to start writing the first draft of this, I happened to be at a book festival with my dear friend, the incredibly talented author Sarah Mlynowski. Sarah asked what I was going to do next, and I mentioned that I was doing something that would partially be set in Israel. Sarah asked if I knew there was a group called PJ Library that was planning to take twenty authors on an all-expenses-paid trip to Israel the next March. This was news to me. A few seconds later, Sarah forwarded me the e-mail with the application. The Israel trip happened to overlap exactly with the very dates that my in-laws wanted to take my children on a spring break trip. If it had been off by a week—or even a few days—I couldn't have gone. But the timing was perfect. So I applied . . . and got accepted.

The trip was amazing. Until it happened, I was only going to draw on distant memories of visiting Israel, but thanks to everyone at PJ Library, the scenes in this book are very much based on the experiences I had on that trip. So huge thanks to Harold Grinspoon for his incredible generosity, and to everyone else in the PJ family: Winnie Sandler Grinspoon, Catriella Freedman, Danny Paller, Meredith Lewis, Chris Barash, Tasha Flagg, and Pnina Solomon.

Particular thanks must be given to our guide, Jonty Blackman, who put up with me sitting next to him at the front of the bus and pestering him with hours of questions—and to the great writer Alan Silberberg, who accompanied me on my attempt to explore every square inch of the Old City of Jerusalem. (We didn't see all of it, but we sure saw an awful lot.) But I also had a great time hanging out with Kim Brubaker-Bradley, Mara Rockliff, Elena K. Arnold, Lin Oliver, Erica Perl, Marla Frazee, Jamie Kiffel-Alcheh, David Adler, and Gail Carson Levine (who would honestly do push-ups any time you challenged her to, no matter where you were).

Of course thanks are due to Sarah Mlynowski, who not only got me on that Israel trip, but who also was kind enough to read an early draft of this book to make sure Charlie Thorne was a believable young woman.

Finally, thanks are due to my incredible family, for their continued support through what has been a difficult year: Ciara Howard, Suz Howard, Darragh Howard, Barry Patmore, Carole Patmore, Alan Patmore, Sarah Cradeur, Jane Gibbs, Ronald Gibbs—and the two most special people in my life, Dashiell and Violet, who accompanied me to explore many of the places in this book. In fact, one of the first excursions I ever had with Dashiell was loading him into a baby carrier and hiking around the spot where the finale of this book takes place. (I told you I'd had this idea for a really long time.) Every time I worked on that sequence, I would think back to that day. It's amazing to see what incredible people my children have become since then.

Dash and Violet, I love you more than words can say.